FEAR TO TREAD

by Michael Gilbert

"Mr. Gilbert seems to me the best of the good English mystery writers we're reading today. *Fear to Tread* brings us what we expect of him—attractive writing, expert storytelling. Highly pleasing."   —Eudora Welty

"This is a mighty fetching thriller."
—*New York Herald Tribune Book Review*

FEAR TO TREAD

Michael Gilbert

PERENNIAL LIBRARY
Harper & Row, Publishers
New York, Hagerstown, San Francisco, London

A hardcover edition of this book was originally published by
Harper & Row, Publishers.

FEAR TO TREAD. Copyright © 1953 by Michael Francis Gilbert.
All rights reserved. Printed in the United States of America.
No part of this book may be used or reproduced in any manner
without written permission except in the case of brief quotations
embodied in critical articles and reviews. For information
address Harper & Row, Publishers, Inc., 10 East 53rd Street,
New York, N.Y. 10022. Published simultaneously in Canada by
Fitzhenry & Whiteside Limited, Toronto.

First PERENNIAL LIBRARY edition published 1978

ISBN: 0-06-080458-0

78 79 80 81 82 10 9 8 7 6 5 4 3 2 1

Contents

FEAR TO TREAD

It may also be true that there have been changes for the worse in the national attitude to wrong-doing and that a man who steals does not incur the same measure of public reprobation which he would have done in the past. . . .

SIR FRANK NEWSOM
To the Chief Constables Association
November 6, 1952

NOTE: The characters are fictitious. The problem is not. The cutting quoted on page 182 appeared in a well-known London newspaper this year.

ONE

South of the River:
An Uncalculated Inspiration

When Wilfrid Wetherall learned that the boys called him "Wellington" Wetherall he was not displeased. He was an admirer of the Duke, and he had no doubt that it was his references to this hero in the course of his history lessons that had planted the idea. A headmaster had to have a nickname. It could have been a good deal worse.

There were physical resemblances, too, in the bony structure of his face, the jut of his nose, the spare frame and forward-bending carriage. It finished there. Nobody, not even Wetherall himself, imagined that he had the Wellingtonian character, useful though it would have been in the daily difficulties which beset the headmaster of an understaffed, overpopulated secondary day school for boys in the southwest of London.

The room in which he was sitting did not much resemble the traditional headmaster's study. It was almost without adornment. The walls were painted (as were the walls throughout the school), the bottom half in pastel green, the top half in primrose, with a horizontal dividing band of dark green. These were the colors which the consultant

1

psychologist to the School Planning Committee had stated to be most conducive to study and relaxation. After six years' practice, Mr. Wetherall found himself able to ignore their message. The floor was covered with dark linoleum. The furniture and fittings were those of a managing director who did not believe in frills.

The modern, iron-framed windows looked bleakly north and east; but there was compensation for this in the sky-line of distant masts and cranes where the river swung south, into Limehouse Reach.

Mr. Wetherall replaced on the table a letter he had been reading, and sighed. It was a thing he often found himself doing. The letter was from a Mr. Turvey who considered (with an optimism which, in Mr. Wetherall's view, bordered on lunacy) that his son might have a chance of a university scholarship.

Swing doors creaked outside.

They were swing doors which, in the first innocent youth of his associations with the school board, he had managed to get installed to cut off the end of the passage and so afford a little privacy to his study and the administration office on the other side of the corridor.

Five deliberate steps, and a knock.

"Come in," said Mr. Wetherall. "Oh, it's you, Croke, do sit down."

"I won't sit down," said Mr. Croke, "because I shan't be a minute. It's Mr. Barlow."

"Not again? We had him last week."

"He won't let his son start calculus."

"I can't find it in me to blame him," said Mr. Wetherall. "I have never been able to see the faintest glimmerings of sense in it myself."

"It's in the Higher Board Syllabus," said Mr. Croke, rather stiffly.

"Oh, quite so, quite so. Why does Barlow's father object to it?"

"He says that calculus leads to the splitting of the atom."

"I see. How unfortunate. He's an ardent pacifist, too, isn't he?"

"Extremely ardent."

"Why not tell him that as the atom has been split once already it is most unlikely to be split again in our lifetime. Then if that doesn't work I'll have a word with him."

"It would be useless, I suppose, trying to persuade him that the differential calculus has no connection whatever with nuclear physics?"

"Quite hopeless. You remember what he was like about Guy Fawkes."

"Yes. Well, all right, I'll try."

Mr. Wetherall resumed his contemplation of the skyline. There was something romantic, he thought, about masts along a tideway.

Miss Donovan came in from the Administration Office across the passage. It should perhaps be made clear that the Administration Office was an even smaller room than Mr. Wetherall's study and had been originally designed— the matter was uncertain—either as a very small extra staffroom or a very large cloakroom. Miss Donovan was simply Peggy, who was the sister of Sammy and of Patsy Donovan, and whom Mr. Wetherall had known, on and off, since she was a slum child of five. She was now seventeen and looked neat, competent and twenty.

"It's this milk," she said.

"What about it?"

"It's the return."

"What's wrong with the return?" Mr. Wetherall was cautious. He knew the power of returns. "Have we shown more milk than we drank, or drunk more milk than we showed —incidentally that's rather a good example of the difference between the aorist and perfect tenses, isn't it?" Mr. Wetherall made a note for his grammar class.

"The figures come about right with a little cooking—"

"Adjustment."

"Adjustment. But now they want them showed—shown,

I mean—in two separate lots. 'Milk served' and 'Milk Drunk.' "

"What the devil," said Mr. Wetherall, "do they think we do with it? Throw it at each other?"

"They've done that before now," said Miss Donovan.

"Show the totals as the same in both headings. If they don't like it, it's up to them to object. If they object perhaps we shall see what they're getting at."

How would the Duke of Wellington have dealt with this?

"There's the boxing lists. I'm just going to put them up."

"I'd like to see them. Schools Area Final. That's tomorrow afternoon, isn't it? Where's it to be this time?"

"The Co-op Hall. Starting four o'clock."

"That's that rather dim place north of the Elephant, isn't it?" Mr. Wetherall made another note on his desk pad. "Is Sammy still in?"

"He surely is," said Miss Donovan. "Eighty-eight and under. He had to sweat off four ounces to make the weight."

"He ought to try standing on his head," said Mr. Wetherall.

The telephone rang.

"Who—oh, Mrs. Ambler. How are you? Your husband —I'm sorry to hear that. Laryngitis? He does seem to have bad luck, doesn't he? No, of course he can't turn up if he's feeling bad. I'll manage somehow."

"Though why," he added, having rung off, "these things always happen to Mr. Ambler on Tuesday morning is more than I can make out. I suppose I'll have to take his class myself. I really couldn't know less about it."

Mr. Ambler was the visiting drawing master.

He became aware that Miss Donovan was still with him. "Is there anything else, Peggy?"

"Well, yes, Mr. Wetherall, there is. It's Sammy."

"Hullo, what's this?" He came out of the clouds with a jerk. A thing to do with boys could be important.

"He's been in trouble with you lately, I know, Mr.

Wetherall. But it isn't really his fault. It's that new master. He was quite all right with Mr. Rollinson, but—"

"Look here," said Mr. Wetherall. "I can't have this special pleading. If Sammy gets sent up for anything, I shall hear about it from him. Besides I haven't seen him here for some time."

"You'll be seeing him," said Miss Donovan.

Left to himself Mr. Wetherall picked up his pen, started to write such a letter as would deflate, without irritating, Mr. Turvey, then put his pen down again and looked out of the window.

Creak of double doors, seven short and rather nervous steps along the passage.

"Come in," said Mr. Wetherall.

It was a boy of fifteen. The hair which might, in Miss Donovan, have been described, at a pinch, as auburn was here unblushing carrot.

"What is it, Donovan?"

"I've got a book, sir, from Mr. Pelley."

"Oh, dear," said Mr. Wetherall.

It should be explained that (unlike our great public schools in which, having paid a great deal more money, a boy is privileged to be beaten by almost anybody older than himself) in most state schools the headmaster enjoys a monopoly of this form of punishment. If a form master wished for a boy to be so dealt with he entered his name and offense in a book and sent the boy with the book to the headmaster, who attended to the matter and recorded the result in a further column. These rather incongruous civil service trappings did nothing to allay Mr. Wetherall's distaste for the barbaric rite which followed.

"What is it this time?"

"Impertinence," said the boy.

"Yes, I can read. I'm asking what actually happened."

"Well, sir," Donovan charged his lungs with a deep breath, "Mr. Pelley said something wasn't cricket and someone asked him what it meant and he said that cricket was the most important game in a school and if you said a thing wasn't cricket you meant that it wasn't done and I said cricket wasn't the most important game in this school by half boxing was and he said that in any decent school cricket was the game that mattered and I said well cricket's a sissy game what's the good of being able to play cricket if a chap came up in the street and tried to take your girl friend away and then," concluded the narrator putting his finger unerringly on the real heart of the offense, "people laughed."

"I see," said Mr. Wetherall. (Curse Pelley and his old school tie.) "It doesn't seem perhaps a very serious offense" (got to back the man up all the same, very young) "but it was certainly impertinent. I think, in the circumstances, I'm going to set you enough work to keep you busy after school, during sport time. Tomorrow's a games day—"

Alarm flared.

"Not tomorrow, sir."

"What—oh, it's the boxing tomorrow, isn't it?" Considering the nature of the offense it would have been very fitting to deprive the boy of his boxing, but he knew himself to be incapable of such chilly logic. "Very well, on Wednesday then." He made a note in the book. He was quite aware that he was being weak. "And look here," he said. "I don't want any more of this. You're coming up here a lot too much. You're growing up now. You've got to think before you say silly things. Next time you'll get hurt—"

"Yes sir," said Donovan cheerfully. Next time was a long way ahead.

It was a warm October day and even the brick and mortar of S.E.17 responded grudgingly to the ancient magic. The South Borough High School for Boys is in the middle of the quadrilateral formed by the Old Kent Road, the New Kent Road, the Camberwell Road and Peckham High Street. It is a square half mile which is almost indescribable because it lacks the first element of description, which is character. It is made up of two or three hundred streets of uninspiring houses; seven churches and twenty-seven chapels; two very small open spaces, created by some bygone town planning enthusiasm and a dozen larger ones opened up by the German Air Force, but even these are subdued to the general pattern of uneasy neatness; the rubble is stamped flat, the yellow bricks are piled into neat heaps. It is an area which lies in the middle of things greater than itself but takes nothing from them. The Old Vic Theatre on the north, the Oval cricket ground on the west, the roaring goods yards of Bricklayers Arms and Crossways and the passenger stations at Waterloo and London Bridge. In this depressing arena the only arteries of life are the High Streets, where the blood flows red from chain store to chain store; where the social center is the butcher's queue and the spiritual temple is the Gaudeon Super Cinema. Away from the High Street the splashes of color are pubs, late and lonely flowerings in reds and greens and golds.

Mr. Wetherall made his way to the Old Kent Road and boarded a No. 53 bus, going south. Twenty minutes later he got off at the stop after Deptford Broadway. He was on the fringes of Blackheath. Not Blackheath proper, which lies at the top of the hill, around the open space, but near enough to it to put it on his notepaper. Postally Brinkman Road was in Blackheath, if spiritually in Deptford.

The Wetheralls leased the top floor of No. 20. The house, which had suffered subdivision in the thirties, was owned by a doctor, and though he was twenty years retired from active practice a faintly antiseptic smell still clung to the lower floors. Above the doctor lived two Japanese. Above the Japanese, the Wetheralls.

Immediately Mr. Wetherall got home he knew that something was amiss. Alice Wetherall was in the kitchen, her hands folded and her lips pursed.

"It's too bad," she said. "Major Francis' food parcel hasn't arrived."

"Oh, dear. Perhaps it's lost—"

"You know how regular he's been. When it was a week

late I began to wonder. I wrote to the railway on Friday. This came this morning."

It was hardly a letter. A printed memorandum. "Unable to trace the package in question—was there any proof of posting?—admit no responsibility."

"It doesn't look very helpful," admitted Mr. Wetherall. "I might ask Major Francis next time I write. It's rather awkward, though. Supposing he had decided not—"

"It's been stolen," said Mrs. Wetherall.

"Stolen?"

"By those railways. Didn't you see that bit in the paper last Sunday? No. It was the Sunday before. About all the parcels they were losing. Food parcels chiefly, and cigarettes. Why should they be allowed to? What do we—what do we pay our fares for?"

He thought for a moment she was going to cry.

"Never mind," he said. "I expect we can manage. We'll have a meal or two out for a change. Why don't we go to Luigi's tonight?"

"I'll think about it. Come and get your lunch now before it gets cold."

"That's to say, if the journey won't be too much for you—"

"Now don't you fuss," said Mrs. Wetherall, more cheerfully. She had, of course, been fussing herself, but like most women found instant solace if she could accuse someone else of it. "It's the principle of the thing that upset me. It's *our* parcel. Why should they be allowed to steal it? Can't we do anything about it, now they're nationalized?"

Instead of attempting to unravel this tangled piece of logic, Mr. Wetherall said he would ring the police immediately after lunch.

He knew that he was not at his best on the telephone. He was very slightly deaf, and was apt to get flustered. The Sergeant in charge of the station was plainly neutral. He was not obstructive, nor was he helpful. He took particulars. He spelled Mr. Wetherall's name wrong, then got it right, then got the address wrong. He, also, wanted to know if there was any proof that the parcel had been dispatched, and when Mr. Wetherall had to admit that there was not, he lost most of his remaining interest. He said he would do what he could. He added that he was afraid there was a lot of pilfering on the railways.

When Mr. Wetherall was on the point of leaving the house (it would, in many ways, have been easier to have his lunch at a restaurant near the school, but with his wife in her present condition he liked to get back as often as he could) he remembered their plans for the evening.

"I'd better meet you at Luigi's," he said. "I'll have to go straight there. Ambler's ill again, and I've got to take his drawing class this afternoon. That'll mean putting off my specials until after tea, so I shall be late anyway. I'll see you there at seven."

"Do we want to go to Luigi's?"

"Why," said Mr. Wetherall, surprised. "We've always liked the food there so much. Do you want something a bit more classy?"

"Silly," said his wife. "It's only that I heard the other day—I think it was Mrs. Ormerod. She was saying that Mrs. Lewis told her—something about the food not being quite clean."

"I'd rather believe my own eyes," said Mr. Wetherall mildly, "than something Mrs. Ormerod said to Mrs. Lewis."

"Well, I always thought it was very nice, too."

"Luigi's let it be, then. If you observe so much as a single cockroach in the minestrone, we can always go on somewhere else."

"Don't be horrid," said Mrs. Wetherall.

There are people who cannot draw. Mr. Wetherall was one of them. In a way this was odd, because he had a good appreciation of line and an eye for the beauty in unlikely places. It was his execution which was hopeless. He often wished that the training he had received, a scrupulously careful training which had covered every conceivable subject from Bible study to eurythmics, had dealt with this important matter. For he was convinced that it was important. For one thing, the boys enjoyed it, and that was half the battle in any school subject. Furthermore he was certain, in an instinctive way, that it did them good.

His usual solution to the problem was to announce that the hour would be devoted to free inspiration, then to allot a suitable subject (the choice was not easy. He still remembered some of the unfortunate results when he had asked the senior class to exercise its imagination on the subject of a pig in a poke) and leave them to it.

That afternoon, after some thought, he selected "A Street Accident" and retired to the master's desk to correct history papers.

For half an hour there was silence, broken only by some hard breathing, the scrape of feet and the squeak of pencils. Red crayon seemed to be in demand. At the end of this time Mr. Wetherall climbed to his feet and toured the classroom to give an interim judgment on the results.

In the back row, somewhat to his surprise, he found a boy with an untouched sheet of drawing paper in front of him. It was Crowdy, a quiet creature whom he liked; according to Mr. Ambler, something of an artist.

"What is it?" he said. "No inspiration?"

"I was just wondering, sir," said Crowdy, with a blush, "what a car would look like upside down."

"Why not draw it the right way up, and then turn the paper round?"

Crowdy looked up with faint scorn and said, "I didn't mean resting on its back, sir. I meant the moment it hit the road, after being turned over. Why, the wheels might still be spinning—like this."

He picked up the pencil and quickly drew four or five lines. Thinking it over afterward Mr. Wetherall was prepared to swear that it was not more than five. And in front of his eyes an accident was born. He could see at once what must have happened. The car, cornering too fast on a greasy road, had turned, first onto its side and then right over. He could see by the crumpling of the coachwork and the distortion of the body how powerful the impact must have been. The drawing was foreshortened and the nearest wheel, unnaturally large, was spinning; it was actually spinning in front of Mr. Wetherall's eyes.

"Yes," he said. "Yes. I see what you mean. I should go on with that. It looks very promising."

He walked back to his desk aware that, in a small way, the thing might have happened which every schoolmaster dreams will happen to him. That he may be privileged to act midwife at the birth of genius; to watch the infant Keats scratching his fingers through his hair and his nib through his first halting sonnet; to listen to the stubby, chilblain-covered fingers of the young Beethoven stumbling along the octave. It is the most intoxicating thought a schoolmaster can have. Mr. Wetherall felt partially intoxicated as he went back to his desk.

He made one more round, toward the end of the hour, and commended several of the more dashing efforts. They were none of them lacking in incident. In one a fire brigade had become involved with a squadron of tanks. In another a lady had been cut completely in two. Crowdy had blocked in a little background, but had done nothing much else to his sketch. It was entirely in hard pencil, in line, with no shading at all.

"Cleanly, sir, you went to the heart of the matter," he found himself saying as he collected the drawings and dismissed the class.

That wasn't quite right. It wasn't "heart of the matter."

"Cleanly, sir, you went to the core of the matter."

It was a poem in some paper or literary magazine. Mr. Wetherall had a good visual memory, if he cared to use it. Sometimes for a bet, he would read once, and then repeat, a whole paragraph of prose. More often it was scraps of verse that stayed in his mind.

This came now, out of its pigeonhole.

> *A calligraphic master, improvising, you invent*
> *The first incision, and no poet's hesitation*
> *Before his snow-blank page mars your intent:*
> *The flowing stroke is drawn like an uncalculated*
> *   inspiration.*

That was right. That was absolutely right. No hesitation. No fumbling. "An uncalculated inspiration." Come to think of it the poem was not really about drawing. It was a description of a famous surgeon, in the theater, performing a difficult operation. But the simile was just. As Mr. Wetherall looked at the clean lines of the sketch he felt an inner certainty that the hand which had drawn them must one day claim recognition.

Then his practical sense asserted itself. Crowdy would be sixteen at the end of the summer. The next step was therefore important. After some thought and a hunt through a well-used address book, Mr. Wetherall took up his pen and wrote:

> I've got a boy here who looks as if he might be useful to you. I'm no art expert, as you know, but he draws a neat, clean line and has lots of self-confidence. He's leaving here in July. Would your people like to take him on? The only thing is, I'm afraid there's no question of apprenticeship. His family have got no money at all, so he'll have to be paid something, even when he's learning. I expect he can run errands and pour out the tea. How's Wright getting on? Best wishes to your wife and family.

The latter was addressed to the Managing Director of Lithography & Artists Services, Ltd. It was on occasions such as this that Mr. Wetherall, who was an inverted snob of a not uncommon type, was thankful that he had been at Oxford and had made, and kept, a few useful friends.

After tea, which was brought in by Miss Donovan—her heart was kind, but her taste in pastries was more flamboyant than Mr. Wetherall's—and after dealing with the not unjustified complaints of Mr. Edgecumb that the Examination Sub-Committee had introduced elementary physics into the curriculum while the Finance Sub-Committee had allowed no expenditure of any sort on equipment, and after devoting an hour to the special coaching of four candidates for future university scholarships, and after reading and signing fifteen papers produced by Miss Donovan, Mr. Wetherall sat back in his chair, looked at the clock which now said half past six, and sighed once more.

He was wondering, and not for the first time, whether he was really suited to his job. He liked boys. He enjoyed teaching, particularly the teaching of the less precise subjects, like history and English. On the other hand he found the routine of administration and management increasingly distasteful. Committees terrified him.

Having allowed plenty of time, he naturally picked up a bus at once, and arrived at Deptford Broadway with ten minutes to spare. All its lights were blazing, but Luigi's had a deserted look, and when he got inside he saw that only one of the tables was occupied, by a depressed-looking couple who were talking in whispers. Three months before, at that hour, the place would have been crowded.

Mr. Wetherall sat down at his usual table, opposite the service door, and picked up the handwritten menu. So far as he could judge the food was as varied and attractive as ever. At that moment Luigi came through the door. His name, actually, was Castelbonato but the South Bank called him Luigi on the same simple principle that led them to call all German waiters Fritz and all French hairdressers Alphonse. His family had been in England for two generations. His turn of phrase was still apt to be foreign, particularly when he was excited, but his accent was purest cockney.

"What's up, Luigi? Have you been frightening the customers away?" Then he saw the look on the little man's face and felt sorry for him.

"What'll it be, Mr. Wetherall?"

"I think I'll wait for my wife."

The couple at the other table signaled for their bill. Luigi went over to them. When he came back he did a thing he had never done before and which, in a trained restaurateur, gave a little indication of how upset he was. He sat down in the chair opposite Mr. Wetherall.

"You can have what you like," he said. "Chicken—duck—I'm shutting up tomorrow."

"What's it all about?"

"No customers." Luigi waved his hand round the empty room. The bright lights. The clean cloths. The fresh flowers.

"What's it all about?" said Mr. Wetherall again.

Luigi took a deep breath.

"They bin saying my food's dirty. They bin coming along here making a fuss. Fortnight ago they come along and find a dead beetle in my ravioli. In *my* ravioli. Who would be likely to put such filth in, I ask you, them or me? They throw it in my face. A whole plateful—"

"Who—?" began Mr. Wetherall.

"Do not ask who. Ask why. I'll tell you. I used to take food from them. There's no secret. Bacon and sugar. All took it, you understand. I wasn't the only one. If we couldn't get it other place, we had to get it from them. Then I wanted to stop, you understand?"

"I don't—"

"They asked too much. Bacon and sugar and butter and tinned meat are good, but they are not good at five and six and seven shillings a pound. You can reckon it up for yourself, Mr. Wetherall, you know what I charge. In the West End, perhaps. That's West End prices. Not here. So I said I must stop. Then they warned me—"

Luigi suddenly cut off the torrent of his speech, and Mr. Wetherall at last got the chance to say, "Who are these people you're talking about, Luigi?"

Luigi was not listening. He had his head half turned, and in the silence that followed they both heard, beyond the service door, the outer door of the kitchen open and shut softly.

Luigi jumped to his feet and went out through the serving door.

At that moment Mrs. Wetherall arrived, five minutes late and full of insincere apologies.

They had, as Luigi had promised, an excellent dinner, but Mr. Wetherall did not find himself enjoying it.

TWO

South of the River:
The Uses of Lithography

Next morning Mr. Wetherall asked Miss Donovan for her elder brother's address.

"Patsy?" said Miss Donovan. "Why, he lives home now, Mr. Wetherall."

He was on the point of expressing his surprise when his experience of the South Bank and its problems checked him. There could be reasons why Patsy Donovan and his young wife would have given up their house and gone back to live with one or other of their families, but Peggy might not want to discuss them.

Patsy was a Detective Sergeant, attached for C.I.D. duties to Borough Police Station. Mr. Wetherall had known him, as a boy, in the mid thirties, at the Battersea school at which he had been teaching. Battersea had been Mr. Wetherall's first impact with the light-hearted, tough-minded, precocious young male who hangs out south of the river. When the wheels of circumstance had brought Mr. Wetherall to the South Borough Secondary School and Sergeant Donovan to the Borough Police Station they had improved this acquaintanceship. More than once they had

16

been able to be useful to one another. It was nearly a year since they had last had occasion to meet.

"Will he be off duty now?"

"He'll be asleep right now," said Peggy. "He'll be up by eleven. Should I ask him to come round—?"

"No. I'm off until lunch. I'll go and see him."

As Peggy was on her way out she stopped for a moment at the door and said, "It's some time since you seen Patsy last, isn't it?"

"Yes."

"You'll find him changed a bit."

"We are none of us static," said Mr. Wetherall.

"I suppose that's right."

"A doctor once told me that you change your blood and your character completely every seven years."

"There now!" said Miss Donovan. "I'd better fetch you those milk returns and you can sign them up before you go."

The Donovan house was one in a row of the oldest houses in the district, a miracle of eroded brick, decaying wood and blackened stone, a sepulcher, whitened daily by the power of Mrs. Donovan's arm. Mr. Wetherall went round to the back and found the Sergeant at breakfast in the kitchen. He was alone in the house, for his mother, though over sixty, still went out to do a morning's work at a block of offices near the Elephant, and Mr. Donovan had long ago drunk himself into an expensive grave.

"Why, come in."

Mr. Wetherall got his first shock when Sergeant Donovan spoke, and another when he got up and the light fell on his face.

"I'm sorry. I seem to be disturbing your breakfast."

"That's all right, Mr. Wetherall. Pleased to see you. Sit down."

The voice was hard. The red-headed boy and the big, well-made, pleasant young man had both gone. In their place was this heavy, and somehow rather dangerous-looking person.

"Some time since I've had the pleasure of seeing you, Mr. Wetherall."

"I expect we've both been busy."

Mr. Wetherall was playing for time. He was wondering whether the new Sergeant Donovan could help him. Might it be better to temporize?—something about Sammy or Peggy—anything would do. He was aware that the Sergeant was looking at him steadily over his teacup.

In the end he said, "I came across something last night that I didn't much like. There wasn't anything I could do about it, but I felt it might help if I passed it on. It was at Luigi's—"

He told the whole story.

It was difficult to say if Sergeant Donovan was interested or not. He sat very still while Mr. Wetherall was talking and at the end he said: "Your idea about this, is it that someone's been starting a whisper about Luigi's food?"

"That's what he says."

"To run him out of business?"

"I suppose so."

"Anyone whose restaurant does bad, Mr. Wetherall, could think up a story like that. It'd be a sort of excuse, wouldn't it?"

"But he said they actually came and pretended to find insects and dirt in his food. They made a fuss in public. That sort of thing—"

"Why would they do that?"

"He said that he used to get food from these people— black market stuff, I suppose. Then they put their prices up, and he couldn't pay. So they said, if he didn't pay they would drive him out of business."

"Well now," said Sergeant Donovan. "Who are 'they'? Who are these people he's talking about?"

"He didn't say."

"Any suggestions?"

"No. He just said 'they' and 'them.' You could see he was nervous about them. In fact, if he hadn't been so angry about it I don't think he would have said anything."

"I can believe that bit all right," said Donovan, with rather a tight smile. "Did he actually say that it was black market food he'd been buying?"

"Not in so many words—I mean, I couldn't swear to it in a court of law."

"You won't be asked to do that," said the Sergeant, reading Mr. Wetherall's thoughts accurately. "It's not Mister Luigi What's-his-name you've got to worry about. He's just the meat in the trap. He's the worm on the hook. Once people like him start fooling round with funny stuff they always end up in trouble, one side or the other. It's the people who supply the Luigis that I'd like to have a quiet word with. Or the people who supply *them*. Just a quiet word."

As he spoke he moved across to the window, so that the light fell on a white line of scars which ran down, stretched and taut, from cheekbone to chin, so that for a moment the jaw seemed to hang from it, like a puppet's jaw on a thread. When the Sergeant turned back into the room he spoke more mildly.

"So far as doing anything about this goes," he said, "I'm L Division. Luigi's place in Deptford Broadway, that's R."

"Is it?" said Mr. Wetherall. The geography he had been taught had not included the frontiers of the London police authorities.

"However, I'll see if anything can be done. I might put a word in the right quarter. But my best advice to you, Mr. Wetherall, is to leave it alone. They're not a nice crowd, the people behind this. Not a nice crowd at all."

"Thank you," said Mr. Wetherall. "I'm sure if anything can be done you'll do it."

As soon as he got back to the school he sent for Peggy.

"What's it all about?" he said.

"All what, Mr. Wetherall?"

"Your brother—living at home. What's happened to his wife? And what's happened to him? He looks ten years older than when I saw him last—you must know what I mean. If you think," he added with belated caution, "that it's none of my business, say so. But I've known you all for a very long time, and if it's just that he's had a row with his wife, or something like that, and there's anything I can do to help—"

"It's not a row, Mr. Wetherall. She's dead."

"Good heavens," said Wetherall stupidly. "I am sorry. I'd no idea. Of course, that explains it. What a pity. Such a nice girl."

He found that Peggy was looking at him, in the steady way that her brother had done. He felt a growing sense of embarrassment.

"Silly of me," he said, "jumping to conclusions. You must forgive me. What happened to her? It was very sudden, wasn't it?"

"She didn't just die," said Peggy slowly. "She was killed."

"Killed?" Mr. Wetherall was really startled.

"I don't think there's any reason I shouldn't tell you about it. It was in the papers. You know they had one of the houses in Lower Marsh. Some men broke in one night. I expect they knew Patsy was away on duty. Doris was alone in the house. They tied her up and gagged her with a towel. They bust the home up. They didn't take much. Just some papers and a little money."

Peggy stopped, and Mr. Wetherall tried to say something, but failed. The truth was that the idea of violence frightened him. At second hand it made him feel rather sick.

"They tied the towel over her mouth too tight. She was suffocated. She was dead when Patsy got home to her."

"How horrible. How absolutely horrible. Did they catch the people who did it?"

"They haven't caught them yet."

"Have they any idea—?"

"Patsy says he knows who it was. But he can't prove it. You know his job is something to do with stealing from the railways, and the long-distance lorries—"

"If he knows," said Mr. Wetherall, very much distressed, "if he knows, surely—"

"Knowing isn't proving. There was one particular lot he was mixed up with. He didn't say much about it. He'd been pretending to take bribes, and they thought he was bought and sold so they got talking a bit freely in front of him. What they did was meant as a sort of warning to him not to pass it on—they never meant to kill Doris."

"It was murder, whether they meant to kill her or not."

"I suppose it was," said Peggy. She seemed unexcited about this aspect of it. For a moment Mr. Wetherall wondered if she might have been making the story up. He dismissed that thought. Nobody could have made up a thing like that.

"Has he told anyone about his suspicions? If the police only knew, surely they could do something. It would give them a line to go on."

"They had an Inspector from Scotland Yard on it. He didn't get very far."

"You're not answering my question," said Mr. Wetherall testily. "Did Patsy tell them what he suspected—what you've just told me?"

"He couldn't, Mr. Wetherall. Really, it was just suspicions."

"So he didn't say."

"No."

"Somebody ought to."

Peggy looked up in alarm.

"I don't think Patsy would like that."

Mr. Wetherall could hardly fail to recognize it. He had heard it twice that morning. It was the red signal. It was the notice which said "Keep Out. Trespassers will get hurt." The dullest man, and Mr. Wetherall was far from dull, cannot live his life in South London without becoming aware of certain facts. He was not a romantic. He was well past the age when one considered crime to be an adventure, or a puzzle, or a joke. He recognized it for what it was, a pathological growth, bred of poverty, rooting and flourishing in the weak and diseased cells of the body. He had been to too many dingy police courts to speak a word for the adolescent victim in the dock, had attended too many tearful mornings after the brave nights before, to think of crime as anything but an affliction: something akin to cancer or insanity; something which, in a perfect world, would not exist, but in the present state of imperfection you had to deal with as best you could.

He also knew that you could live among crime without being affected by it. There were plenty of doctors and parsons and schoolmasters who did it without a second thought. He himself knew a garage where a lot of things were done which had nothing to do with the repair of motor cars. He knew cafés which would not serve an unknown customer. He knew at least two receivers of stolen goods. But it stopped at knowledge.

Crime would not interfere with him, provided that he did not interfere with it. That was the limit of the sufferance.

In the end he said rather weakly, "All right, Peggy. I expect you're right. Are you coming to the boxing?"

"You try and keep me away," said Peggy.

When he arrived home he was so unusually silent that his wife, after a number of unsuccessful efforts to obtain his attention, asked him what was the matter, and after some deliberation, he told her a certain amount.

"It's nothing to do with you," said Mrs. Wetherall.

"So two other people have informed me already this morning."

"Well, is it?"

"Not really, I suppose," said Mr. Wetherall. "Except, if you see a thing going wrong, you ought to try and put it right."

"Sergeant Donovan's old enough to look after himself."

"He didn't look after his wife very well."

"It was an accident," said Mrs. Wetherall. "Just the same as getting run over by a bus."

"All right, I agree. But if you thought the bus driver had done it on purpose, surely you'd want him prosecuted."

"If he really knew who these people were," said Mrs. Wetherall, "and if he had any real proof against them, he'd have them arrested. He's a policeman."

"Yes. He's also an Irishman."

"I don't—"

"When he was a boy, he always liked to handle things himself. Sammy's the same. And Peggy, for that matter. It's a Donovan habit."

"What do you want to do?"

"I don't know. I wasn't very happy about one thing. Peggy told me that her brother had got into the confidence of one of the gangs by pretending to take bribes. Well, that's all right in theory, but in practice it must be a very fine line between pretending to take them, and actually taking them—if you see what I mean."

"Yes," said Mrs. Wetherall doubtfully.

"He pockets the money either way, you see. He may be saying, I'm only doing this to fool them, and sooner or later I'll pay it over to the Police Orphanage, but—"

"I see what you mean," said Mrs. Wetherall. "You think that's why he daren't tell anyone who they are—"

"It could be one of the reasons, couldn't it?"

The Co-operatius Hall, on the Walworth side of the Elephant, had been built as a swimming pool. During the winter months the pool was boarded over and the space thus created became available for dances, gym displays and other feats of endurance. Or (with a small stage at one end and chairs) for theatrical performances, lectures, debates and revivalist meetings and (with tiers of benches round a movable ring) for boxing and all-in wrestling. In none of these transmogrifications did it really look like anything but a converted swimming pool. It might, Mr. Wetherall considered, have served as a working model for democracy, for it meant different things at different times and all its seats were equally hard.

Nevertheless it was convenient—and cheap.

He made his way there through the October fog which had come up at dusk. In fog and in darkness the South Bank seemed more tolerable. Its outlines were softened. The lights from the shops and the naphtha flares from the booths made brave splashes of light. The lamps behind the red curtains gave an impression of snugness to the inconvenient little houses.

The hall was packed. The South Borough High School had two other boys besides Donovan in the Area Finale and Mr. Wetherall had meant to go round to the changing room and give them a last-minute word of encouragement. Then, because he had an understanding mind, he sat down in his seat. They would all, he realized, be going through agonies of nervousness, one's first public boxing match was an ordeal beside which any future ordeal, from the dentist's to the electric chair, must pale into insignificance. Anyway, their trainer, a competent and taciturn man, would be with them.

The master of ceremonies entered the ring. "Three rounds of two minutes—no applause during the rounds, please—highest traditions of sportsmanship—no clinching, holding or gouging—best man win," and two tiny boys entered the ring from opposite sides, one with a red sash round his waist, the other with a blue. For the allotted two minutes, and in the most spirited and creditable way, they did their best to destroy each other, and then the bell rang and they sank back into their corners. Mr. Wetherall was close enough to the ring to hear the nearest of the seconds, a gray-haired, earnest man in a sweater, saying, "Ride off his leads on your arms, and cross to the right side of his face," and Blue Sash saying, "O.K., Mr. Braithwaite," when the bell sounded again.

At the close of the bout Blue Sash was proclaimed winner (though whether as a result of the advice he had received, Mr. Wetherall was too inexpert to decide), and his supporters in the hall were threatening the stability of an entire section of the seating, when Mr. Wetherall became aware of his neighbor.

He smelled him first.

Parma violet and after-shave lotion. Then his eyes took him in. Black hair, a white face, and a striking suit of clothes—bold pattern, thick cloth, rolled lapels, stuffed shoulders. A metal green tie. Pointed brown shoes. All the success signals. Looking again it occurred to Mr. Wetherall that he knew him. Pollock, Postgate, Partridge. It began with a P. He conducted a mental roll call. Parry, Parsons, Price. That was more like it. Not Price, though. Prince!

He was so pleased at getting it that he spoke the name aloud. The man turned slowly, and seeing his full face, on which the flesh was beginning to hang, he realized that the man was older than he had first imagined—and also that he was blind in one eye.

All the same, he was sure he was right.

"I'm so sorry," said Mr. Wetherall. "I thought—"

What he thought was lost in a fresh outburst of cheering.

"Can't hear."

"I said," he shouted, "that I thought—"

"Why, it's Mr. Wetherall."

Prince shot out a fat white hand, at the end of a thick wrist. Gold cuff links winked against silk shirt cuff. "How's tricks? Been finding any dead kittens lately?"

This was a reference to a long forgotten, and not very happy episode in Mr. Wetherall's early teaching career at Battersea, and he laughed half-heartedly.

"That's right," said Prince. "Keep the little sods in order. Spare the rod and spoil the child. And between you and me"—Prince leaned forward and a bow wave of Parma violet came ahead of him—"a little more stick in the schools and we shouldn't have so much joovenile delinquency."

"Oh, quite," said Mr. Wetherall. "And what have you been doing since I saw you last?"

"In and out of the ring. You seen my eye? Lost that fighting. Mug's game. Near as a nicker lost the other one too. Then I stopped. S'all right for boys and amachoors. Does 'em good. Not professional, though. They know too much, those professional boys."

"Eighty-eight pounds and under," announced the master of ceremonies. "In the read sash, Peter Dawkin, Walworth Secondary School. In the blue sash, Sam Donovan, South Borough Secondary School—"

From the back of the hall Mr. Wetherall heard the Donovan family giving tongue.

Sam sat in the corner, pretending to listen to what his second was saying, his red hair in striking contrast to his white singlet. Then the bell sounded and the fight was on.

It was the sort of fight which often results where one of the parties has a balance on science and the other a balance on courage. At the end of the first round the front of Sammy's vest was almost as red as his hair. At the end of the second, he had a fast-closing right eye, and even the Donovan family were beginning to sound anxious. In the middle of the third round Sam seemed to collect himself, and hit his opponent once, very, very hard, in the face. After that the opposition crumbled, and he came out a handsome winner.

Mr. Wetherall attended only partly to the fight. He had seen Sammy perform too often to have any serious doubts as to the result. The more active part of his mind was concerned with the man sitting next to him. Everything about him said Money. But not, he felt, very good money. Surely a half-blind boxer, one who had never reached the first flight and had now slipped out of the game altogether, could not be earning a great deal. He might have other jobs, of course.

At that moment—the mass hysteria making all normal speech impossible—Prince leaned across and shouted, "Good boy, that."

"Very," said Mr. Wetherall.

"One of yours, ent he?"

"Yes."

"Plenty of guts."

"It's a thing that runs in the family."

"Patsy's Sammy Donovan's brother, ent he?"

"Yes. Do you know Sergeant Donovan?"

"I've heard of him," said Prince with a grin. "Patsy's a bright boy, too." He consulted an expensive watch. "I gotter run now. Quite like old times seeing you again. Ever you're up west you must come and have a drink at my club."

"Er—certainly," said Mr. Wetherall, slightly surprised. "I'm afraid I don't know—"

"The Atheeneum," said Prince. "Just ask for the Bishop of London. Ta ta."

"One hundred twelve pounds and under," said the announcer.

Mr. Wetherall sat looking thoughtfully after the back of the retreating Prince.

Mr. Wetherall did not go directly home after the match. By making a slight detour he could visit the school, and there were some exam papers he wanted to pick up. He would have to correct them at home (a form of overtime from which schoolmasters suffer a good deal, without the corresponding advantage of getting paid at overtime rates). He collected the papers and found a letter, which had evidently arrived by the evening post. It was from the Managing Director of Lithography & Artists Services, Ltd., who said that he would be only too pleased to take on Crowdy as a paid junior assistant at a starting salary of £3.0.0. a week and how was Mrs. Wetherall keeping?

It capped the end of a rather successful day. All of his boys had won their bouts and now it looked as if he had done what he could to place Crowdy's foot on the bottom rung of the ladder—that narrow, unstable, overcrowded ladder which leads up to eminence in the arts.

Warmed by this glow of altruism he decided that he would break the good news to the Crowdy family at once. By making a further small detour he could go past their house, and then catch his bus one stop further along.

Outside, the fog had thickened. He made his way into the old Kent Road, crossed it and, after a moment's hesitation, chose one of the side streets running along the northern side of the Bricklayers Arms railway goods yard. As he went by, he stopped for a moment to look through an open doorway at the complicated hell within. A huge, concrete-floored building with concrete loading ramps round three of the sides. Single unshaded electric lights fighting a losing battle with the fog. Vans loading and unloading. Hurrying figures, the familiars of the place, in leather peaked caps, and overalls, which might originally have been of any color, now blackened to a drab uniformity by grease and dirt. Above the throng, in detached hutches round the perimeter, the dispatchers and parcels clerks, slapping on labels and making entries in books. And, all around, an ocean of parcels, packages, bales, boxes, coops, crates and cartons: things tied lengthways in bundles, things wrapped in sacks, things wrapped in straw. Where, among all this, might one tiny food parcel be lying?

He became aware that a railway policeman was standing just inside the entrance, watching him.

"They're very busy tonight," he said.

"You ought to see them at Christmas," said the policeman.

"Well, good night."

The policeman said nothing to this.

The Crowdy house was discovered without much difficulty. It was a thin and dirty house, in a terrace of thin and dirty houses. The front door, at the top of a flight of steps which spanned the area across a flying buttress of concrete, was ajar. Mr. Wetherall pulled the bell but this proved to be a waste of time, since it was quite obviously not attached to anything. He knocked, without result, pushed the door open and went in.

Usually he was most scrupulous about such things but he felt that, as a bearer of good tidings, it would probably be forgiven him; also he was late for his supper.

He found himself in a narrow hall, bare of all furniture

and walled with a glazed paper which looked like oilcloth and was yellow from age rather than design. There was a narrow strip of carpet on the floor, worn nearly through, but sufficient to deaden his footsteps as he made his way toward a crack of light in the doorway at the end.

It would be the family room. He stopped again to knock. There was a sound of a chair scraping, and a rather startled voice said, "Who's that?" He pushed open the door. Crowdy was alone in the room. He was sitting at a table with a piece of paper pinned out in front of him and he had been doing something with pens, steel rulers and India ink. From where Mr. Wetherall stood he could see the end of one word—it looked like "-AGE" followed by "PA-" which was the beginning of another word. Crowdy's face was as white as a sheet. He stood, saying nothing.

"I'm sorry to butt in," said Mr. Wetherall. "I only came to tell you—"

He got no further. The door behind him burst open. Before he could turn he was seized by the collar and run out into the passage. When he got free and managed to turn round, he saw that it was Mr. Crowdy. He had only met him once before. His first idea was that he was drunk.

The heavy face was dark red, the eyes staring.

"Get out of here and stay out. Keep going."

"Really, I—"

"Bloody snoopers."

"I only came in to tell you—"

"Who asked you to come in?"

"Well, no one—"

"Then go out and keep out. And keep your bloody great nose out of my house. Sticking it in where it isn't asked for. Snoopers, schoolmasters—"

Conscious that the steep front steps, with a drop into the area on either side, might not be the best place for a harassed retreat Mr. Wetherall broke clear and ran from the house. When he reached the pavement he turned. Mr. Crowdy had not followed him. He was standing in the doorway—his face still red and his mouth working.

"I must protest—" began Mr. Wetherall.

"Keep it for the boys," said Mr. Crowdy. The door slammed.

Mr. Wetherall walked very fast down the street. His breath was coming in gasps, as if he had been running. His heart was thudding and his mouth felt dry. Real, deliberate, unprovoked rudeness can be quite as shocking as physical violence. He felt as if his face had been smacked. He walked for ten minutes before he could trust himself to get onto a bus.

Ayton mumbled something which sounded like "Ruddy lot." "Keep it for the boys," said Mr. Chowne. He continued.

Mr. Wetherall walked very fast down the street. He

THREE

South of the River:
Jock's Pull-In for Carmen

A historian looking back on Mr. Wetherall's life from the vantage point of complete knowledge would easily see that the key to almost everything of importance in it was a quiet, inoffensive, persistent obstinacy.

For instance, had it not been for obstinacy he would have been a form master—might have been a housemaster —in some leading school.

On leaving Oxford in 1923 he had spent the regulation eighteen months at a teachers' training college and had then taken a post as history master in one of the smaller public schools. On arrival, his first surprise had been the discovery that he had apparently done the wrong thing in going to a teaching college at all. It was, he discovered, to his credit that he had spent four years at Marlborough, and even more creditable that he had followed this up with a further three years at Oxford; but the attempt to fit himself for his chosen career (a gilding, as it were, of the perfectly formed lily) by actually learning to teach was not an asset at all. "After all," as a large undergraduate just down from Brasenose had remarked, "there's nothing to this teaching business. If you play a decent game of rugger they won't rag you—and all the stuff you've got to teach them's in some book or other. You've got a copy. They haven't. That's all there is to it."

When Mr. Wetherall started, mildly, to talk of the technique of instruction it began to be rumored in the staffroom that he was odd.

Now all this, in the normal way, would have mattered very little. In fact the hearty young man from B.N.C. left at the end of the term to devote his undoubted talents to stock farming in Canada, and Mr. Wetherall might quite easily have settled down and become, in a few years, as ivy-covered as the school tower itself. But it was at this point that his obstinacy stepped in. He argued that, having devoted time and money to a training which was apparently not required in the job he was in, he had better find a job in which it *was* wanted. In other words, having acquired an asset, he would take it to a market where it had value. He therefore departed, at the end of 1926, for a job in a secondary school in Hornsey.

It was neither an easy place nor an easy period for such an experiment, but on the whole he had enjoyed it very much.

He had become an intellectual socialist; had picked up and in turn dropped the Communist Party and, later, the Oxford Movement; had found himself agreeably able to despise his friends who taught in luxury schools; and had started writing detective stories. When these were published in magazines, which was rarely, so much of the proceeds as his literary agent allowed him to keep formed a welcome addition to the Burnham Scale—all the more welcome when he met and, after a courtship conducted chiefly at the Promenade Concerts, married Alice Golightly.

Here again his obstinacy took charge, for when his friends combined to assure him that marriage was quite impossible on an assistant master's salary, he at once confounded them by obtaining the headmastership of a junior school at Enfield.

On the outbreak of war he made several quite genuine attempts to get into the fight, but being shortsighted, nearly thirty-eight, and in a reserved occupation, he had experienced very little return for his patriotic feelings and had been evacuated, with his school, to Leamington Spa.

In this dreary time he must have done reasonably well, for it was on his return to London in 1946 that he was offered the headmastership of one of the largest and most up-to-date secondary boys' schools in London, the South Borough.

Mr. Wetherall, who was genuinely modest, wondered more than once why the choice should have fallen on him.

At breakfast, on the morning following his visit to the Crowdy house, he reflected on the happenings of the night before. Seen through the filter of a night's rest, and in the calmer light of morning, they had lost a little of their sting.

He thought, on the whole, that Mr. Crowdy had either been drunk, or had been suffering under the stress of a strong emotion. Working-class parents did odd things. He remembered one who, whenever he had had a row with his employers, used to come and weep in the school playground; and another who, at the bidding of some obscure complex, periodically sent his two small boys to school dressed as girls and his two girls to theirs dressed as boys.

No doubt a word with Crowdy would straighten things out.

The postman had brought a letter from Mr. Bullfyne, his literary agent. It was an ominously large envelope and contained, as he had feared, the rejected manuscript of *Death by Big Ben.*

"You might like," wrote Mr. Bullfyne, who seemed to take a sadistic pleasure in passing on such comments, "to hear what Messrs. Huddle and Stockton have to say about your story."

Mr. Wetherall glanced through the criticisms. It was as he had feared. "Too theoretical—must have more action—

does anyone ever really solve a mystery by sitting about in a dressing gown?"

"I was afraid that dressing gown business was getting a bit dated," he said.

"Why not make him play a violin?" suggested his wife.

"I think that's been done too," said Mr. Wetherall.

When he reached the school he was plunged at once into a sea of administrative worries. Gang warfare had broken out in the lower forms. The cleaners were on strike on account of the mess in the cloakroom. Mr. Wetherall thought he detected a connection between these two recurrent items. He made a note on his pad, "Beat McClure. Sack Mrs. Parsons." The Schools Medical Officer of Health proposed to visit him to discuss compulsory inoculation against chicken pox.

It was the eleven o'clock break before he got round to thinking about Crowdy, and sent Peggy to fetch him. She returned five minutes later to report that there was no sign of him.

"What's happened to him?"

"He didn't turn up this morning. I expect this may be something to do with it. Roberts brought it. He lives in the next street to Crowdy."

Mr. Wetherall opened the envelope. It was one which had apparently been delivered to Mr. Crowdy with some Pools literature, and Mr. Crowdy had simply crossed out his own name and address and had written on it, in a curiously clerkly hand, "The Headmaster." The note inside was brief. It said, "My son has chicken pox and will not be at school for approx. 3 weeks. Yrs sincerely."

"Hmp!" said Mr. Wetherall. "Is there any chicken pox in the Bricklayers district, Peggy?"

"Search me," said Peggy. "There's whooping cough in the Albany Road and mumps at Waterloo."

Mr. Wetherall said "Hmp" again. He took down a fat and shabby folder, alphabetically indexed, ran his finger through it, and picked out a card.

Crowdy's father, he saw, was described as a dispatch

clerk, employed by British Railways, and working at Crossways goods station.

He slipped the card back into the folder and placed with it the note he had just received. He was about to throw the envelope away when he saw something written on the back, also in Mr. Crowdy's handwriting. "Jock's Pull-In for Carmen." After a moment's thought he put the envelope with the letter.

After that he taught the senior class an hour of unusually absent-minded history and, finding that he had an early class that afternoon which prevented him going home, slipped out to get himself some lunch.

Outside the side gate he bumped into Luigi. The little man was in wait for him.

"Oh, Mr. Wetherall."

Mr. Wetherall withdrew himself from a reverie of Mr. Crowdy, the Schools Medical Officer of Health and the Duke of Wellington.

"Mr. Wetherall, I got to speak to you."

"Privately, do you mean?"

"Yes. We speak private."

Mr. Wetherall hesitated. He wanted his lunch. Then he said, "All right, Luigi, come along." He led the way back into the school and opened the door of a small classroom on the ground floor that he guessed would be empty at that hour.

"We can sit down here for a minute if you like," he said. Luigi collapsed into one of the desks. With his wide eyes and his hair on end he looked not unlike a large, nervous schoolboy but Mr. Wetherall felt no desire to laugh. Luigi was suffering from a complaint which he could diagnose without difficulty. He was afraid. He was empty with fear, like a deflated brown paper bag.

"What is it?" he said.

"Mr. Wetherall, you must stop it. I should not have spoken to you." He hammered the top of the desk in his earnestness. "You must stop it at once."

"Stop what?"

"It was stupid of me. I was mad. I said certain things—" he swallowed hard—"they were not true. Now you must stop."

"Look here," said Mr. Wetherall. "I want my lunch. If you can't talk sense, I shall have to ask you to go. What am I supposed to stop?"

"You went to see Sergeant Donovan?"

"Well—yes, I did."

"You went also to see Mr. Crowdy. I know. You must not do it, Mr. Wetherall. Please."

Mr. Wetherall was trying to adjust himself to the slight nervous reflex which everyone must experience when they find that, unknown to themselves, their movements have been of interest to others.

"I suppose it's no good telling you," he said at last, "that there was absolutely no connection whatever between going to see Sergeant Donovan, and Crowdy."

"Mr. Wetherall, please don't do it. I—I shall get into trouble. I been in trouble already."

"Yes," said Mr. Wetherall. He could guess about that trouble. It was not necessarily the sort of trouble which would leave a black eye or a split lip: but it was real trouble, all the same.

"All right," he said. "Whatever it is you think I've been doing, I promise I won't do it again."

Luigi's relief at this rather qualified concession was astonishing. "That's right," he said. "Now we all forget about it, eh?" He jumped up, shook Mr. Wetherall's hand, and shot out of the room.

Mr. Wetherall followed, but more slowly. He hardly noticed what he was given to eat for lunch.

He was fully aware of the curious strands of his own character. But the fact that he recognized them, as any toper or drug addict may recognize and deplore his own weaknesses, did not make him competent to counteract them.

He knew, for instance, that he was afflicted with the most malignant type of obstinacy. Did fate so much as nudge him in one direction, he would automatically strive to move in an opposite one. He could no more help doing this than a frog's leg could help jumping when an electric current was passed through it. It was immaterial that this opposite direction might be one in which he had no real desire to go—one in which every rational faculty told him he ought not to go. It was the spirit which used to take Christian martyrs into the arena, and which forces small wage-earners to thrust themselves twice daily into impossibly crowded underground trains. It has led to quite a few unsuitable marriages.

After paying the bill he walked back in the direction of the Crowdy house. It would have been no use asking him why he did this, because he had no idea himself.

The street was empty and quiet, and the house looked inoffensive. Mr. Wetherall knocked, waited, knocked again and then waited for a long time. I'll count twenty, he told his conscience, and then if no one comes I'll give it up. He had reached fifteen when he heard a faint shuffling, as of slippered feet. Then the door opened a few inches and a very old woman looked out, a faded, dusty amalgam of whites and grays and blacks.

"Is Mr. Crowdy at home?"

"No, he ent," said the old lady.

"Is his son in the house?"

"No, he ent in neither."

"Is there anyone at home?"

"Not except for me there ent a creature in the house."

The lie was at once given to this statement by the appearance of a sleek black cat, which shot through the narrow opening and disappeared down the area.

"There now," said the old lady, "Tibby's out. He won't come back now till tomorrow morning."

"Do you know where they are?"

"They all gone to work."

"What?" said Mr. Wetherall. "The boy as well? But he's—"

"He's gone fifteen," said the lady, who seemed to have

her wits about her. "Why shouldn't he work? I started earning a wage when I was eight," she added.

"I—well—it can't be helped." Mr. Wetherall felt frus-
trated. "I'll come back this evening."

"You're the schoolmaster, ent you?"

"Yes."

"I'll tell him you called." She parted her gums in a smile
which might have been malicious, but was probably merely
friendly.

Mr. Wetherall walked back to the school, deep in
thought. When he got there he sent for Peggy.

"Do we know anyone on the railway?" he asked.

"Plenty, I should think," said Peggy. "It's a favorite job
round here."

"Crossways?"

"I'll have a look. Any particular sort of person you had
in mind?"

"Well—I don't want a boy who just joined last week as
a porter. Someone with a bit of seniority—"

Peggy was back within five minutes. "William Fisher's the
man you want."

"Bill Fisher. Yes." Mr. Wetherall had to go back nearly
twenty years to place him. A fat, cheerful boy, always late
for school but popular with everyone.

"He's administrative grade," said Peggy. "I think that
means some sort of staff manager. And he was at Crossways
when we last had a note of him. That's the number. Extension 341."

Extension 341 admitted that it had heard of Bill Fisher.
It rather thought he had left Crossways and gone to Waterloo. It suggested an extension number at Waterloo.

This extension was even more helpful. It thought Fisher
was definitely at Waterloo. It suggested another extension.

Here Mr. Wetherall found his man.

After he had introduced himself he mentioned what was
in his mind. Like all schoolmasters and clergymen he was
skilled in asking extraordinary favors of comparative strang-
ers. He decided to stick, as closely as possible, to the truth.

"You see," he said, "this boy—he's just leaving—I'm not happy about him. Crowdy's the name. He's got some sort of job on the railway—at Crossways, I think—with his father. I wanted to talk to someone who could give me the form—"

"Delighted," said Fisher. "Was there anything particular you had in mind?"

Mr. Wetherall said it was difficult to talk about it over the telephone.

Fisher thought this over. What, he suggested, did Mr. Wetherall say to a talk over a bite somewhere that evening.

Mr. Wetherall said that would suit him very well.

"I'm off at six," said Fisher. "I usually have a snack at a place by the Elephant—I don't suppose it's much in your line—Jock's Café. A lot of railwaymen use it."

Something stirred in Mr. Wetherall's memory.

"Jock's Pull-In for Carmen," he said.

"That's right. You know the place? Say six-thirty."

"Splendid," said Mr. Wetherall. "Splendid." He rang off. He had the distinct feeling that he might have started something. The odd thing was that, at the time, he felt quite pleased about it.

Jock's Pull-In was more pretentious than its name suggested. It was a long, bright room, full of marble-topped iron-legged tables. It was crowded with railwaymen, mostly outdoor men and drivers. The place had its own car park, formed of a blitzed site, at the back of the restaurant, and this was packed with vans and trailers.

Fighting down the feeling that he was making his way into a club to which he did not belong, Mr. Wetherall steered a course down the center gangway and got in behind one of the few empty tables.

He studied the menu which offered "Egg and chips, Sausage and chips, Bacon and chips, Steak and chips. Or Mixed, with or without tomato."

That seemed fair enough.

"Eggs, bacon, sausages and chips," said Mr. Wetherall to the girl. "No tomato."

"And coffee."

"Yes—and coffee."

"And bread and butter."

"All right. And bread and butter."

The girl disappeared and Mr. Wetherall took a quick look round the crowded room.

The proprietor was a fat man, with jowls like a bulldog, small bloodshot eyes, and a thin fringe of gray hair which lay like a moat round an island of mottled flesh. The customers called him Pop.

He was serving one section of tables himself, as well as handling the cash register. There was a second girl who operated the tea and coffee urns and served another section of tables. The girl who had taken his order seemed to be just a waitress. The three of them were running the place on their own, though there were no doubt slaves behind the service door slicing countless hundredweights of potatoes, and frying numberless eggs and sausages and rashers of bacon in unfathomable seas of fat.

It was clearly not a place for people without a talent for hard work.

When the food arrived it was excellent. Mr. Wetherall added a name to the mental list which all Londoners carry of good and unexpected eating places. The rashers were real thick, prewar ones with an even division of fat and lean. The butter was real butter.

At that moment Bill Fisher arrived. It took him a little time to reach the table, because he seemed to know almost everyone in the room.

"Well, and how are you, Mr. Wetherall? Nice to see you. You've got yours, have you? That's right. You start away. Pop always does you well here. You oughter try his steaks—"

"Steaks?" said Mr. Wetherall faintly.

"Steaks it is. And not gee-gee neither. Ah—there's the girl. And how are things tonight, Miss Russell?"

"The name, Mr. Fisher, is Bessie."

"Well, there now. And I thought it might be Jane. You

know, Bessie, with a figure like yours you oughter be on the stage."

"It's only the linoleum that keeps me from the boards, Mr. Fisher."

"Smart too," said Mr. Fisher. "Better than Bob Hope. Makes up her own gags. I'll have the same as this gentleman, Bessie."

"It's a popular place," ventured Mr. Wetherall.

"The Railwayman's Arms, you might call it. Or the Van Drivers' Home from Home. It's handy, see. And Pop used to be on the railway. In the old London Brighton and South Coast. He used to walk in front of the engine with a red flag, didn't you, Pop?"

"That's right, Mr. Fisher. I used to clear the cows off the line. Always glad to see a friend of yours—"

The last part of the sentence seemed to have a question mark at the end of it.

"More than a friend," said Fisher. "This is my old schoolmaster. Many's the time he's tanned the hide off me, Pop."

"I expect you earned it."

"Of course, I earned it. I was the worst boy in the school."

"Well, any time you pass, Mr. Wetherall, just drop in. I can give you as good to eat here as anywhere up west."

"Thank you very much," said Mr. Wetherall. "I'm sure you can." If he spoke a little absently—and if he also failed to hear some of the early part of Fisher's conversation —it may have been because he was trying to work out how Pop had suddenly become aware of his name.

". . . just a paster," said Fisher.

"I'm sorry, I didn't quite catch that."

"He was a label sticker. Worked in the Forwarding Office."

"Who did?"

"Old Crowdy," said Fisher patiently. "The chap you were asking about."

"And that was at Crossways?"

"That's right. All the stuff that comes in goes through the Forwarding Office. The clerks mark it up—Special Delivery, C.O.D., Carriage Forward—whatever it might be. Pasters we call 'em."

"I see," said Mr. Wetherall. He explained, with some suppressions, the details of Crowdy's case.

"Seems a bit of a waste to me," said Fisher. "If the boy's got talent, like you said."

"He's over fifteen," said Mr. Wetherall. "I can't stop him if he wants to go—or rather, if his father wants to take him."

"Dispatch clerk isn't much of a job. Mind you, it's cushy. He won't come to any harm. But he won't get fat on it, neither. If he's got a good headpiece he wants to get onto the administrative side. Like," Fisher added without any shrinking modesty, "me."

"Yes," said Mr. Wetherall. "I was afraid it might be rather a dead end."

"Can't you talk to his old man?"

"I tried that," said Mr. Wetherall. He told Fisher something about that.

"Well, that's a rum go, if you like," said Fisher. "Old Harry Crowdy fly off the handle. I'd never have thought it of him. With another chap I'd suggest he might have been tight, but drink don't take Harry Crowdy that way—it mellows him. That's the way it is with some people—"

"Look here," said Mr. Wetherall—he didn't mean to say it abruptly; it was just that the thought had come into his mind rather suddenly—"is there really such a lot of stealing on the railways?"

Fisher didn't answer that immediately. When he did there was a noticeable shade of reserve in his voice.

"There's quite a bit," he said.

Mr. Wetherall realized that some explanation was due. "It's not just curiosity," he said. "I lost a food parcel myself last week."

"You're sure it was sent?"

"That's what everybody says," said Mr. Wetherall. "That's

what the police wanted to know. Yes. I am sure. But I couldn't prove it."

"You've been to the police, then."

"I reported it. They weren't very enthusiastic."

"They wouldn't be," said Fisher. He laughed, but he didn't sound amused. "It's tricky. If they put a foot wrong on a thing like that they get up against the union."

"Oh," said Mr. Wetherall. It was a new factor.

"There's a lot of pilfering everywhere. Docks, road transport. Warehouses. I don't suppose the railwaymen are worse than anyone else. It's just that they got special opportunities. A lot of the stuff they handle's scarce stuff. There's a market for it, see. And it isn't like putting it in a warehouse. If it goes from a warehouse you know who's responsible. On the railway it goes through a lot of hands."

"Yes," said Mr. Wetherall. "There are bound to be losses. I can see that. But is it just a lot of casual pilfering or is it organized?"

"Sauce," said a voice.

A tall man had drifted up, as silently as a snowcloud. Mr. Wetherall got a fleeting impression of a scrubbed red face, close-cropped hair, light blue eyes, and a pair of large red hands. One of these hands came over Mr. Wetherall's shoulder and picked up the sauce bottle from the middle of the table.

For just a moment longer than was absolutely necessary the newcomer remained there, leaning on the table; he looked at Fisher, who opened his mouth to say something then shut it again.

Then the man was gone, as suddenly as he had come, threading his way back to a table at the door.

"Why should he bother to come all the way over here?" said Mr. Wetherall. "There's plenty of sauce on the other tables."

"Oh, he's a character," said Fisher shortly. "Guardsman, they call him. Believe he was in the Guards once." As he spoke, and with great rapidity, he was pushing the last few chips into his mouth. Now he swallowed the remains of his coffee, stood up, said, "I'll settle with Pop next time. I've got to run now—" and he was gone.

Mr. Wetherall sat still. He suddenly felt very much alone.

Panic is a curious thing. Like the tide advancing over a salt marsh, it comes by strange channels. One moment it is not there. The next and it is everywhere.

Suddenly everyone in the room seemed to be talking louder than was necessary. One group at the door, where the Guardsman sat, with his arm half round the man next to him, was particularly noisy.

Mr. Wetherall looked round. It seemed to him that people were avoiding his eye.

He forced himself to sit back in his chair and to breathe slowly. It was like being at the top of a precipice. If you sat quite still, after a time, confidence returned.

The girl was serving the table next to him. He called her, and found he had to call twice, because his mouth was dry. She came quite readily.

"How much?"

"Eggs, bacon, sausages, coffee, bread and butter. That's four shillings."

Mr. Wetherall had two half crowns ready in his pocket and he slipped them to the girl. "Keep the change," he said, "and tell me is there anywhere here I can telephone?"

"Through that door." She pointed to a door in the corner, beyond the service door.

When the girl had gone Mr. Wetherall picked up his half-empty cup and sipped at the cold coffee. "I shall count ten," he said to himself.

Then he put the cup down, got quickly to his feet, and walked to the door. Beyond it was a passage, dimly lighted. He went along it. At the end the passage turned. To the right were some stairs, going down. On the left was a door, clearly an outside door. Mr. Wetherall put his hand to the handle and uttered a prayer, which was answered. The door was not locked. It led out into the car park.

As he went through it and closed it behind him, he

thought he heard footsteps coming along the passage he had just left.

There was no light at all in the car park. He could make out the shapes of lorries all about him, and he felt his way past the tailboards of two of them, and then along between the side of a third one and the wall. He felt safe in the dark. He stood while his breathing steadied, and he wondered if he had been behaving like a fool.

There was a long, spreading fan of light. Someone had opened the door. Then footsteps on the gravel. It was two men. They came straight out, walked to the front of the lorries and stopped a few paces away from where Mr. Wetherall was standing, squeezed between the outside lorry and the wall.

"As long as they aren't going to move this one—" he thought.

The nearer man was Pop. He recognized his voice, without being able to hear what he said. Then, as the other man moved, his nose picked up a well-known scent. It was Parma violet. That could mean Prince. Mr. Wetherall hardly felt surprised. If Pop was engaged in buying black market food there was nothing extraordinary in Prince being one of the people selling it to him.

They were using a torch inside the cab of the next lorry but one. The murmur of voices went on. Then the cab door slammed. Pop said, "Where are you for? The Aldershot Ladies?" And Prince's voice, quite amiable, saying, "Mind your own bloody business, Pop." Headlights flicked on, the engine started, the lorry moved forward, swung right, right again and was gone. Pop walked slowly back and slammed the door behind him.

Mr. Wetherall wasted no more time. A minute later he was in the High Street, walking fast.

It was nearly eight o'clock. The shops were shut—except for the greengrocers which seemed to observe laws of their own. But there was still plenty of life. The last-house queue was moving into the cinema. The pubs were cheerful splashes of light.

On impulse Mr. Wetherall stopped at the first pub he came to and went in. It was small, snug and almost empty, and there was a coal fire. He bought himself a brandy and drank it. It tasted all right. He ordered another and took this one to the fire and sat down.

He had things to think about. If he went home his wife would talk to him and that would stop him thinking about them. He could not, by any stretch of imagination, talk to her about it. He had discovered that early in his married life. Although he was very genuinely in love with her, he could not talk to her about things that mattered. Perhaps all married people were like that.

The figures of Prince and the Guardsman belonged to another place. A separate place. A place which must be kept separate. It was a world in which Pop and Bill Fisher and Sergeant Donovan moved easily. It was their jungle. It had no connection at all with Brinkman Road and the water rate and the butcher's bill. It must have no connection.

How on earth had he himself got involved in it? It had started with a food parcel. How absurd to take so much trouble over a food parcel, which might contain anything from dried apricots to black-currant syrup.

Prince, who had come in softly and seated himself at the table, opposite to Mr. Wetherall, nodded his agreement. "Look for yourself," he said.

There was the food parcel, open on the table. Mr. Wetherall looked into it. He found himself able to do this without changing his position, merely by elongating his neck. It was an odd sensation. The contents of the parcel were disappointing. Bottles and bottles of black-current syrup.

A hand fell on his shoulder, and he found himself being shaken roughly.

". . . go an' fall into the fire," said a voice.

"Grmph," said Mr. Wetherall.

"Never have let him have that second brandy if I'd known," said the barmaid. "Respectable-looking party, too."

"What do you mean?" said Mr. Wetherall. "Just fell asleep."

"You can't fall asleep in here."

"Allow me to explain."

"Fresh air's what you want."

Mr. Wetherall found himself in the High Street. He was no longer depressed. His little nap must have done him good. He felt fit and wide awake.

He decided he would call on the Crowdys.

By the time he reached the area of the Bricklayers Arms a little of the warmth of the fire and the brandy was out of him. Nevertheless he persevered. He climbed the steps. The front door was shut this time, but there was a light showing through the fanlight. He knocked. Almost at once, footsteps approached and the door swung open and Mr. Crowdy, in shirt sleeves and slippers, stood blinking out into the night.

"Oh, it's Wetherall."

No sooner had he spoken than Mr. Wetherall realized two things. The first was that Mr. Crowdy was very drunk. The second was that Bill Fisher had been perfectly correct. Mr. Crowdy was a man whom drink mellowed.

"Come in, Wetherall. I was hoping you'd call back. Come right in."

"I can't stay—"

"I was a bit short last time. Come right in here and sid-down. A bit put out. I'd like to say I was sorry."

"Oh, that's quite all right," said Mr. Wetherall. "Well, only just a drop." He was not a very experienced drinker but he realized that rum and brandy were unlikely to go well together.

"I was upset. Trouble at work. Plenty of trouble about these days. Don't have to go out and look for it."

"I'm sure you're right."

"Let me tell you something. Take one step off the middle of the road and you're up to your neck in the muck."

Not being quite sure what this new departure was about Mr. Wetherall contented himself with a sympathetic grunt.

"The truest saying ever spoken. What a tangled web we weave."

"When first we practice to deceive," concluded Mr.

Wetherall, with a feeling that he was taking part in some round game.

"That's right. Practice to deceive. That's it."

Mr. Crowdy's great red face was glowing under the conflicting pressure of drink, self-pity and an overmastering desire to confide in somebody. Indeed, there is no telling what he might not have said if Mr. Wetherall had not unfortunately changed the subject by asking, "Where's Peter?"

"In bed," said Mr. Crowdy. "Where-else-woody-be-this-timer-night?"

"I really meant, why isn't he coming to school?"

"Got chicken pox."

"But hasn't he been going to work with you at the station?"

"That's right."

"But how can he go to work if he's got chicken pox?"

"It's not the infectious sort."

"Well," said Mr. Wetherall, doubtfully. "If it isn't the infectious sort why doesn't he come to school?"

"Can't come to school with chicken pox. 'Gainst the law."

It occurred to Mr. Wetherall that he was not making much progress. He also recognized, with the inner clarity of a man who doesn't drink very much, that although he was sober at the moment one more glass of rum was going to finish him.

He got up, shook hands with Mr. Crowdy and, without being conscious of any precise interval of time, found himself in the street looking up at a policeman.

"Nice night, officer," he said affably.

"Lovely, sir," said the policeman. "Were you going anywhere?"

"Going to catch a bus. Have you ever considered, officer, what a prolific word 'catch' is? Catch a bus—catch a mouse—catch a crab—"

"Perhaps I'd better come with you," said the policeman.

"Delighted," said Mr. Wetherall. What a pleasant man! As they walked Mr. Wetherall told him a number of interesting and little-known facts about Wellington's campaigns in the Peninsula. On the bus he went to sleep. The conductor, who knew him by sight, woke him at the right stop.

When he reached the house he found his wife waiting on the stairs. As soon as she saw him she burst into tears.

"Now then, Alice," said Mr. Wetherall sternly. "What's all this about?"

"I was worried."

"I'm often late on Wednesday. And you knew I was getting my meal out—"

"It was the man—"

"What man?"

"A man telephoned, about an hour ago. He said he hoped you were all right."

"What sort of man—"

"He hadn't got a very nice voice," said Mrs. Wetherall. "I asked him who he was and why should he think you weren't all right. He just laughed."

"Laughed, did he?" said Mr. Wetherall thoughtfully.

"Yes. Then he rang off."

FOUR

The Morning After

Mr. Wetherall went to school on Thursday morning with one fixed intention. That was to forget about the events of the last three days.

The weather was helpful to such resolution. After the fogs and uncertainties of the previous days it was an autumn morning which could have sat as a model for all autumn mornings. The sun shone down through a layer of mist which filtered the sunbeams into defined and spiky rays. The sky seemed pale and drained of color. It looked like the background of an Italian religious painting.

On his desk Mr. Wetherall found a note that Colonel Bond had telephoned and would telephone again. Peggy had added "Received 9:12" and Mr. Wetherall looked uneasily at the message.

Colonel Bond was a man who had brought to a high pitch the art of putting other people into their places. It was a technique which Mr. Wetherall had often observed in action. It was founded on the tactical principle of never, in any circumstances, giving an opinion of his own. If a question was put to him so directly that it demanded an answer he would say, "Well, really!" or "I wouldn't know" in tones of such haughty surprise that the questioner often apologized for having been so gauche as to put the question at all. Though he still nourished his military title he had not seen khaki since 1919. As well as being a retired Colonel he was a retired accountant, a retired J.P. and, at the moment, Chairman of the General Purposes Sub-Committee which, under the direction of the Schools Committee, looked after the affairs of South Borough Secondary School.

By and large he was about the heaviest cross that Mr. Wetherall had to bear.

It suddenly occurred to him that the excitements of the past few days had postponed a number of little jobs that he had intended to put in hand before his next meeting with the Colonel. There was the revised program for evening "Supplementaries"—always a ticklish matter; there was the minute on staff discipline (the Colonel had encountered one of the junior masters smoking in the corridor); there was the census of boys with unremoved tonsils—

"A lady to see you," said Peggy.

"Oh."

"No need to straighten your tie. This girl friend won't see seventy again. I put her in the small classroom. She wouldn't come upstairs. She says it's important."

"All right," said Mr. Wetherall.

In the classroom—it was the same one in which he had talked to Luigi—he found old Mrs. Crowdy.

"He's dead," she said.

Mr. Wetherall looked at her stupidly.

"Fell over a bridge at the main line intersection and broke himself up."

Mr. Wetherall battled with the fear that had got hold of him.

"Peter—?"

"No. No. Not the boy. His father."

"When did it happen?"

"This morning. He goes off to work at six with the boy The boy's back home now. I come straight along—"

She had come straight along, on her feet. An adventurous journey for an old lady. When in trouble, go to the school-master or the parson.

"Rent's paid to the end of the week," she said, "then we'll have to move."

Mr. Wetherall looked at her helplessly.

"What are you going to do?"

"I shall be all right." She spoke with the authority of one who has survived for three quarters of a century the level of bare subsistence. "It's the boy—"

"I can give him a bed. For a night or two, anyway. After that I can probably fix something." It was the sort of arrangement he had had to make more than once before, in the recurrent crises which occurred in the lives of his pupils. "What about family?"

"I'm all the family he's got," said the old lady. "I never heard he had no other. His mother was from Wales. Might be some family there. They'll take some getting hold of."

"That's all right. I have to ask. I've seen trouble caused that way before." He got a bit of paper and wrote on it "I, Mrs.—first name'll do—Amelia Crowdy, being the paternal grandmother and, to the best of my knowledge, the only surviving relative of Peter Crowdy, agree to placing him in the custody of the headmaster of South Borough High School until such time as permanent arrangements can be made for him."

He read this out to Mrs. Crowdy, who repeated "paternal grandmother" proudly to herself, nodded her head and signed her name with surprising clarity.

"You know my address," said Mr. Wetherall. "There, I'll write it down for you. Tell Peter to get his things together and go straight along. He can take a bus. I'll telephone my wife—"

When she had gone he went back to his study. He placed the paper in the Crowdy folder, noticing as he did so the last letter which Mr. Crowdy had sent him and the envelope with the scribbled note on the back "Jock's Pull-In for Carmen." In the press of events it had slipped his memory. Now he pulled the envelope out and sat looking at it.

"Sergeant Donovan," announced Peggy formally. She spoiled the effect by adding, "Wipe your feet, Patsy, there's a boy. I just swept the carpet this morning—"

"Come in, Sergeant. Put the engaged notice up, would you, Peggy."

"I shan't keep you long, I hope."

"About Crowdy?"

Sergeant Donovan turned sharply. Some feeling showed in his eyes.

"Who told you that, Mr. Wetherall?"

"I had old Mrs. Crowdy round here just now. Poor old soul. She says she can look after herself. I've taken the boy off her hands till we can fix something."

"I see." Sergeant Donovan sounded disconcerted. He had come to say something, to take a certain line with Mr. Wetherall, and he was out of his stride.

"Was it an accident?"

"I suppose you could walk over a three-foot parapet if you had enough on your mind."

"What sort of thing do you mean?"

"That's something I hoped *you* might be able to tell *me*," said Sergeant Donovan, "seeing you've been twice to his house lately."

"Three times," said Mr. Wetherall. "I was there last night, too."

"Ah. Were you now?" Something which, by a stretch of the imagination, might have been the beginning of a grin broke the grim face. "You wouldn't by any chance have been the talkative gentleman that Timmins saw back to his bus about half past ten?"

"I was not aware—"

"Highly instructive, I'm given to understand. It's all in his book. You didn't know that policemen were authors, did you? Everything that happens to them, big or little, it all goes into the book. Makes funny reading sometimes—"

"No doubt," said Mr. Wetherall stiffly.

"Well now, what did you and Mr. Crowdy find to talk about?"

"Let me ask you a question for a change. Why are you interested in Crowdy?"

"We're always interested in people who get themselves killed." The smile gapped again.

"Yes," said Mr. Wetherall. "But he hadn't been killed last night. Were you watching him? How did you know I'd been to see him?"

"Peggy told me."

Mr. Wetherall considered. He didn't believe it. But it was just conceivable that it was true.

"All right," he said. "For what it's worth, I'll tell you about it. I first went to see Crowdy on the night of the boxing—that was Tuesday night. I went to tell him that I'd fixed up a job for Peter—that's the boy. He threw me out. For absolutely no reason at all, that I could see. He wouldn't have schoolmasters snooping and prying round his house. That sort of thing. I thought at the time he was drunk. I don't think so now. I believe he was frightened."

"Ah," said Sergeant Donovan. "Yes."

"Next day Peter didn't turn up at school. There was some cock and bull story about him having chicken pox. I went round in the afternoon to find out about it. There was only old Mrs. Crowdy in. She said come in the evening, so I went round again, after I'd made a few inquiries about him first." He told Sergeant Donovan about Bill Fisher and Jock's Pull-In for Carmen. He omitted any mention of his own panicky conduct, but otherwise he gave him a fair account of it all. "That was last night. I saw Mr. Crowdy. There was no mistake about it that time. He *was* drunk."

"Did he have anything to say for himself? It's a thing people do sometimes when they're drunk—talk."

"Nothing very sensible. He talked in a general way about

the dangers of stepping off the straight and narrow path. He might have meant something, or he might just have been philosophizing."

"That's another thing they do when they're tight," agreed Sergeant Donovan noncommittally.

"Now look here," said Mr. Wetherall. He tried to remind himself that the formidable person in front of him had once, not so very long ago, been a boy to whom he had taught the dates of the Kings and Queens of England. "I insist on knowing what this is all about."

Sergeant Donovan got up.

"You asked me if I thought it was an accident," he said.

"Yes."

"If it *was* an accident, all I can say is it's not the sort I want happening to me."

"What?"

"I don't think Harry Crowdy fell off that bridge, Mr. Wetherall. Experienced rail men don't fall off bridges— even if it's a bit dark or slippery, and a mist about. Nor I don't think that the train which went over him afterward did all the damage. I think he was thrown over. And if you want the truth, Mr. Wetherall, I think he was broken up before he was thrown."

"Broken up," repeated Mr. Wetherall stupidly.

"A pick helve or a spade," said Sergeant Donovan. "Not nice," he added, as he walked over to the window.

Mr. Wetherall said nothing. He was thinking of Mr. Crowdy, as he had seen him the night before, red-faced, stupid, well-meaning, drunk—frightened.

"Why would anyone do that?" he said at last.

"They're a nasty crowd," said Sergeant Donovan. "I'd say they're the nastiest we've seen in England for some time. And when money's the object, they aren't going to pull their punches. But all the same, I can't see them doing a thing like that, to a harmless old packet like Crowdy unless—well, unless they knew he was stooling."

"Stooling?"

"Informing. There's almost nothing they wouldn't do to an informer."

"This is Fawcus," said Colonel Bond. "We hope to persuade him to join our committee. He's had a lot of experience of educational problems."

Mr. Fawcus was a small pink man with gray hair, very neatly parted, and rimless glasses. Mr. Wetherall shook hands with him warily and asked, "Where—for your sins— did you teach?"

"I have never—ah—actually taught at a school," admitted Mr. Fawcus, "but I have had a certain amount of experience of them. I was for many years on the governing council of the Kim-Alla School in Northern Nigeria—"

"I see," said Mr. Wetherall.

"And I was adviser on schools to the Government of Hyderabad."

"Mr. Fawcus has strong ideas on the modernization of education, haven't you, Fawcus?"

Mr. Fawcus raised himself a couple of times onto his toes—a purely symbolic gesture, demonstrating the strength of his ideas—and said, "Speaking for myself I should like to see all curricula founded on a flexible basis of stenography, shorthand, double entry bookkeeping and elementary commercial law—only elementary, of course. Can't turn boys into jurists. No, no. Just a basis of accountancy and a basis of law. What do you think, Colonel?"

"Well, really," said the Colonel. "What do *you* think, Wetherall?"

"I may be old-fashioned," said Mr. Wetherall, "but I must confess that I hold the opinion that education is a general training of the mind for *all* vocations. I'm sure you agree, Colonel?"

"I'm just a plain man of action," said the Colonel. "Not one of your long-haired theorists. What do you say, Fawcus?"

"In a limited sense—"

"After all," said Mr. Wetherall, "once you start on that line, where are you going to stop? If you try to foresee what job each boy's going to do in life, and then get his poor little nose straight down to that particular grindstone, you're back in the days of child labor and the Factory Acts."

"I think you exaggerate," said Mr. Fawcus. "In my experience—"

"—Silly old fool," said Mr. Wetherall to his wife, when he managed to telephone her. "Lock him in for an hour with one of my junior forms and he might begin to understand what education's about. After all that I shall be too late to get back for lunch. Has Peter Crowdy arrived?"

"Yes. He's here."

"Is he all right?"

"I think so. He's very quiet."

"I'll get home as early as I can this evening."

When Mr. Wetherall got home he found his wife and Peter Crowdy sitting in front of the fire.

He thought at first that the scarlet patch in each of the boy's cheeks might have been caused by the heat of the room, but then he realized that he was wrong. Although outwardly his pale-faced, reserved, polite, awkward self, there was now something at work inside. It was something bitter and shocking and only partly understood.

The first thing the boy expected was to have to answer questions. His defensive position told Mr. Wetherall that. Accordingly he asked him none at all. He talked for a time, in his easy way, to both of them, and soon after supper he sent Peter to bed.

"What's wrong with that boy?" said Mrs. Wetherall.

"Shock, wouldn't you think? Losing his father—"

"Yes, I know. But it's something more than that—I thought—I don't know."

Mr. Wetherall badly wanted to talk to someone about things. It would have been nice to talk to his wife, but the ice of years is not easily broken.

He supposed that there might be marriages, not just

workaday, good-enough, bread-and-butter marriages like his own, but the true and lovely thing itself where no barriers existed and no reticence was possible.

His mouth was open to speak when the telephone rang in the hall.

It was Sergeant Donovan.

He said, "Have you got that boy there, Mr. Wetherall?"

"Yes, I've just sent him to bed."

"Best place for him. I rang up to warn you not to be surprised if you saw a couple of characters hanging about in the street. One of them might even be me."

"Why? What's up?"

"Nothing in particular. We don't want to lose this one, do we?"

"No," said Mr. Wetherall. "Of course not. But has anything in particular—"

He was speaking to a dead telephone. Sergeant Donovan had gone.

He made his way slowly back to the sitting room.

"Who was it?"

"Patsy Donovan."

"Oh." Mrs. Wetherall went on with her knitting without comment. Not long afterward she rolled it all up into an untidy bag and went off to bed. Before he followed her, Mr. Wetherall went into the kitchen, got up on a chair, felt inside the cupboard in the corner and turned off the gas at the main. He did this quietly and almost guiltily, but he did it nevertheless. Whatever Sergeant Donovan might say, in his opinion Peter Crowdy's worst enemies were inside his own head.

Later, in bed, Mrs. Wetherall said, "That telephone's a very loud speaker. You can hear every word from the drawing room. Don't tell me if you'd rather not, but—"

Fortified by the friendly darkness he lay back and told her everything.

At the end of it, and for perhaps the first time in their married life, she managed to surprise him.

"You always resented missing the war, didn't you?" she said.

"Yes, I did," said Mr. Wetherall. "Why?"

"It looks as if you've got one on your hands now."

Then they both went to sleep.

FIVE

Soho: The Aldershot Ladies

Nothing happened that night.

Mr. Wetherall woke, for no reason at all, at five o'clock and tiptoed into the room next door. Peter Crowdy was sleeping peacefully. He then went out into the passage and looked out of the end window. It was difficult to be certain, but he fancied that somewhere among the shadows between the street lamps a man was standing. He got back into bed and, feeling that he was not going to get any more sleep, he composed his mind to his problems.

It occurred to him that he could do with a bit of help. It was all very fine and large for Alice to talk about war, but wars were fought by armies; and armies had Transport and Supplies and Signals and Provost and Intelligence services. The latter in particular. What he most needed at the moment was an Intelligence Department.

Even as he considered it a name came into his head. Todd. Alastair Todd. "Sweeney" Todd, the demon of Fleet Street. So pleased was he with this inspiration that he at once fell asleep, with the smile still on his lips, and he awoke to find his wife shaking him and telling him that she had called him twice, that his toast was burnt to a cinder and don't blame her, and did he want to be late at the school?

"That's all right," he said. "Not going in this morning. Too much to do."

After breakfast he made three telephone calls. The first was to Peggy, telling her that he hoped to be in sometime during the afternoon. If anyone important wanted him she must say that he had a touch of pulmonary gastritis.

"It was pulmonary gas works last time," said Peggy.

"All right, I'm going to a funeral. Near relative."

He rang off, dialed Long Distance and spoke for some time to a man called Ap-Lloyd, whom he seemed to know very well.

After that his address book came into play again and he dialed a number at Wimbledon.

The telephone at the other end went on ringing for quite a long time, but Mr. Wetherall persevered. Finally there was a "clunk" and a sleepy voice said, "Todd here."

"It's Wetherall."

"Who?"

"Wilfrid Wetherall."

"Good God," said the voice. "I thought it was the News Editor. No one else would have got me out of bed. What the hell do you want?"

"Some information."

"What's in it for me?"

"Just at the moment," said Mr. Wetherall firmly, "nothing. Eventually, I really think, possibly something quite big."

"Hump," said the voice. "The last time you asked me along, if I remember rightly, was when the Reds broke up that Fascist meeting in Thorneycroft Street and I got a black eye."

"And a good story."

"Is this as big as that one?"

"Bigger than that."

"Crime?"

"I imagine so."

"All right. It's not really my pigeon now, but fire away. Only try and make it snappy, because I haven't got my slippers on."

"Well, this is what it is. I want to find a place—I imagine it would be a restaurant or a night club, or a pub or something like that. The only thing I know about it is that those who are in the know call it the Aldershot Ladies."

"You don't want much, do you? Aldershot Ladies?"

"Yes."

"Ring you back."

When Peter Crowdy had repacked his one suitcase—he had pathetically few clothes but among them a set of good silk shirts a size too big for him—Mr. Wetherall took a cautious look out into the street.

He could see no one but the milkman and the lady from next door holystoning her front step. It was hard to be sure. A lot of people were passing and repassing at the end of the road where the High Street crossed it.

He decided that a Wellingtonian simplicity was to be the order of the day. He went back to the telephone and rang up a Mr. Atkins. After inquiring about Mr. Atkins' family (it seemed that Mr. Atkins, too, was an ex-Battersea pupil) he asked him if his cab was available.

"On the spot," said Atkins.

"Then would you please bring it round to the end of Brinkman Road? Don't turn in. Park it fifty yards up in the High Street, facing north."

"Quick getaway," said Atkins. "What is it this time, Mr. Wetherall? Police after you?"

"That's right. Exactly ten minutes from now. And keep the engine running."

It was eight minutes later when he and Peter let themselves out of the front door and walked down Brinkman Road. A man came out of the telephone box on the corner as they passed it, but otherwise their arrival seemed to cause no flutter. They crossed the road. The taxi was there all right. Atkins was leaning half out of the driver's seat, apparently doing something to his windscreen wiper.

As they came level, Mr. Wetherall exclaimed, "Well now. Just the thing. Let's take a cab." He pulled the door open, pushed Peter in, threw the suitcase in and jumped after him. The cab started with a wrenching jerk which threw them both onto the back seat, twiddled around a corner, slipped along a side street, turned right and left half a dozen times and emerged unexpectedly into the Walworth Road.

"Clean as a ruddy whistle," said Atkins cheerfully. "Didjer see 'em all running?"

"I'm afraid I hadn't time to look."

"Three of 'em. Let 'em run. Won't catch us now. Where to?"

"Waterloo," said Mr. Wetherall.

When Mr. Wetherall eventually got back to the school that afternoon he found a few matters waiting his attention. Colonel Bond had called and would call again later. Sergeant Donovan had rung up, and had said that he would try to catch Mr. Wetherall that evening before he left. An unknown gentleman had telephoned, but had refused to state his business. Fifteen boys had been sick. The stew at lunch was suspected.

"Quiet morning really," said Peggy.

The telephone started again.

"Todd here. That business you were talking about this morning. What is it? Competition or something?"

"It's a sort of competition," said Mr. Wetherall guardedly. "Have you got the answer?"

"I'm not sure. 'Two Aldershot Ladies,' so my colleagues tell me, is a term used by the lower-income groups in connection with their pastime of darts."

"Darts?"

"Yes. Like skittles. All possible combinations of skittles have got names."

"I thought you said darts."

"I was drawing an analogy. Most of the doubles on a dart board have got names, too. You know, like 'double-top'—that's double twenty, and 'double-bottom'—double three. And 'double-one'—"

"Up in Annie's room."

"That's the boy. I've got a young chap in the office here who's a bit of an expert. He knows them all. They're most of them sort of rhyming slang. 'Two tens' becomes 'two fat hens' and 'two eights' is 'china plates' and so on.

"Yes. But why Aldershot Ladies?"

"Two fours."

"Why—oh—"

"Got it?"

"I think so," said Mr. Wetherall guardedly.

"I had someone search the directories. We've got rather special directories here. There's a roadhouse called the Two Fours at Leytonstone. There is—or rather there was, I fancy it's shut down now—a night club called the Twice Four and there's a pub in Lauderdale Street, near Dean Street, called the Double Four."

"That's three possibilities."

"Two, actually. I think the night club really is defunct."

"Yes. And come to think of it, it wouldn't be a night club. The man who said he was going there—it was about eight o'clock in the evening."

"All right. I'll look at the other two and let you know."

"It's very kind of you," said Mr. Wetherall.

"That's the way I'm built," said Mr. Todd.

After he had rung off Mr. Wetherall looked at the list of people who were threatening to call on him and decided that the simplest way of avoiding them all was to go home to tea. After tea he took his wife to the cinema. When they got home Mr. Ballo, the Japanese lodger on the floor below, told them that the telephone had been ringing on and off the whole evening.

Mr. Wetherall, who was feeling mildly defiant by now, got busy with a screwdriver and undid something essential

in the telephone connector box. After that they went to bed
and had an undisturbed night.

Next morning, as was her custom every other month,
Mrs. Wetherall was paying a visit to her mother, who lived
in Kent. She usually stayed away for two nights.

"I'll be back on Tuesday morning," she said. "You're
sure you'll be all right?"

"Certain," said Mr. Wetherall.

At two o'clock that afternoon a repairman arrived,
detected the fault, and put it right. He asked Mr. Wetherall
if the trouble had happened before.

"No," said Mr. Wetherall. "Positively the first time."

At three o'clock Todd rang through.

"I don't think Leytonstone's much good," he said. "I
wasted an afternoon there yesterday. It's called a roadhouse, but it's really a buttered-toast and homemade-cake
sort of place, kept by an old sweetie with two Dandie-Din-
monts and a fearful squint. I took a pot of tea, and a plate
of toast that cost me about a bob a slice, retail. If it's
really a hidden headquarters of crime, then all I can say
is I'm losing my touch. Anyway, I didn't spot anything. The
Lauderdale Street pub looks a bit more promising. I had
a drink there last night. It's full of dim types, but that
doesn't mean anything, because all Soho pubs are like
that. Nobody tried to sell me anything. There's rather a
pretty barmaid—"

Mr. Wetherall reflected.

"Alice is stopping with her mother tonight and tomorrow
night," he said. "Perhaps I could go up and have a look at
it myself. I might see someone I recognized."

"You might. Or someone might see you."

"No harm in dropping in for a drink."

"I suppose not," said Todd. "It isn't a *den*—I mean, you
don't have to sew your pockets up before you go in.
Equally it isn't the sort of place you'd choose to take your
Aunt Flossie for a quiet evening."

"I used to go to Soho quite a lot before the war," said
Mr. Wetherall. "There was one little restaurant—what was

its name —Pagani—Busoni—something like that. They did the most beautiful, *dry* vermicelli, in butter—"

"Soho's full of places with names like Pagani and Busoni. But they're in the four main streets. This pub is side street. Definitely side."

"I'll keep out of trouble—I'm only going to look—"

"All right," said Todd. "Ring me up on Tuesday and let me know how you get on."

When Mr. Wetherall said that he knew Soho quite well he was, so far as he was aware, speaking nothing but the truth. Before the war he had been patron of many of its good, cheap restaurants; lately he had not had much time to visit them and had therefore not been saddened by their decline in goodness and increase in price. When he was walking in that part of London he liked to arrange his route so that it lay through Soho. He was attracted by the different, foreign world that started at Wardour Street, full of shops which seemed to cater for the catering trade itself; shops which sold nothing but carving knives or weighing machines, or wholesale port and sherry glasses or chef's glasses or chef's uniforms; wine bottlers and coffee grinders, odd delicatessen stores and even odder chemist shops. And the restaurants themselves, from the famous ones in Dean Street and Greek Street, to the lesser known but more exciting ones which flanked them, down to the cafés where out of work musicians, resting artistes, and stage hangers-on sat for hours over single cups of coffee, talking to their friends and waiting for the union to fix them a job.

But when he reached Lauderdale Street, at about nine o'clock that Monday evening, he realized that he was in yet another Soho, of which he knew little. It was the Soho of the side streets, where the people who were at your service in the main streets lived and moved through their oddly regulated lives: lives which started with sundown and ended as the day was breaking.

It was like getting behind the scenes at a theater. What appeared, from the front, to be handsome and well-lighted and lifelike here dissolved into a jumble of meaningless odds and ends. Once behind the neon glare of the restaurant fronts and gorgeous rank of commissionaires, you were in the kingdom of working dress, and half lights, and whispers.

At first sight the Double Four looked so uninviting that Mr. Wetherall nearly turned back. It was like no pub he had ever seen before, even in his own part of South London (where, indeed, they were usually glittering oases of light and life and respectability).

The windows and doors, which had been boarded against the blitz, were still nailed up. What had once been fresh woodwork was now between dark brown and black, oily with twelve seasons of fog and neglect. Someone had playfully spiked the head of a rabbit on the area railing. A dim light from behind an old blackout slit illuminated the words SALOON BAR.

As he was hesitating a door swung open further along the street and a man came out. In the light of the door, before it shut again, he had time to take in such diverse items of dress as a kilt, a duffel coat and a bowler hat. Then the newcomer was advancing toward him. He seemed to be carrying a small corpse under his left arm. As he came up to Mr. Wetherall he put out his right arm, wrapped it round Mr. Wetherall's shoulder, and said, in a voice in which the stage Scotsman fought an unequal fight with the cockney, "That's the boy. Were you taking a wee drappie? Come awa' in. I had just the same thought mesel'."

Having no free hand he kicked the door open and surged into the saloon bar with Mr. Wetherall obediently in tow.

Inside it wasn't so bad. It was warm, and there was a good deal of light, some overhead and some from behind the bar, where a string of painted electric bulbs suggested some bygone Christmas decoration which no one had troubled to remove.

"Whass yours?"

"No, really."

"Double Scots, Miss. And the same for my friend."

"Really, you're very kind—"

"Not at all," said the Scotsman. "I took an in-stan-taneous liking to you the moment I saw you." He removed the corpse, which turned out to be an old set of bagpipes, from under his arm and laid it out carefully on the plush-covered settee.

"With or without?" said the barmaid.

Mr. Wetherall thought that this might be the girl Todd had mentioned. She had a sort of stage prettiness. Anywhere but in that awful bar she could have looked attractive.

"I never drown good usquebaugh," said the Scotsman. "Warrerbout choors?"

"Oh, I'll have some soda water," said Mr. Wetherall. "Plenty of soda water, please."

The Scotsman disposed of his drink with a twist of the forearm and since he looked faintly expectant Mr. Wetherall ordered two more. His own went down more slowly. He had time to notice that it was very good whisky.

"Scots wha' ha'," said his new friend. He got through his second drink at creditable speed, too. Mr. Wetherall bought him a third, but left himself out of the round.

"It's a braw bricht moonlicht nicht," observed his friend, and this seeming to exhaust his fund of compulsory Scots axioms, proceeded more rationally. "It's a long time since meself set eyes on you, Hector. Where have you been hiding?"

"I—"

"It was boat-race night, twa years syne. Not, and it wasn't though. Don't tell me. It was the steps of St. Paul's, on Hogmanay."

The thought affected him so powerfully that he sang a whole verse of "Auld Lang Syne," in a strong tenor voice. This brought the proprietress onto the scene from the private bar.

She wasn't just one more woman. It was quite clear that she was Somebody.

The barmaid started polishing an already clean glass,

and the Scotsman discontinued his singing and said, "How's tricks, Annie?"

"Quiet enough till you come in. What do you think this is? Second house at the Empire?"

It was her eyes that you noticed first. The white was very white and the brown was very shiny and brown and the whole was set so far forward that you had a feeling that she could see, like the caterpillar, both forward and backward without moving her head. Her hair was black and coarse and tightly drawn over her head.

"Do I know your friend?"

"Friend indeed. It's me Cousin Hector, all the way fra' Aberdeen."

"The back of a picture postcard's the only place you've ever seen Aberdeen," said Annie.

The voice had an overlay of professional bonhomie but there was clearly a whip in reserve.

"You're unkind——" He looked so disconsolate that Mr. Wetherall bought him another glass of whisky, which cheered him up a lot.

Meanwhile Annie was trying to place Mr. Wetherall. You could almost see her, like a factory hand testing parts for gauge, fitting him into various sockets and slots, giving him a twist here and a twist there, and deciding that he didn't quite measure up.

Private detective? Not nearly tough enough.

Journalist? Not enough bounce and savvy.

Commercial traveler? Could be. Not really smart enough.

Dirty old man on the prowl? Wrong sort of eyes and mouth.

In the end she abandoned finesse and said, "My guess is you're a journalist. Am I right?"

"I——"

"He's my second cousin Hector," said the Scotsman, "and he travels in corsets."

"Anyone who'll stand you a drink's your second cousin," said Annie.

"You insult me," said the Scotsman gravely.

"As a matter of fact," said Mr. Wetherall, "you're both wrong. I'm a schoolmaster."

"Well, there now," said Annie. "I guessed it was something to do with writing."

"Would you take a drink with me—?"

"I don't mind if I do. It'll be a gin and pep. Two and eleven. That's right. As a matter of fact I daren't drink anything else. This job's death to the lining of my stomach. Overwork and old age—"

"Overwork, perhaps," said Mr. Wetherall gallantly.

"Get away with you. And what are you doing in these parts?"

The question came sliding out of the froth like a blade out of a sheath.

"I was having dinner with someone," he said. "At Bernadi's. But they didn't turn up."

"Stood you up, did she?"

"As a matter of fact, it was a man."

"That's right, dearie." Annie gave a sharp, popping laugh. "Just a joke."

During the next half hour, though customers came and went, Annie never entirely abandoned Mr. Wetherall. She seemed to have become quite attached to him.

In the intervals of nagging the barmaid, serving drinks, and keeping up her side of a marathon argument with an unseen gentleman in the private bar, she leaned over the counter and treated Mr. Wetherall to an account, in serial form, of the progress of her various ailments. The multitude of her afflictions, the skill and unexpectedness with which they attacked her, the occasional triumphs, the deadly setbacks.

"It's standing round on the feet all day," she said. "It draws the humors down into the legs. Many's the time I've gone to bed at the end of the day with a deathly feeling in my—those packets of biscuits are fivepence now, Beryl, do you think we give 'em away—the only things that done me any good was pads of heated cotton wool and regular doses of Bangalore Broth—I expect you've heard of it—it's the essential germ of wheat and nine other vitamins in emulsified form—and there's a picture on the packet of a woman had symptoms just like mine and three tablespoon-fuls of Bangalore Broth finished her right off."

"Extraordinary," said Mr. Wetherall. "I can't remember that I've ever seen it advertised."

"Advertised," said Annie scornfully. "When a thing's as good as Bangalore Broth you don't need advertisement. There's a place in North London where—I can't hear you, dearie."

"I said," said a voice from the private bar, "that when we went off the gold standard prices went down, not up."

"Well, they're going up now, all right, you must admit. Cranky, see. What'll it be, dearie? This one's on me."

Mr. Wetherall accepted a small whisky, and looked round for his friend, and found that he was asleep on the settle with his head on his bagpipes.

"You don't want to worry about him," said Annie. "He's just a cadger. Plays the bagpipes to the queues in Leicester Square. Between you and me he's not a Scotsman at all. His name's Higgins."

"It's funny the people you run across," said Mr. Wether-all. "I've been a schoolmaster in London most of my life, so I dare say I notice it more than most. I'm always running across boys I've taught. I can't always place them straight-away. The other day I sat next to one at a boxing match. At first I couldn't think of his name. Then I got it—Prince."

If Mr. Wetherall had happened to look up at that moment it is quite possible that he would have saved him-self a lot of trouble. If he had seen the sudden, wary look that passed over Annie's face, sweeping away the surface animation, as water hardens again when a ruffle of wind has passed: if he had seen this and been able to interpret it, it seems likely that he would have gone straight home.

"Prince," said Annie. "That's quite a common name."

"Used to be a boxer, so he tells me. Then he lost an eye."

"Yes," said Annie. She had her back to him and was restacking a small pile of cigarette packets. "And you were his schoolmaster, were you? It's a small world, isn't it?" She turned round. "What school would that have been?"

"Actually it was in Battersea."

"Battersea Park, Battersea Park," said the Scotsman, "Oh, the bonny bluebells of Battersea Park."

"You've woken up, have you?"

"Awake, my love, and thirsty."

"Perhaps I might—" began Mr. Wetherall hospitably.

"Now don't you do it," said Annie. "You've stood him plenty of drinks already. It's time he bought you one."

Mr. Higgins shot her a dirty look.

"Really," said Mr. Wetherall, "I've still got—"

"That's right," said Mr. Higgins rapidly. "Always finish one glass before you start on another. I'll buy myself a drink this time." He took out a wallet which seemed to contain more pound notes than Mr. Wetherall had ever seen in one wallet before, and said, "Make it half a pint of mild."

This was to the barmaid. Annie had disappeared into the private bar.

When she came back she was her old cheerful self again, and she told Mr. Wetherall a number of surprising things about the functions of the kidneys. Mr. Wetherall, who had really begun to enjoy his evening, was sorry when the clock hand reached eleven.

"Time, gentlemen," said Annie.

"Your clock's fast," said a small man in the corner.

"So what?" said Annie. There seemed to be no adequate answer to that. The small man removed himself from his corner and drifted off.

"Will I play you a wee tune on the pipes?" suggested Mr. Higgins.

"No."

"A lament for the closing of the day. Written by the great Rob Roy himself when they refused him a last drink at the Railway Tavern at Ardrishaig."

"Come along now. We don't want any trouble—your friend's going. You'd better go with him."

"All right," said Mr. Higgins. "All right. All right."

Outside in the street he linked his arm through Mr. Wetherall's and said, in the tones of one who has had a bright and daring idea, "Why don't we go and have a drink?"

"The pubs will all be shut."

"Och, and awa' wi' ee," said Mr. Higgins. "There are plenty of clubs." The idea sounded vaguely attractive. Club, to Mr. Wetherall, meant the United Universities where he occasionally took tea with a friend. He had never in his life visited a night club, or even contemplated such a thing.

As they turned into Dean Street a name caught his eye. "Bernadi's." There was something odd about it. No lights. A notice in the window.

"It's no good trying there," said Mr. Higgins. "Closed for repairs and renovations."

"Oh." Mr. Wetherall had suddenly remembered something. It took him a moment to put his finger on it. Hadn't he told Annie that he was dining at Bernadi's with a friend? She must have known—

"How long's it been like that?"

"Months and months. Come along."

Obediently Mr. Wetherall moved after his new friend.

Like a shadow, a tiny sense of disquiet moved with him.

Mr. Higgins' ideas on how to look for a club in Soho had the merit of simplicity. You looked into every basement until you saw a light. Then you went down and knocked.

After one or two unfortunate mistakes they found themselves at the door of the Minstrel Boy.

"Come on," said Mr. Higgins. "This one's all right."

"Don't you have to be a member?"

"Of course I'm a member. Come *on*."

At the bottom of a further flight of stairs they found

a youth seated beside a table, with a cash register and a magazine devoted to racing pigeons.

"Are you the Minstrel Boy?" inquired Mr. Higgins.

"No, he's gone to the war," said the youth sadly.

"With his wild harp slung behind him," suggested Mr. Wetherall.

"That's right. Members?"

Mr. Higgins said, "Certainly."

"Gotcher cards?"

"Left them at home."

"Five bob each," said the youth, "and you can become members all over again."

"Scandalous," said Mr. Higgins.

Mr. Wetherall paid and they went in. It seemed to be a popular sort of place, even if it did not quite square up with Mr. Wetherall's idea of a night club. No floor show, no band, no orchids, no champagne, and, rather to his disappointment in his exalted state, no female uncovered above the knee or below the neck. As much as it looked like anything else on earth it looked like an up-to-date, well-run station buffet. There were a number of tables, all occupied, and a counter at one end which was dispensing coffee and hot snacks. A wireless set was relaying dance music from a foreign station. Everyone seemed to be talking at the top of his voice.

"More room further on," said Mr. Higgins. He plunged through the doorway and they found themselves in another cellar.

This had a small bar made entirely of looking glass, and a lumpy settee round its wall, and a choice of three further doors.

The first one they looked into contained a very large table, on which was a gramophone and round which was a circle of young men listening to the gramophone. Everyone looked up angrily when they came in, so they went away. The second door led down two steps into an even lower cellar, full of tables, at which men with beards sat playing chess. In this room no one looked up at all. The third room was almost empty. They selected a table and sat down.

They sat for a long time while nothing much happened.

"Perhaps it's run on the cafeteria system," suggested Mr. Wetherall. "Do you think we ought to help ourselves?"

"Certainly not," said Mr. Higgins. "Assert yourself."

He picked up a glass ashtray and clashed it on the table top. Since the table was a metal one the noise was considerable.

A middle-aged man at a neighboring table, whom they had supposed to be a fellow patron, put down his evening paper and asked what he could do for them.

"I would like some hot sausages and some beer," suggested Mr. Wetherall.

"How much of each?"

"Twenty sausages and a gallon of beer," said Mr. Higgins. "And make it snappy. The proprietor's a friend of mine."

"Very good," said the middle-aged man. He left the room.

Five minutes later he came back with two big steins and a pitcher of beer, and asked, as he put it down on the table, "Would either of you gentlemen be Mr. Wetherall?"

"Certainly not," said Mr. Higgins, before Mr. Wetherall could open his mouth. "My name's Freeman. This is my friend Mr. Hardy."

"O.K. O.K.," said the man. He withdrew.

Mr. Higgins poured himself out a lot of beer and drank it. "Never does to tell 'em your name," he said. "Probably find it's someone you owe money to."

Even at that time of night Mr. Wetherall found it difficult to believe that his few and modest debts would have pursued him to a club in a cellar in Soho. Something was happening in the main room. Voices were being raised and questions were being asked. The sense of unease, which had been in the background since Dean Street, suddenly took a decisive step toward him.

The waiter reappeared. He looked worried.

"Please come and talk to the gentlemen," he said. The words were plainly addressed to Mr. Wetherall. Mr. Higgins had settled down on the sofa in his favorite position, with his bagpipes under his head.

In the outer room by the counter stood two men. They were both above ordinary height and wore belted raincoats and soft hats which yet contrived, somehow, to look like a uniform.

"Mr. Wetherall?"

"Yes."

At that they looked at him. It was a bleak, dispassionate look which he was to remember afterward.

"I'm afraid we must ask you to come along with us."

"Where to? And what's it all about?"

"West End Central Police Station," said the man who had spoken first. He had reddish hair and a strong, red face, like a rough-riding, hard-drinking farmer. One of his eyes had a tiny spot of yellow in the iris. He lowered his voice slightly. "If it's any interest to you, it's about Crowdy."

"But I—"

"We don't want any trouble here, do we?"

"I suppose not," said Mr. Wetherall. Since he had made his mind up, all he was concerned with was to let no trace of it show on his face. "Do you mind if I get my coat?"

"Sure." The red-faced man nodded to his companion. He was a younger man, with a pale face under thick black hair. He followed behind Mr. Wetherall, but not too quickly or too closely for what Mr. Wetherall had in mind. As he reached the door leading into the room where he had been sitting he quickened his pace, jumped through it, shut it behind him, and slipped home the bolt. It was a strong bolt: he had happened to notice it as he came out, and on it his impromptu scheme depended.

He was only just in time. As the bolt went into its socket a body thudded into the door from the other side.

At the noise, Mr. Higgins, now the only other person in the room, sat up sharply and cried, "Wassat?"

"Burglars," said Mr. Wetherall breathlessly.

"I'll give them burglars."

"They're after your bagpipes."

"Over my dead body."

The door shook again and a lump of plaster came out of the wall.

There was another door, in the far corner. Mr. Wetherall opened it and looked out. It led to a short, dimly-lit passage. There were further doors opening off it. The one on the left proved to be locked. The one on the right led to a coal cellar. As he tried the third, at the end of the passage, there was a crescendo of crashes behind him and above them the faint, defiant squeal of bagpipes.

The third room was a small, dirty lavatory. Mr. Wetherall went into it, and shot the bolt. It wasn't much of a refuge. The door was flimsy and the bolt small. He climbed onto the seat and tried the window. It was a ramshackle casement, its panes covered with whitewash, and it looked as if it had not been opened in twenty years. Nevertheless it moved, reluctantly, a few inches.

Mr. Wetherall was slim, and fear lent him the necessary agility. A few seconds later he was through the window and standing in a small area. It was really no more than a pit, acting as air shaft to three or four houses. Overhead he could see the bars of a grating against the night sky. From the noise behind him it seemed that his pursuer was busy breaking down the cellar doors. It would not be long before he turned his attention to the lavatory.

Mr. Wetherall stumbled forward across the area, which seemed to be knee-deep in bottles. Logic told him that there must be at least one corresponding window on the other side. There was, and it was tightly shut.

It was not a moment for half measures.

He groped down and picked up a bottle. With it he knocked out the top pane of glass then thrust his hand through and undid the latch. He pressed the bottom casement up, only discovering as the blood ran down his palm that he had by no means removed all the glass. In the excitement he felt nothing.

A light sprang up in the lavatory behind him.

He fairly dived through the window into warm, fluffy darkness.

It was an inhabited room. There was some sort of carpet on the floor. It smelled like a bedroom. At that moment the light came on. It was a bedroom. There was a very old man in bed. He sat up, clasping the flex of the light switch to his thin, night-shirted body, and stared at Mr. Wetherall.

"It's all right," muttered Mr. Wetherall. "Just reading the meters."

The man appeared to be deaf. He simply sat and stared, with his mouth wide open.

With a strong feeling of unreality upon him Mr. Wetherall tiptoed to the door, opened it, and went through, shutting it quietly behind him. He had seen a flight of uncarpeted stairs ahead, and he went up them. Another passage not quite so dark. He guessed he was back on the ground-floor level now. There was a door at the end of the passage, and it was obviously a street door. It was fastened.

First he fumbled with the top bolt, then the bottom bolt. There was a chain in the middle, which he finally got off, at the cost of a clattering jangle.

A woman's voice said something from the room to the left of the door.

Mr. Wetherall worked with clumsy speed in the dark. There was a Yale lock, which he fastened open on the catch, and finally a big handle, which he turned.

The door still refused to move.

A shaft of light lit up the passage. The door on the left had opened. A dark woman, with her hair in curlers, looked out.

"Henry. It's a burglar." Her voice sounded tiny and far off.

"I'm not a burglar," said Mr. Wetherall. "I'm trying to get out. Get *out*. Do you understand?"

The woman gaped at him, with exactly the same air of disbelief he had already seen on the face of the man in the cellar. Then she said faintly, "The key's beside the door."

Mr. Wetherall looked up, and there it was, a large, old-fashioned key. He took it down, fitted it into the lock and turned it. The door opened and he stepped out into the street.

Two seconds later he realized, with a sense of apprehension, that it had all been a waste of effort. He had been running like a rabbit in a circle. The men who were after him understood the geography of Soho better than he did. They were waiting for him in the street.

"Just along here," said the red-faced man, as calmly as if nothing had happened since the last time he had spoken.

They turned into a short cul-de-sac between high buildings. The red-faced man held him by one arm, just above the elbow. The younger, black-haired man walked beside him, whistling very quietly, his hands in his pockets. As they turned into the cul-de-sac a lamp on the corner lit up his face. It was not a very good face, and Mr. Wetherall remembered where he had met it before. It was the man he had seen coming out of the telephone kiosk at the corner of Brinkman Road on the morning he had taken Crowdy to Waterloo.

"Where are you taking me?" he asked suddenly.

"That depends on you," said the red-faced man. As usual he did the talking. "We don't want any trouble. It's people like you who make trouble."

"What is it you want?"

"A bit of information. Where have you put that boy?"

"Which boy?"

"Don't stall. Which boy? Which boy? Do you kidnap three a week?"

"Are you police officers?"

"That's right," said the red-faced man. "We're police officers. Now just answer the question."

"I don't believe—" began Mr. Wetherall.

It came from behind, a jolting blow of agonizing force and precision, into his side, below the ribs and above the hip. He tried to turn, but the grip on his arm was too strong for him. He tried to speak, but his voice had gone.

"Better answer the question," said the red-faced man. "You don't want to upset Sailor. Once you upset him he gets excited. He likes doing it, you know."

Mr. Wetherall got his breath back.

"I can't tell you."

The second blow was on exactly the same spot and was harder. Mr. Wetherall felt a red-hot pain stabbing through the growing numbness. And again.

"St. Christopher's Home for Boys." The words seemed to be jerked out of him.

"Where's that?"

"At Woking."

"All right," said the red-faced man. As though it was a signal, something heavy caught Mr. Wetherall on the side of his head. At the same moment the grip on his elbow loosened, and he dropped forward onto his knees.

The black-haired man kicked him twice on the side of the head.

"That's enough," said the other man.

"I haven't started yet," said the black-haired man. It was the first time he had spoken. His voice was educated.

"I said that's enough." The red-faced man leaned down and flicked the wallet out of Mr. Wetherall's inner pocket. Then with the same neat, studied movement, he took a flask out of his own pocket, unscrewed the lid, and emptied the contents down the front of Mr. Wetherall's coat.

He looked down at the crumpled figure on the pavement. Something seemed to be amusing him. "Looks as if he's had quite a party," he said.

The two of them walked away. As they went the black-haired man trod hard on the back of Mr. Wetherall's outstretched hand. Doing it seemed to cause him some sort of pleasure.

In the distance a woman began to scream.

It was this screaming that Mr. Wetherall noticed first. Then the warm salty taste of blood in his mouth and behind his nose. Then sickness. Then the hurt in his hand. Then the hurt in his side and back.

The woman had stopped screaming and was bending over him.

He had lost his glasses. He must find his glasses. He was helpless without them.

"Here they are," said the woman. "What a smell. You bin drinking?"

One of the lenses was cracked across, but the glass was all there. It was while he was putting them on that he first became aware of the state of his face. His right ear was numb, but felt enormous.

"I saw them," said the woman. "The brutes." Mr. Wetherall blinked up at her. She had a fat, good-natured, sketchily painted face.

"You ought to get home, you know," she went on. "You let a copper take one sniff at you and he'll run you in just as quick as he'll swear your character away next morning."

Mr. Wetherall had not associated the smell of spirits with himself. He had imagined it came from the woman. Now he noticed his sodden reeking shirt front.

"Oh, dear," he said. "Oh, dear. What shall I do?"

"You ought to get a taxi and go off home."

"Yes. That's right." Home seemed infinitely desirable. "Would you be so kind—I wonder if you could find me one?"

"Oh, I'll find you one all right," said the woman. "Have you got any money to pay for it, that's the thing."

It was then that he discovered that his wallet was gone. The loss suddenly unnerved him completely. He started to shiver.

"Money gone too," said the woman. "Well, that's a fix and no mistake."

He forced his undamaged hand into his trouser pocket. There were a few coppers and some silver. He could hardly hold them for the shaking. "That won't get you far. Have you got a friend who could lend you some—?"

Mr. Wetherall took hold of himself with an effort.

"Yes," he said. "If you can find me a taxi I shall be all right. Just as far as Fleet Street. Then I can borrow some more money—"

"All right," said the woman. "I won't be a minute. There's always a cab behind the Casino." She looked at him doubtfully. Mr. Wetherall had begun to shiver again.

"Hold onto yourself," she said. "I won't be a jiffy."

SIX

Fleet Street: Night

Alastair Todd was playing cards with two friends. He was in his office on the first floor of the chocolate-box building toward the southeast corner of Fleet Street that houses that great and justly celebrated daily newspaper, the *Kite*.

He was a round, cheerful person with a fringe of brown curly hair lying like a halo of camel's wool above a chubby face. He looked a little younger than he really was. How he had attained to the responsible office of a subeditor on the *Kite* was a bit of a mystery to his friends.

He had come to journalism by curious byspaths, as do most members of that exciting, disorganized profession. At the age of twenty he had been ranked as the second-best squash player in England and (in the opinion of many) the greatest rackets player in the world. He had a small allowance, dispensed to him by a guardian, and no desire to do anything other than play those two games. It was the tiresome recurrence of summer which had defeated his program. Finding that his keenest opponents fell off as the temperature rose into the eighties, he had started to fill in the lengthening intervals between matches by writing about them; and he had very soon been signed up by the *Morning Toast,* which specialized, as you will remember, in accurate and informed accounts of all gentlemanly sports.

On the decease of that paper he had joined the *Kite,* and its editor (a man from Newcastle who believed in no game but soccer) had suggested that he turn his attention to crime. He could, if he wished, said the editor, continue to write a short, seasonable column about squash and rackets, but crime, as he pointed out, had the advantage of being an all-weather activity. So Todd had turned placidly to crime and, employing some of the finesse which had kept his opponents guessing on the court, had turned out to be a moderately successful reporter.

After the war, which he spent in the Air Force, he had been welcomed back to the paper by the new editor (a Yorkshireman who believed in no game but cricket) and had been put as assistant to the man in charge of the feature page. On the retirement of this hero shortly afterward, with peptic ulcers and delusions, he had stepped quietly into his place.

His companions that night were the chief crime reporter on the *Kite,* a man called Jones, whose nickname was "Mattress"—a name which no one could understand until they met him, when they realized that it was the only name possible—and a crime reporter from the *Kite*'s companion paper, the *Balloon,* a very serious young Irishman called Hoggarty.

Todd was waiting up, principally, for a notice from the dramatic critic on the current first night. He expected this to be in his hands well before midnight since Duncan, like most of the critics employed by the *Kite,* wrote his reviews in outline before he got to the theater and filled in his conclusions during the first interval.

There was a knock.

"This'll be it," said Todd. "We shall have to call it a day. That's two and six you owe me, Mattress. Give me two bob and sixpence to Hog and we're square."

It was a messenger.

"Two men for you, Mr. Todd."

"Two men?"

"One's a cabby, and the other—well, he's in a bit of a mess."

"Sounds just right for the feature page," said Jones.

"It'll be Duncan," said Hoggarty. "I expect the leading lady got hold of him. You ought to have seen what he wrote about her last piece—"

"Bring 'em up," said Todd. "You two had better fade."

A few minutes later he was staring, in speechless astonishment, at Mr. Wetherall.

"I'm very sorry to bother you," croaked Mr. Wetherall, "but could you oblige me with the loan of ten shillings? I haven't enough on me to pay my fare."

"Your fare," echoed Todd faintly. "Were you thinking of going somewhere?"

"I'm going home."

"Yes. Of course. But look here, old boy, are you sure you want to go home in that state—your wife—do sit down."

This was just in time. Mr. Wetherall's legs had hinged under him.

"What's the bill so far?"

"Three and ninepence," said the taximan, "and demmage to me upholstery."

"I expect it'll wash off," said Todd. "It's only blood."

"Suppose it will," said the taxi driver. He was plainly divided between a desire to make some money out of the situation and fear of offending such a power for good and evil as a subeditor of the *Kite*.

"Here's five bob," said Todd. "That should cover it. Put your name and license number down on that bit of paper, and if there's a story in it I'll see you get a mention."

The taximan retired, and Todd got onto the house telephone and asked for Mrs. Weaver.

"Could you bring some hot water and lint and sticking plaster and that sort of thing?" he said. "No—not exactly a street accident, but something pretty like it. Yes, shock too, I should think."

The *Kite* was apparently used to tackling emergency first aid. Mrs. Weaver, a brisk woman, who had patched and bandaged her way through the blitz, dressed Mr. Wetherall's multiple injuries. It was his right hand that caused her most concern.

"There's bones broken," she said. "He'll have to see a doctor over that."

"All right. But he's not dying?"

She sniffed disapprovingly.

"He ought to be in bed."

"It's no good sniffing," said Mr. Wetherall, with an irritability which showed that he was recovering. "I didn't drink that whisky. It was upset over me."

"If you say so," said Mrs. Weaver, gathering her first-aid kit together.

"Come in," said Todd. "Oh, here's the tea. Thank you, Brice. Just the thing for shock. Hot, weak and sweet. I'm not sure I won't have a cup myself. Here you are."

Mr. Wetherall accepted it gratefully.

"Now," said Todd. He moved across and casually turned the key in the lock. "Now, don't you think you had better tell me something about it?"

"Yes," said Mr. Wetherall. "I really think I'd better do that."

It was such a difficult story to tell. It had an end but no beginning. Or rather, when looked at closely, it had too many beginnings. Important things like Crowdy, the Donovan family, Jock's Pull-In for Carmen. Unimportant things too, like Luigi and the missing food parcel. It was interrupted, once by the arrival of the expected first-night report and twice by queries from the compositors' room, but in the end it was done.

When he had heard it through, Todd went over to the cupboard and got out a special bottle of whisky, and out of it he poured, in silence, two careful tots, and handed one of them to Mr. Wetherall.

"Charge your glass," he said. "The toast is the small boy who thought it *such* fun fiddling with the detonator of the ten-thousand-pound bomb."

"It's as bad as that, is it?"

"Have you got the faintest idea what you're doing? No. I thought not. Well, how can I begin to explain? You're touching the edges—you're playing round the fringes—of almost the only really organized piece of nonsense in England. It's so big that it seems to be invisible to the naked eye. It hasn't even got a real name. In this street, where we know about most things a jump ahead of the British public, we just call it the food game. It's a growth. It's also an organization. It's big business. It's so big it's almost respectable."

"Oh," said Mr. Wetherall. He was holding his glass in his left hand, swirling the tacky liquid slowly round.

"I can't even tell you how it works. It's like the British constitution. It's got no rules. You can only tell it's there by results. And those you run into every day of your life. Have you ever wondered why the restaurant where you have your supper can serve you three rashers—three walloping thick rashers—of bacon, while your wife and you shared a thin rasher between you for breakfast? Or why there's a full sugar bowl on the table? To say nothing of the rows of expensive cakes and pastries in the window, all made of butter and sugar and eggs. Or where your favorite Soho restaurant gets the ingredients for that lovely Steak Toreador? Or why, when you've finished eating the steak, you can buy a hundred of your favorite cigarettes from the headwaiter? Or why, when your wine merchant, who's a man and a friend, and whom you've been patronizing for years, can't get you more than half a bottle of Scotch at Christmas (and that's a favor) you can drink a good Scotch, to your heart's content, in the X Club and the Y Club and the Z Club?"

"I'm not a great clubgoer," said Mr. Wetherall. "But—yes, I did wonder once about the bacon."

"The answer is so simple that I can give it to you in one

word. Redistribution. It used to be called Black Market, but that's a word that was misued so much in the first five or six years after the war that it lost most of its meaning— and anyway, this is more specialized. Redistribution. It's so simple. Think of a lorry hurtling down the Great North Road, with a dozen sides of bacon swinging in the back. That's about nine thousand bacon rations. If it gets to its destination, which is some absolutely reputable wholesaler, it will be split up among the retailers, who will sell it to you and your wife and nine thousand other citizens and no one will make more than about a farthing a pound profit, because that's the way it's meant to work. But what actually happens? The driver stops for a snack. He and his mate get out. No doubt they remove the ignition key, or lock the cab, or take other sensible precautions. But what's all this? Before they are through their second cup of tea—Wirra! Wirra! Goblins about! The lorry has started up and driven itself away."

Todd broke off, then added in an unexpectedly serious voice, "You know, the thing I find really unpleasant about that bit is that although a lot of drivers who are robbed are innocent and unsuspecting victims, in other cases the lorry *may* have stopped at that particular time and place because a little envelope reached the driver at an accommodation address that morning with ten crisp pound notes and a few simple instructions inside. However that may be, the result is the same. Instead of coming into the shops the bacon is sold at its *real* price to half a dozen restaurant and club owners, who may themselves be essentially honest men, but have got their customers to satisfy and can't afford to have bacon off their menu if the next-door chap has got it on his. Then you and your wife and other citizens go in and have a jolly good helping of bacon at three or four shillings a plateful and glad to get it. See?"

"Yes," said Mr. Wetherall.

"Multiply that instance by a few thousand, and you see how Redistribution works."

Todd helped himself to another cup of tea, long since cold.

"There's nothing particularly novel about it. The only new thing is that the idea is getting around in informed circles that the old business has come under some sort of central management. Just after the war it was fairly haphazard. That's why I called it a growth. In those days, if you were lucky enough to steal a dozen sides of bacon and get away with them, your troubles were only beginning. You had to find somewhere to store them—you couldn't keep them under the bed; and you had to look round for people to sell them to, with the risk that one of your customers might be a fool with more conscience than sense who would go to the police; and you had to get the right price for the stuff, and see that the money was really paid to you, as promised. Well, Redistribution deals with all that. Guaranteed markets, guaranteed prices. You sell to them. They deal with the Luigis of this world."

"They deal with the Luigis all right," said Mr. Wetherall absently.

"This isn't only generalization," said Todd. "It's got a moral as far as you're concerned."

"I'm glad it's got a moral." As long as he sat quite still his aches were just bearable.

"I can explain it most easily by asking you a question. Why did what happened to you tonight have to happen at all?"

"It seemed perfectly simple to me," said Mr. Wetherall.

"That's because you've got a simple mind. It isn't really straightforward. If you were bothering this crowd at the circumference, I refuse to believe that their methods would have been so direct or so drastic. They get lots of that sort of bother. Restaurant proprietor A complains that ditto B is getting stuff off the ration. A goes to the nearest policeman or food official and screams Black Market. The authorities, if they take A seriously, have B watched. Maybe they can't prove anything. *Then A notices that his own custom is mysteriously beginning to fall off.* If he's a wise man he takes the hint and drops his complaints against B. Or perhaps there's a retailer, C, who gets caught handling stolen food. That's easier still. C is cut out of the system altogether. He's no good to them. He's been found out. He can whistle for the stuff. But—and here's the point—A, B and C don't get beaten up in back streets. That sort of treatment is reserved for people who get rather nearer the center."

"Then I must have been right on the hub," said Mr. Wetherall.

"Don't you believe it," said Todd cheerfully. "If they'd really wanted to see you off you wouldn't be sitting in front of this fire drinking whisky. You'd be in the casualty ward of the Middlesex Hospital with screens round you. All the same—you may have hit on something. It might be something to do with that boy—Crowdy. They seem to have slipped up over that. I suppose they'll be down at Woking watching him like hawks from now on—"

"They might," said Mr. Wetherall. "Always supposing they know where he was."

"But I thought—"

"I told them the first thing that came into my head. I don't suppose there *is* a St. Christopher's Home at Woking. I made it all up."

Todd whistled softly. "The devil you did," he said. "Well, that's quite a point, isn't it? You had them on the wrong foot there, all right." He got up, picked up the ruler from the desk, and with it shaped a very delicate backhand drop-shot up the left-hand wall of the room.

"But then again—supposing that Crowdy business was just a blind. Something they said to take your mind off the real object of the exercise. Supposing you went somewhere or saw someone or heard something tonight that you weren't ever intended to. Supposing you got behind the scenes and saw the strings moving—"

"Do you think it could have been that Scotsman?"

"Might have been. I should have thought it was more likely someone in that pub. After all, that was the name you were working on. Or that club. Or just one of the basement doors you happened to knock on. You seem to have thrashed around a good deal."

As well as he was able to for an aching head, Mr. Wetherall reflected.

"I don't think I was actually followed to Soho. I don't know. It's difficult to be sure—"

"There's no certainty about it. You'll have to wait until the police pull in those two toughs. That may tell us something."

"Until—"

"If you give the police as good a description as you've just given me," said Todd, "it shouldn't be too difficult. There are only a limited number of professional bullies in London and most of them are on the books."

"You think I ought to go to the police—?"

"Not tonight," agreed Todd. "But very first thing tomorrow morning, of course you must. You'll be putting yourself hopelessly in the wrong if you don't. You've got nothing to hide, have you? You're a law-abiding citizen. You've been assaulted. You inform the police, and sit back and wait for your assailants to be lined up for you to identify."

"All right. But if by sit back you mean that I'm to stay out of this thing from now on, I'm afraid you've got it wrong. I certainly couldn't drop it now. To start with I don't approve of physical violence—"

"You don't—" Todd looked at his friend, and suppressed a desire to smile. Mr. Wetherall was peering earnestly over his broken glasses, apparently unconscious of the fact that one side of his face was red and blue from forehead to chin, that his lip was split, that one hand was heavily bandaged, and that his suit was an unspeakable travesty of its once respectable self. "You don't," he said, "approve of violence?"

"I've always been against bullying, too. It's a thing I've been very strict about in any school I've taught in."

"Quite so," said Todd. "Well, all I'm suggesting is that just at the moment you ought to keep in the background a bit. You're a marked man now and if there is any secret to be discovered in the Soho area it won't be you who'll turn it up."

"What do you suggest?"

"I thought, just for a start, that perhaps I might hang round that pub in Soho. They can't assault *all* their customers."

"You're sure you won't get into trouble?" said Mr. Wetherall earnestly.

"That's all right," said Todd. "I'm not rugged, but I'm supple. I used to be reckoned one of the best dodgers in London. You're about all in," he added suddenly. "I'll get you a taxi. Or better still, Hoggarty lives in your part of the world. I'll ask him to run you home. The sooner you're in bed the better."

"I expect you're right," said Mr. Wetherall.

An hour later, as Todd was preparing to pack up for what was left of the night, the house telephone rang. He listened for a few moments and said, "Have you any idea what the old boy wants?"

The voice at the other end had no idea.

Todd went out into the corridor, took the lift up three floors, and went through a swing door marked "Private." A stepping up of the chromium, pressed rubber and indirect lighting indicated that he was approaching a higher authority.

He went through another door, and a middle-aged woman who was sitting at a desk said, "Straight in, Mr. Todd, he's expecting you."

"Did you realize, Aurelia," said Todd, "—I only mention it in case no one has ever broken it to you before— that you sound exactly like the *compère* at a Roman circus, saying, 'This way for the lions.'"

"That's your conscience," said the woman. "As a matter of fact he's in rather good form."

Duncan Robarts was the greatest editor that the *Kite* had ever had; at that time the brightest star in the night sky of Fleet Street. Yet "star" was hardly the word. Of heavenly bodies he most resembled a planet. There was no twinkle about him. He shone, with a steady, lowering power, and lesser bodies moved in their orbits under his influence. His private intelligence system was remarkable, and he knew every least member of his staff, and liked them all. The moment he ceased to like them, they ceased to belong to his staff. It was as simple as that.

"Come in, Alastair," he said. "Sit down. Tell me, now, who was that man you salvaged?"

Todd told him, as succinctly as he could.

"You were friends before, were you? What sort of man is he?"

Todd considered carefully before he answered.

"He's a likable person," he said, "and remarkably adult for a schoolmaster. In ninety-nine situations out of a hundred I should say he would behave in the decent, woolly way that his class always do behave."

Robarts was small and thick and he sat so hunched over his desk that he looked almost deformed.

"In the hundredth case," Todd went on, "if his blessed principles happened to be involved, and if he saw what he conceived to be a duty ahead of him, and if he got the bit between his teeth—well, I don't know of anyone with wrists strong enough to hold him."

Robarts swung his chair round suddenly, hopped out of it, and moved across to the fire.

"It's not quite our usual line, is it? What are you planning about it?"

"I don't know, sir. I thought of spending a little time on it myself, but I don't—"

"You think it's too big to tackle?"

"I certainly think it's too big for Wetherall to tackle."

"Don't you be too sure of that," said Robarts. He had his hands behind his back and he flirted his coat tail up and down like a sparrow in the spring. "The Liverpool race gang got broken up before the war—but I don't need to tell you about that—"

"No indeed," said Todd, fingering a white scar on the side of his jaw.

". . . because one stupid, obstinate, frightened little cockney bookmaker refused to play ball and got himself kicked to death behind the grandstand at Aintree. And the biggest racket in organized prostitution that this country has ever seen came to grief when one girl—one absolutely innocent girl—was arrested in Regent Street for soliciting and refused to back out by the easy exit that was offered to her—plead guilty and pay ten shillings—and stuck her toes in, in the face of every filthy threat that was made until—well, you know that story too."

"Yes," said Todd, "I know that story too."

Outside, a long way down, they could hear London coming to life. The lights were going out and the wheels of day were beginning to turn.

Robarts walked back to his desk and sat down. "Don't get us officially involved unless I tell you," he said.

SEVEN

West End Central

When Mr. Wetherall crawled back to consciousness next morning he found that most of his resolution had drained away. His right hand was an aching lump. His head was opening and shutting in hellish rhythm, and the first thing he did on leaving his bed was to be sick. After this he felt a little better and put some coffee on, using his left hand. Then he shaved and (very slowly) dressed.

The only grain of comfort was that, since it was a Tuesday, he need not be at the school until after lunch. Apart from this, the difficulties loomed in successive and aspiring crests.

First, he must have his hand dressed and set at the hospital. Then he must see the police. Then he must get hold of some money. And send his suit to the cleaners. And think out what to say to his wife when she came back that evening.

On the hall mat he found a further letter from Mr. Bullfyne.

"I have had no luck so far," said Mr. Bullfyne, "in placing your short story 'The Chimes at Midnight.' I myself

enjoyed it, and it was well written, but you might like to
see the comments of the editor of *Home Detective* which
I enclose."

Mr. Wetherall said something uncharitable about the
editor of *Home Detective*, but he had never yet had the
strength of mind to throw away such an enclosure un-
opened.

"It seems to us," said the editor, "that although Rupert
Fraser [the name under which Mr. Wetherall wrote] has
talent, he seeks to describe scenes of which he can have
no first-hand knowledge. If he would abandon his attempts
to describe night life, gangs and physical violence and
would devote himself to those sides of life—"

"Tcha," said Mr. Wetherall.

Divisional Detective Inspector Clark inspected Mr.
Wetherall with distaste.

"Where did this happen?" he asked.

"In a street off Dean Street, in Soho."

"When?"

"At about eleven o'clock last night."

"Then why wasn't it reported before?"

"I was in no condition to report it," said Mr. Wetherall,
indicating his hand which, plastered and strapped at the
hospital, lay like a whitewashed football on his lap.

"May I ask what you were doing in Soho at eleven
o'clock last night?"

"It doesn't seem to me to be entirely relevant, but if you
must know, I'd been having a few drinks—at a public
house."

"I see."

Inspector Clark managed to vest these simple words
with such a bottomless depth of innuendo that Mr. Wetherall wriggled afresh on his chair.

"Were you alone?"

"I started the evening alone. I finished it in the company
of a man who stated that he was a Scotsman. I understand

that his name is actually Higgins, and he earns his living by entertaining queues in Leicester Square."

Inspector Clark was beyond comment. To gain time he wrote down Leicester Square on the corner of his blotting pad. "Perhaps you would describe the men again—the ones who you state attacked you."

Mr. Wetherall described them again.

"Have you any idea why they should have attacked you?"

"Well, they took my wallet."

"Yes. Any other idea?"

Mr. Wetherall's mind stalled at this question, like a tired horse at a high fence. It had taken him an hour when he had talked about it to Todd the night before. How could he begin to explain it all over again to this large angry person?

"I—yes—" he said. "I did think that there might have been other reasons, but they're rather complicated ones. I don't want to waste your time."

Inspector Clark sighed. The expression on his face was more eloquent than speech. If, said his expression, fools get muddled up in matters they don't understand, and if their warped minds invent tortuous reasons to explain their imbecile conduct, then it was his unhappy duty to listen to them. That was the sort of work he was paid for. The job for which he drew his inadequate salary.

No treatment could have been better calculated to provoke Mr. Wetherall's familiar spirit.

"Well," he said more cheerfully, "if you're really sure you've got time for it, I *will* tell you about it."

It proved easier a second time, and in ten minutes he had reproduced, with very few omissions, the story of his doings during the previous week.

Mr. Wetherall had not been instructing classes for twenty years for nothing and one thing was apparent to him as he spoke. His audience might have started cold but it was warming up. The interruptions became fewer and fewer and the Inspector's careful parade of indifference became more and more perfunctory. At the end he was listening with more than interest. There was an undercurrent of stronger feeling.

"So it seemed to me," Mr. Wetherall concluded. "Although there isn't any direct proof, I know—this part is really only guesswork—but it did seem possible that the men who assaulted me were—"

A curious thing occurred at this point. He had been intending to finish the sentence by saying, "—were part of the crowd who run this food racket." Instead, at the last moment, and for no reason at all he changed it: "—were part of the crowd who murdered Sergeant Donovan's wife."

If he had produced a hand grenade, extracted the pin from it, and dropped it casually into the wastepaper basket, the effect could hardly have been more remarkable.

Inspector Clark jumped to his feet, turned extremely red, glared down at Mr. Wetherall, opened his mouth as if to say something, shut it again, and sat down with an effort at self-mastery that was so obvious as to be almost ludicrous.

Then he said, in a choked voice, "Will you kindly leave Sergeant Donovan out of this?"

"I'm sorry," said Mr. Wetherall. "As a matter of fact I didn't mean to mention Sergeant Donovan at all, but he happens to be a friend of mine—"

"I don't want to hear anything about Sergeant Donovan."

"Oh, all right," said Mr. Wetherall. "It was just a thought. Let's all forget about it, shall we?"

Before the Inspector could say anything further there was a knock on the door and a sergeant came in and put a note on the desk. The Inspector read the note, snorted, and said to Mr. Wetherall, "It looks as if we might have something for you soon. You said that one of those men called the other Sailor?"

"Yes."

"You're sure of that?"

"Well, as sure as I could be in the circumstances. There was quite a lot going on."

The Inspector looked at him with distaste.

"You realize," he said, "that if we arrest these men yours is going to be almost the only evidence—"

"The waiter in that night club ought to be able to identify them—"

"He might identify two men who called for you. That won't prove that they were the ones who assaulted you—"

"No—" said Mr. Wetherall, doubtfully. His head was aching, and he was disliking Inspector Clark more and more every moment. "There was a girl too—"

"A prostitute?"

"Yes—well, I'm afraid she probably was, but she seemed a kind creature."

"I'm afraid her identification wouldn't carry very much weight."

"I wouldn't know," said Mr. Wetherall, suddenly feeling he had had enough. "Perhaps it would and perhaps it wouldn't. But I can't help feeling that if you would concentrate a bit more on helping and a bit less on making difficulties, we should get on faster—"

"My duty is to assess the evidence, and see if there is a case on which we can act."

"Then assess it. Don't act as counsel for the defense."

"I don't think we need trouble you any more at the moment," said Inspector Clark, standing up.

He did not offer to shake hands. Mr. Wetherall fumed his way out into the street.

It was half past twelve and the sun was out. When he had recovered his equanimity it occurred to him that he might get some lunch before going back to school.

In spite of his aches his mind was tolerably clear, and as he sat at the café table, awkwardly ladling soup into his mouth with his left hand, he was hammering out a proposition.

Sergeant Donovan had been engaged in cases to do with food stealing. His wife had been attacked and (though possibly accidentally) killed. Sergeant Donovan hinted that he knew who was responsible, but he had not passed on the information to his superiors. Now he, Wilfrid Wetherall, had almost certainly run into the same crowd—or a branch of the same crowd—and had got into trouble. Yet any suggestion that the two cases were connected was anathema to the police. Or was anathema to Inspector Clark—who might not be the highest court of appeal.

It did not make sense.

And yet, in another way, it did.

"Cottage pie, mashed potatoes, anything that doesn't need cutting up," he said to the waitress.

"You hurt your hand?"

"It was trodden on by an elephant," said Mr. Wetherall. The girl rewarded him with a smile, and he suddenly felt better.

His good humor stayed with him until he got back to the school and found Colonel Bond there.

The first disconcerting thing about the Colonel's behavior was that he made absolutely no reference to Mr. Wetherall's appearance. Even allowing for the tidying up process which he had undergone in hospital that morning, it was, as he was aware, remarkable.

However, if the Colonel was going to play at not noticing anything, it was hardly Mr. Wetherall's place to bring the matter up.

They discussed staff discipline and the revised timetable for the coming term and the difficulty of obtaining reliable charladies at reasonable prices—reasonable, that is to say, so far as the pockets of the Education Committee were concerned.

At the end of it, and as he was on the point of leaving, the Colonel said, with ponderous casualness, "I hear you had some trouble in the West End last night."

"Yes," said Mr. Wetherall guardedly. "Yes, I did."

"Robbery, I suppose?"

"I'm afraid so, sir. I lost my wallet."

"Extraordinary," said the Colonel. "I've been living in

the West End for twenty years, and no one has ever taken my wallet."

"You must have been lucky."

"Just a question of—er—keeping one's wits about one," said the Colonel. "These chaps will always take advantage of you if—if they see half a chance."

While he had been speaking, he had been edging toward the door, and before Mr. Wetherall could think of any suitable reply, he had gone.

Mr. Wetherall sat staring after him.

Five minutes later Peggy came in.

"Well, you've done it this time," she announced.

"Done what?"

"Got 'em all talking about you."

"And just what," said Mr. Wetherall, "are they saying?"

"It goes by age groups. The younger ones say that you got lit up and took on three policemen outside the Wandsworth Tube. But Sammy won't have that—and he's got a lot of supporters."

"Sammy?"

"He says you got your face caught in Tower Bridge when they were winding it up."

"I see."

"The bigger ones say you went on a spree in the West End and got beaten up by a gang in Soho."

"They do, do they," said Mr. Wetherall thoughtfully.

The telephone rang.

"West End Central Police Station. Is that Mr. Wetherall?" said a woman's voice. "One moment please." Then a man's voice. "Superintendent Huth here, Mr. Wetherall. Could you come over here as quickly as possible, sir? I've got Inspector Clark with me here. We have two men we hope you may be able to identify."

"Yes—I think I could—"

"I'll send a car for you."

"All right," said Mr. Wetherall. "But for heaven's sake don't send it to the school, or you really will start something."

"I'll tell them to pick you up at the corner of the road," said Superintendent Huth.

The police had done their work well and fairly. The room seemed to be full of large men with reddish hair and open-air complexions and thinner men with white faces and black hair.

Despite the competition Mr. Wetherall picked out the two men as soon as he came into the room, and he saw from their expressions that they knew him and knew that he had recognized them. The red-haired man looked indifferent. The young one had a calculating look in his eyes which Mr. Wetherall found disquieting.

"Just line up there," said Superintendent Huth. "Now, Mr. Wetherall. Would you have a good look at them all. Do you see anyone you know?"

"Yes," said Mr. Wetherall. He indicated the two men.

"You have seen these men before?"

"Yes."

"Where was that?"

"Well—last night—in—I can't remember the name of the street. In Soho. They are the two men who attacked me."

"You're quite sure?"

"Yes, quite sure. I saw them twice, once in the full light, and then in the street. I particularly noticed this one—" he pointed to the red-haired man—"had a tiny yellow spot in the iris of his left eye."

Superintendent Huth moved across and looked into the red-headed man's eye with the gravity of a West End oculist. A police sergeant with a notebook wrote down, "The man identified had a yellow spot in his left eye," and looked gratified.

"And what about this one?"

Mr. Wetherall stared at the white-faced man, who stared back.

"Yes," he said. "There's nothing in particular about this one, but it's him all right."

"You're sure?"

"Oh, quite sure."

"All right," said Superintendent Huth. "The rest of you can go, and thank you very much. Would you come this way, Mr. Wetherall?"

He found himself in the Superintendent's office. The Superintendent had a shock of white hair and a hard but mobile face. Mr. Wetherall liked the look of him. At the moment he was sitting at his desk with the tip of his tongue showing out of one corner of his mouth, writing. He wasn't being rude. It was just that he had a lot to do and the moment for Mr. Wetherall's further assistance had not yet come.

After a few minutes, Mr. Wetherall's curiosity got the better of him.

"Who are those men?" he asked.

Superintendent Huth withdrew his tongue, placed one broad forefinger on the paper as if to pin down the thought he had been interrupted in penning, and said, "Hired bullies. The big one's name is Whittaker. His friends call him Red. The thin one, I think, is Jackson. No one seems to know anything for certain about him except that he was in the Navy during the war and was dismissed from the service for kicking a Maltese stoker to death."

"A sailor?"

"That's right. Sailor Jackson."

"And they work together."

"They and one or two others."

"Would a man called Guardsman be one of the others?"

"Could be," said the Superintendent.

"And Prince?"

"Which Prince?"

"An ex-boxer, with one eye."

"Again, could be. He's in the same trade." The Superintendent looked, for a moment, as if he were going to go on writing. Then, instead, he laid his pen carefully in the pen tray, tilted back his chair, and gave Mr. Wetherall a long stare.

"You seem to know a lot of these people," he said.

"Well, you see," said Mr. Wetherall, "I'm a schoolmaster. As a matter of fact I used to teach Prince. He was a horrible little boy."

"He hasn't gone uphill since. Did you teach the Guardsman too?"

"No. I met him in a café. Jock's Pull-In near the Elephant."

"Jock's Pull-In?" said the Superintendent. He looked as if he were going to say something about it, but changed his mind. "I suppose you meet a lot of queer types in your job. That's really the only difference between us. You get 'em young. We get 'em afterward."

"Not all of them, I hope. By the way, what will happen about those two?"

Again the Superintendent paused before answering. He was, thought Mr. Wetherall, being perfectly friendly but never, for one instant, coming off his guard. Possibly all policemen were like that.

"It depends what the others make of them," he said.

"The others?"

"We haven't been able to find the girl, but there's a busker called Higgins, and we've got the doorman and the waiter from the Minstrel Boy."

"I see," said Mr. Wetherall. "That's quick work. They all saw the men in a good light. And they're not the sort of faces it's easy to forget."

"It's quite surprising," said the Superintendent, "what some people can forget if they give their mind to it."

At this moment the door opened and Inspector Clark came in. He walked straight over to the desk.

"No go, sir, I'm afraid."

"None of them?"

"None of them."

Both men turned and looked at Mr. Wetherall, who went first hot then cold.

"Do you mean," he said, "that Higgins and those two men from the club—that they none of them recognize those two men?"

"That's right," said Clark shortly.

"No," said the Superintendent. "Not quite." He got up from his chair and sat on the edge of his desk. "Mr. Wetherall said, 'They none of them recognize the men.' That's not quite right."

The Inspector looked blank.

"They none of them *admit* that they recognize them. That's more correct, isn't it?"

"Oh, quite, sir. But it's all the same so far as we're concerned."

"It's impossible," said Mr. Wetherall. "There couldn't be the slightest question about it. That big one. Apart from anything else you can't suppose there are two men of just that size and complexion with a tiny yellow spot in his left eye—"

"No doubt," said Clark. "The pity is we shall have to say if we are asked that you didn't mention the yellow spot until you'd inspected the men at close quarters this afternoon."

"Do you believe me," said Mr. Wetherall, "or don't you?"

"It's not a question of believing. It's what we can prove to the court."

"Then you prefer their story to mine?"

Inspector Clark sighed.

"It's not just your story," he said. "They've got alibis. The usual sort. Playing cards with friends. But you can't laugh them away altogether. All right. Perhaps a court's going to prefer your word to theirs. But there's something more they're going to say. They're going to say you were so far under the influence of drink that you couldn't possibly have recognized anyone."

Mr. Wetherall swallowed hard.

Inspector Clark waited for comment, and then went on with a sort of patient reasonableness that Mr. Wetherall found more infuriating than bluster.

"Higgins agrees he had six or eight whiskies, and as you were meant to be standing level turns he's not likely to suggest you had less. And those night-club people say you were behaving queerly—banging ashtrays on tables—"

"That was Higgins."

"And there's a story about breaking a bedroom window in the house next door."

Mr. Wetherall sat still. He was angry. He felt angrier than he had ever felt in his life before, and he was trying to bring himself under control. If he lost his temper all was lost.

At last, when he was sure of his voice, he said:

"I asked you a question, Inspector, which you haven't yet answered. Do you believe me or not?"

"Since you put it to me like that, I think you may have been mistaken."

"All right." He had himself in hand. "That's blunt anyway. Now I'm going to ask a favor."

"Yes?"

"I want a word with Higgins. If he denies these two men to my face, then I'll give it up. But I don't think he will. I don't think he can."

"I'm afraid—" began the Inspector heavily.

"Let him see Higgins," said Superintendent Huth. He had been sitting so quietly that both of them had forgotten him.

"I think he's gone, sir."

"Then send someone after him. You can use this room, Mr. Wetherall. I expect you'd like to see him alone."

But Higgins had not gone.

Seen in broad daylight, and some hours away from the whisky bottle, he was rather a pathetic figure. He seemed to have shrunk inside his clothes. Daylight and sobriety had reduced him to half of himself. It was like meeting one's favorite actor for the first time in front of the footlights.

"Good afternoon, Mr. Higgins."

"Good afternoon, sir. I don't think I ever caught your name."

"I was your Cousin Hector last time we met."

"So you were, then. It was quite an evening, wasn't it?"

He seemed fascinated by the enormous bandage on Mr. Wetherall's right hand. His eyes kept swiveling round to it, and jerking away again, as if he realized that he might be drawn to a forbidden topic.

"Look here," said Mr. Wetherall abruptly. "Why did you tell the Inspector you couldn't recognize those men?"

"I—hmp—" said Higgins. "Well—"

"You saw them perfectly clearly. You must have done. They broke down the door of that room at the club. They not only went through it, they came back again. You must have seen them twice."

"I was lying down. I wasn't feeling very well."

"You were on your feet when I came through."

"Then I must have laid down again."

"Nonsense," said Mr. Wetherall, in exactly the tone he had so often adopted with an obstinate boy. "You're not telling the truth."

"It's very confusing."

"It wouldn't be confusing if you stuck to the truth. What's wrong with you? Are you frightened?"

"Yes," said Higgins, sitting down suddenly on one of the hard chairs beside the desk. "I'm frightened."

Mr. Wetherall felt at a disadvantage.

It was no good saying, "Well, don't be frightened." The fact was there. It was evident in every line of Mr. Higgins' dropped face and huddled body. It was in his twitching mouth and in his eyes, where the whites showed startlingly as in a horse that has been mishandled.

"It's easy for you," said Higgins suddenly. "You don't have to put up with it, like what I do. You've got a house of your own, with a front door, and if there's any trouble you get the blower and send for the police. I'm not like that. I've just got a bed in a room in a house in Lauderdale Street. You could walk into it right now. There isn't even a lock on the door. And I work, nights, in Leicester Square and if they wanted me they'd pick me off as easy as—as easy as knocking back a glass of beer, and think no more about it. You don't know them—"

"Oh, don't I," said Mr. Wetherall.

"It isn't just knocking down and kicking. Have you seen

that Jamaican that runs round with them? 'Pretty' they call him. Pretty! The other night he got in an argument, just over nothing, with another brown boy. And do you know what he did? I'm not telling you the tale—I was there—I saw it. He got out a knife—" Mr. Higgins gestured toward his own inner pocket—"just like that—casual like—like you or me might take out a fountain pen and sign our names—and he cut an inch off the end of his nose."

Mr. Wetherall scratched the end of his own nose thoughtfully, tried to laugh, and found himself clearing his throat instead.

"Did you tell the Inspector all this?" he said at last.

"Certainly not."

"And those night-club people. Are they the same? Is that why they won't talk?"

"It's worse for them. If they made any trouble their place'd get bust up."

There is something both disarming and flattering about a person who admits that he is afraid. It suggests, without precisely stating it, the corollary that you are not afraid yourself.

"Now you look here, sir," said Higgins, observing that Mr. Wetherall was weakening. "You leave those boys alone. They're not worth worrying about. Sooner or later the police'll catch 'em at it and run them all in."

"Well—" said Mr. Wetherall.

"You do that," said Higgins, "and I'll do something for you. It's something—" he held up a dirty hand and spread the fingers—"not that number of people in London know about. Keep your eye on that girl Annie. She's hot—"

"I didn't want you to go away thinking I'm happy about this," said Superintendent Huth, as he said good-by to Mr. Wetherall. "Some time back you asked Inspector Clark if he personally believed your story. You must never ask a policeman that. It isn't a fair question. What he thinks personally doesn't signify. All he's taught to look at is what sort of case he can put up in court next morning."

"All right," said Wetherall. He was tired of the whole

thing. His head was aching again and he wanted to get home. "You may be right. I wouldn't know. I haven't had much to do with police before."

"That wasn't all I wanted to say." The Superintendent was still patient. "I wanted to tell you that if there is any more trouble, I'd like you to get in touch with me straightaway. Either me or Scotland Yard. One of our people there has been handling these food cases for a long time. A lot of them start through me, because Soho's in my manor, but he gets them all in the end. Co-ordinating, you might say. The name's Hazlerigg. Chief Superintendent Hazlerigg. You might care to make a note of it."

EIGHT

To the Editor, Dear Sir

When Mr. Wetherall got home that Tuesday night he felt very tired; tireder than the night in 1939 when he had evacuated four hundred children on a special train to Leamington Spa (which was his previous standard of tiredness).

Since he could not conceal the state of his hands and face, he gave his wife a modified version of his adventures and fell asleep in the middle of her lecture on the folly of people who behaved like schoolboys the moment other people's backs were turned.

The next things of which he was clearly conscious were that the sun was shining, that, judging from the angle of the sun, it was very late, and that he felt a lot better.

"I thought I'd let you have your sleep out," said his wife. "I telephoned that girl of yours and told her you'd be late."

"Splendid," said Mr. Wetherall. A real night's rest had put its blessed curtain down between him and what had gone before. "In that case, perhaps I might have a second slice of toast."

At the school he found Peggy in charge and everything

running smoothly. If he had helped himself to a month's holiday and left the school in her hands he sometimes wondered if anyone would have known the difference.

"That horrible Clayton child," she said, "has come to school again with nits, and it's Nurse's Inspection Day tomorrow. I've locked him in the lavatory till he can be seen to. Here are the draft agenda for your School Board Committee on Friday—and—have you heard anything lately about Patsy?"

Mr. Wetherall was reading the agenda, which contained a new, and therefore suspicious, item and he hardly heard the last question. Then, looking up, he saw the trouble in her eyes and said, "What's that, Peggy? What's wrong with Sergeant Donovan?"

"I just wondered if you'd heard anything."

"Not that I can remember. Why?"

"You've been seeing a lot of the police lately."

"I can't remember anything—no, wait a minute. There was something. When I was talking to Inspector Clark I happened to mention his name and the Inspector looked as if he was going to blow up. What's Patsy been doing?"

"I wish I knew. He won't tell us anything, Mr. Wetherall. He just sits at home. He hardly goes out at all."

"He must go on duty."

"That's just it. He doesn't. I think he's been chucked out."

"Chucked out?"

"Suspended. Something like that. There's an inquiry on."

"Oh, dear." Forebodings came rushing back. "When did it happen?"

"Whatever it was it was this week end. He ought to have gone to the station Monday afternoon and he didn't. Inspector Clark was round to see him that morning, and then he didn't go. He's been sitting there ever since, like a bear with a sore head. If only he'd tell someone about it—" Peggy's sigh comprehended woman's entire view on the stupidity of man—"we might do something to help."

"It may be nothing to do with—all this other stuff," said

Mr. Wetherall. "There's no reason it should be connected.
It may be something quite different."

But he did not say it very hopefully.

It was while he was eating his lunch that he spotted the
letter.

It was in a weekly paper which styled itself Liberal but
which was, in fact, devoted to a pinkish, peevish brand of
intellectual socialism. Although he had long fallen out of
love with its politics Mr. Wetherall still read it for its
literary competitions.

To the Editor,
Dear Sir,

Used we not to pride ourselves, in this country, on
the freedom of the citizen? In these days, even if we
are bound in by a multitude of administrative restric-
tions (some of them necessary, many of them stupid),
do we not comfort ourselves with the assurance that,
at least, we are not a police state?

Now if I were asked to define what is meant by a
police state I should say that it was a country where
the police were not subordinated to publicly elected
representative bodies. Where, in fact, they were an-
swerable, in the last analysis, not to Parliament but to
the Administration.

Is England becoming a Police State?

Let me give you a small example which may be
typical of others.

Last week a police sergeant, in the alleged course of
his duty, but without either a search warrant or a warrant for arrest, forced his way into a restaurant to
question the proprietor on the subject of an alleged
food offense.

When the proprietor proved (apparently) "unco-
operative" he was subjected to brutal physical violence.
So far as I am aware the police sergeant concerned is
still a serving member of the force.

I am prepared to give to the Commissioner of Police

for the Metropolis the name of the restaurant and of the proprietor (who may himself be too intimidated to take any further step in the matter) and the name, number and division of the sergeant concerned.

Is this Liberal-Democratic England? Or are there neo-Nazis in this country as well?

The letter was signed "Mr. Pride" and was addressed from the Augean Club, Pall Mall.

What a scandalous thing, thought Mr. Wetherall, as he stoned a stewed prune and maneuvered it into his mouth. He was becoming very adroit with his left hand. What a shocking thing. It wasn't until he had finished his coffee and was getting up to go that it occurred to him that the letter might have something to do with him.

He sat down again and reread it. There was nothing in it to show. The letter was undated, and the latest, he supposed, that the paper could have received it would have been the beginning of that week. It said, "Last week a police sergeant. . . ." He cut out the letter and put it into his wallet.

He dismissed it from his mind; but it must have stayed in his subconscious and troubled his thoughts, for in the course of a single lesson on eighteenth-century history he managed to allot the Drapiers Letters to Junius and Mrs. Fitzherbert to Charles James Fox.

As he was getting ready to go home that evening Colonel Bond came through on the telephone. He was as soldierly and cryptic as usual, but Mr. Wetherall thought he detected a suggestion that it would be a good thing if the two of them had a quiet talk before committee on Friday.

"We might manage it tomorrow," said Mr. Wetherall doubtfully. "I'm very busy at the moment." Almost the last thing he felt in need of was a quiet talk with Colonel Bond.

"I think we should have a word. People are talking."

"What about?"

"Can't explain over the telephone. Committee's at twelve on Friday. I'll be there at eleven-thirty."

"Oh, very well," said Mr. Wetherall.

When he got home the first thing his wife said was, "He's moved."

His mind full of Sergeant Donovan, Mrs. Fitzherbert and Colonel Bond, he stared at her.

"I felt him this morning. Just after you'd left the house. He gave a little kick."

"Good heavens!" said Mr. Wetherall.

"It's called quickening."

"I'd no idea. I mean, I didn't realize they moved at all until they—er—came out."

"Good gracious, yes," said his wife. "He'll turn and kick now until the last week."

Mr. Wetherall absorbed the information in silence. It had not been brought home to him before that there was a third party actually in existence; a person who could be talked about as if he were alive; a person who would have to be taken into account with the hundred and one other confusing factors in his daily existence.

"There's a letter from Major Francis. Such a nice letter. He wishes we could all go out and see him. His daughter's had a second child. There's a bit about the Winnipeg floods, but he's all right, because he's on high ground."

Mr. Wetherall read the letter, and when he had finished it he folded it up and put it in his wallet, where it lay alongside the cutting containing the letter of Mr. Pride of the Augean Club.

Anyone who did not know Mr. Wetherall might have supposed that the episode was closed.

His bruises were fading. His hand, though still out of action, was comfortable. The medical attention had been paid for by the state, though there was still a cleaner's and a tailor's bill, perhaps a couple of pounds which would have to come out of his pocket. Most men would have accepted Superintendent Huth's verdict and would have written the thing off to experience.

"To one beating-up of moderate severity—forty shillings."

Not Mr. Wetherall.

At twelve o'clock on the following day, Thursday, he took a bus over Waterloo Bridge and got off it at the Aldwych. Then he walked past the Law Courts and Temple Bar, into Fleet Street.

It was not the offices of the *Kite* he wanted, because he turned north off Fleet Street into one of those seventeenth-century courts which have remained almost unchanged since the boy Pepys lived there with his father the tailor, and went to Church at St. Bride's. Successive blocks of offices have grown up round them, but have not destroyed them. Rather, they have preserved them, as Pliocene and Oligocene growths might incrust and protect a genuine Jurassic deposit.

In Hoopmakers Court, up two breakneck flights of stairs, lay the office of Messrs. Bertram and Moule, Solicitors and Commissioners for Oaths, whose sole surviving partner, Mr. Bertram, was Mr. Wetherall's man of law.

The office of Bertram & Moule was arranged with a simplicity which itself reflected a bygone age. It consisted of an outer room, an inner room and a passage. The passage was so full of black boxes that it was impassable, but since it led nowhere this hardly signified.

In the outer room, at a high desk, sat a young man who typed and dispatched the letters, drew up and delivered the bills, kept the accounts, answered the telephone and brewed the tea.

In the inner room Mr. Bertram practiced the Law.

He looked like a gangster. Not the big one, with the machine gun, but the small, cheerful one who holds open the door of the big shot's car.

He listened, in silence and without visible surprise, to Mr. Wetherall's story. Occasionally he closed his eyes. They were his most remarkable feature, set deep in his head, behind countless protecting folds, involute and overlapping as the petals of a rose; and in the middle, when you had lost your way among the bordering ridges and creases, like the treasure at the heart of the labyrinth, a pair of remarkably bright gray eyes.

"What are you going to do?" he said at last.

"Really," said Mr. Wetherall, "that's what I've come to ask you."

"I thought you might have some general idea. Do you want to have a go at the police for failure to do their duty?"

"Oh, no. That wasn't my idea at all. I just thought that if the police wouldn't prosecute these men, I could."

"Technically, yes. On the other hand it wouldn't be easy if the police were against you. But there would be nothing to prevent you starting a civil action against them."

"Then let's do that."

Mr. Bertram cogitated.

"It would be unusual," he said. "We'd have to serve them personally with the writ. I suppose it could be done. If you got a court to believe you, you might even get awarded damages. They wouldn't be easy to collect. Have they got any property?"

"A lot more than I have, I should think. They all go round in silk shirts with gold cigarette cases—"

"That wasn't quite the type of property I had in mind," said Mr. Bertram. "It would be a matter of delicacy to levy a distress against either of the articles you mention. Incidentally, do you know their names and addresses?"

"One is called Whittaker. Red Whittaker."

"Is Red his Christian name?"

"Really," said Mr. Wetherall irritably, "I don't know. That's the trouble with you lawyers. You do nothing but make difficulties. Do you mean to tell me that a man can come up to me in the street and assault me, and I can do nothing about it?"

"If the person who assaults you is a respectable citizen, with a proper name and address, there is, of course, a great deal you can do about it. If he is a person of the—ah— lower or criminal class, your remedies are less accessible."

"Well, I expect you know," said Mr. Wetherall wearily.

"It seems so monstrous and illogical that I'm prepared to believe it's correct."

As he got up to go he added, "By the way, do you happen to know a Mr. Pride?"

"Pride. Yes. The name is familiar."

"You belong to the Augean, don't you?"

"Of course. I knew I'd heard it. Marshall Pride. A tiresome little man. He's always writing to the papers. I trust he's not a friend of yours."

"Far from it," said Mr. Wetherall. "I just happened—"

"You remember the *Hoop* case. That was Pride."

"Not well," said Mr. Wetherall, reseating himself. "What was it?"

"He's no client of mine," said Mr. Bertram cheerfully, "so it's no breach of confidence. Pride wrote a letter which was published by the *Hoop*. It accused Collet—you may remember Collet. He's not an M.P. but he is, or was, a leading light in industry and trades unionism—of a lot of things that were nearly but not quite criminal. Disloyalty, talebearing, sucking-up to his chiefs, allowing bribery in his own department—and, I believe, for good measure it threw in personal immorality as well. It was cleverly written and wrapped up in a lot of high-sounding stuff and it was published under the usual heading—'The Editor accepts no responsibility for the views expressed'—and so on. But as a matter of fact it was fairly well known that the bosses of the *Hoop* had been gunning for Collet for a long time."

"I see," said Mr. Wetherall. "They used Pride as a stalking horse. What happened next?"

"Collet slammed down writs for libel against Pride, and the editors of the *Hoop* and the printers and everybody. There was a technical defense—the newspaper said it had printed the letter in good faith and as a matter of public interest—but Collet got reasonable damages against Pride and the paper. The *Hoop* paid all the damages. Collet faded out of public life—and Pride bought a new car."

"Do you happen to know him?"

"Personally? No. I see him at the club. I don't like him

enough to want to take it further. He's the sort of man you instinctively suspect of having a big, locked cupboard in his bedroom, full of dirty books."

"You don't make him sound very pleasant."

"He's popular enough—if popularity means being asked to every wedding and every cocktail party for fear of what he'd say if you left him off the list."

"If I wanted to meet him, could you manage it?"

"I expect so." Mr. Bertram looked as surprised as his face ever allowed him to look. "I could fix it through Duxford—he's one of his circle."

"It was just a thought," said Mr. Wetherall. "I'll let you know if anything comes of it."

When he got home that evening he found a letter from Alastair Todd waiting for him. It was a short letter, with a bulky enclosure, which turned out to be a sort of report. There was no indication of whom it was addressed to, and it started without preamble.

The Double Four is an odd setup. The saloon bar is quite a normal sort of place, I thought. The only really remarkable thing about it is the whisky, which is Scotch, all branded types and the supply unlimited. After a bit of hinting I was even able to buy a bottle to take away. Price forty-five bob. I half thought it would turn out to be vinegar and water, but it wasn't. No, sir.

The barmaid in the saloon bar is called Ethel, and she's rather a honey. At the moment she's my cover story for visiting the place so often, but if things go on as they are I shall soon be promoting her to the front page.

The private bar really is *private*. There's no fancy-diddle about this. If you go in you're turned out. I tried it the first night and the two Flash Alfs already there simply sat and stared at me as if I was something that had strayed in out of the comic supplement—and no one would make a move to serve me with a drink. I'm not thin-skinned about that sort of thing, but after a bit I saw the point and withdrew. The next day I got there bright and early and went in while it was still empty. Annie—the proprietress (-trix) I'm coming to her in a moment—shoved her head round the partition and said, quite politely, "Not in there, sir, if you don't mind. Plenty of room in the saloon. We keep that one for club members." Grossly illegal, of course, though I fancy it's done in quite a lot of these back-street pubs, only not often so openly.

Well, there it is. If we're looking for the headquarters of a mob, this could be it. I should have thought it was a trifle public for the hatching of schemes and the disposal of swag. Particularly if we're looking for a food-stealing racket. You could no doubt slip a bundle of pound notes over the counter as you paid for your drinks, but not a side of bacon.

I've had four sessions in there so far. Lunch and evening on Tuesday and lunch and evening on Wednesday. No one seems to find such persistence surprising. Why should they? I'd go there for the whisky alone. With Ethel thrown in, it's a walkover.

As I said, after a bit of a false start (I leaned over too quickly and spilled her gin into her lap), we're getting on famously. I'm afraid I'm not the first man in her life. Only last month a commercial traveler, who had been coming there regularly every evening for a month, "offered for her." He was a nice gentleman, steady income, and ever such good manners (*he* never upset her gin). But she had to turn him down in the end, *on account of what he traveled in.* I haven't been able to get out of her what this was, but I have my suspicions.

Last night was my most successful to date (I'm not talking about Ethel, now. My eye's back on the job). It's not possible to see into the private bar direct, but I got wedged up at one end of the saloon bar and there was one of those looking-glass-advertisement contraptions on the shelf that gave me a bit of a view. It was too messed up with gilt lettering to be much use, but I got occasional glimpses, and round about nine o'clock I saw a big, red-faced, red-haired man who looked as if he could have been one of your pals. Circumstances didn't permit of spotting spots in eyes, but I think it was him all right. He had a younger, black-haired type with him and that seemed to match up, too.

Mr. Wetherall discovered, at this point, that his left hand was shaking, and he put the paper down for a moment. "Must be getting tired," he said. But it wasn't that. In a sudden flash of pure intuition he had realized that the black-haired young man was the one who had broken up old Mr. Crowdy, as he lay beside the track. A pick helve or a spade, Sergeant Donovan had said. He picked the paper up angrily and went on reading.

My view wasn't good enough for me to see what they were up to. They left about ten o'clock. I toyed with the idea of following them, but decided that it wasn't the moment for heroics. It was lucky, in a way, that I didn't because I managed to get some gen about Annie that I might otherwise have missed.

Annie is some girl. I don't know when I've met anyone quite like her. She's not what I should call easy to get on with. Her appearance is a bit off-putting and she's got an insulting way of listening to all you have to say and then topping it off with a perfunctory laugh as if you were a child trying to amuse her with conjuring tricks. In fact, I believe I only really heard her laugh once (that was at a joke I should hesitate to repeat in any company) and it was a most extraordinary noise—like a marble coming out of the top of a full ginger-beer bottle.

But she's certainly all there, and she runs that pub in a way that makes Joe Stalin look like a National Liberal. The only weakness I've been able to detect in her is that she seems to be a soft touch for patent

medicines. By means of the same useful-looking glass
I got a glimpse into her private medicine store underneath the bar. From the glimpse I got of it, it was
crammed with every sort of mixture and tonic and
buck-you-up-oh that's ever been sold at nine hundred
per cent profit to a gullible public. Some enterprising
firm must be making a fortune out of her.

However, as I was saying, just before closing time
last night, I got into conversation with an old man. It
might be more accurate to say that he got into conversation with me. He was as tight as a tick, and had
obviously reached the stage where he had to tell somebody something. I just happened to be nearest so he
grabbed me. In the course of a twenty-minute mon-
ologue I never got as far as finding out his name or
anything much about him, but I did gather that he was
deeply in love with Annie, and that Annie would have
nothing to do with him. Dispassionately, I couldn't
blame her. He was a seedy old boy, with a long alcohol-
ic history written in his face.

"She's cold," he said, grabbing me by the sleeve, and
breathing into my face a blast of mustard pickle,
whisky and senile decay. "Cold as a nice-berg. Not
seckshually cold, old man—I don't mean seckshually.
Temperamentarally. Cold as a nice-berg." Did I know,
he went on, why her closest friends called her Icebox
Annie?

"Because she's cold as a nice-berg," I guessed.

"No, no. Not at all. It's a story," he said.

And a story it was. Even now I don't know if I believe it (but the mere fact that people *do* believe it
describes her better than I can do). It appears that
once, in the early days of the Hitler war, Annie had a
husband. She got tired of him, so she "stretched him
with a bottle." No doubt many a wife has done as
much before—and then screeched until the neighbors
or the police rolled up. Not so Annie. Being in the
catering profession provided her with certain amenities

not enjoyed by ordinary folk. She was the owner of several out-sized refrigerators, into one of which she pushed her better half. Thereafter, being, among her other accomplishments, a good rough butcher, she cut him up into very small parcels indeed, which she deposited, from time to time, in the swill bins set up at each street corner by a thrifty government. At the end of three or four weeks she had only the larger bones left, and these she parceled up and dropped off a pleasure steamer at Southend.

The whole thing was, thought the boys, an extremely neat job, with the right professional touch about it. It seems to have raised her no end in their estimation— though it's noticeable that no one has since actually volunteered for her hand.

I'd had about enough for one night, and shaking off old Mustard Pickle I pushed along out and went home to bed.

More soon.

Mr. Wetherall folded up the three or four sheets of typescript. The one he was reading was a carbon copy. It did occur to him to wonder who had got the top copy.

NINE

Ratcliff Lane, S.E.

When Mr. Wetherall arrived at the school next morning he was surprised to find that Peggy was not there.

In all his experience of her this had only happened once before, when she had scalded her hand helping with the weekend wash, and the chaos during the seven days she had been away was something he liked to forget.

He sent for Sammy, and found that he was absent too. There was no time to do any more about this. He went into morning school with vague misgivings.

At eleven-thirty Colonel Bond arrived. An air of mystery hung about his shoulders like a cloak.

Part of the Colonel's technique, as Mr. Wetherall well knew, was to allow the other person to start the conversation. It gave him the sort of tactical advantage which comes from sitting fourth in hand at bridge. It was an innocent gambit which Mr. Wetherall was usually willing to accept, but today he felt obstinate.

The Colonel had suggested the meeting. Let him get on with it and say what it was all about.

"There are matters," said the Colonel at last, "which I do not find it at all easy to discuss."

Mr. Wetherall contented himself with a nod. He was not going to abandon his moral position for a platitude like that.

"I'm a liberal-minded man, Wetherall. I think I may say that a lifetime of experience has made me so. Nobody could spend twenty years in the Army and thirty in a profession and on the bench and remain narrow-minded."

"I suppose not," said Mr. Wetherall.

What now? Smoking on the way to school? Mixed dancing class? Lavatories?

"What a man thinks is his own business. This isn't a police state." Mr. Wetherall looked up. He fancied he recognized an echo. "Liberty of conscience is a fundamental concept. Not a form of words, Wetherall, a fundamental concept. Most of us are in the happy position of being able to go further. We can not only think what we like, we can say what we think. We have no responsibilities. If the man in the street wishes to join—to join—" the Colonel paused for a moment as he let his mind rove over the varied fields of human activity—"the Co-operative Movement, then there is nothing to prevent him doing so."

Mr. Wetherall felt a very faint premonition of what was coming. He decided to force the pace.

"You mean," he said, "that people in positions of responsibility, like yourself, Colonel, or myself, have to be more careful than other people."

"Caesar's wife, Mr. Wetherall, Caesar's wife."

"Good gracious me! I *am* sorry. I had no idea—"

"I was using an analogy," said the Colonel crossly. He looked at his watch. He was being maneuvered into the unthinkable position of being forced to make a definite statement.

"It has been suggested—" he said, "I know the matter is to be raised in committee—is it true that you are—were —a member of the Communist Party?"

The cat was out now, claws and all.

"I was once," said Mr. Wetherall. "I'm not now."

"And you've severed all connection with them?"

"I never had very much connection. I paid two annual subscriptions and attended one or two meetings. Then I decided that they were even more stupid than the other political parties. So I gave them up. That was nearly twenty years ago."

"You paid subscriptions?"

"Two subscriptions, yes."

"To the Party funds?"

"I certainly didn't intend them as a personal gift to the treasurer, if that's what you mean. He was a greengrocer's assistant. A most unpleasant man. Even while I was a Party member he seemed to pick me out nothing but maggoty carrots."

"But he was official treasurer."

"Certainly. What is all this about?"

"As I told you. Miss Toup has given notice that she intends to raise the matter in committee. As chairman I hardly see how I can stop her."

"Short of cutting her tongue out, I doubt if you could," agreed Mr. Wetherall.

"It's very difficult. Of course, the committee would quite understand if you decided not to be present."

"I shall certainly be present," said Mr. Wetherall. He was pleased to find how well he had himself in hand. Two weeks ago such a maneuver would have left him speechless with rage. The events of the last fortnight had evidently toughened him.

"If the matter is going to be discussed," he said, "—though I have yet to be convinced that it is a proper matter for this or any other committee—I should certainly prefer that it was not done behind my back."

"Oh, quite, quite," said the Colonel.

"Well," said Colonel Bond. "That disposes of the midday milk question." He looked at a list of items on the agenda before him, all neatly ticked off. "Unless any member of the committee—?"

He allowed his gaze to rest on each of them in turn; on Mr. Hazel, small and sharp-looking; on Mrs. Griller, who spent all her money on clothes and still managed to look like a badly tied parcel; on Miss Toup, who was thin and rigid and was always unselfishly willing to express her Views on Subjects however Difficult.

It was Miss Toup who responded.

"I gave notice, Chairman, of an additional subject I wished introduced for preliminary discussion."

"Yes, Miss Toup."

"Then perhaps you would kindly introduce it."

Put on the spot in this cowardly way the Colonel cleared his throat, rearranged his papers, and said, "Miss Toup wished the committee to consider the subject of political affiliations so far as they may affect Heads of State Schools."

Mr. Hazel looked surprised.

"Is it proposed," he said, "that we discuss the subject theoretically?"

"Certainly not," snapped Miss Toup. Her nose was a little pink, and she so steadily avoided looking at Mr. Wetherall that the rest of the committee at once stared in his direction.

"Perhaps, then, Miss Toup, you would outline the nature of the discussion you propose," said the Colonel, playing the ball neatly back into her court.

"Certain allegations," said Miss Toup, "have been made, and I consider that the committee should discuss them and, if it thinks fit, make a minute of its conclusions."

"What are you talking about?" said Mrs. Griller, suddenly.

"I thought I had made myself quite plain," said Miss Toup.

"You haven't said anything yet," said Mrs. Griller. "Allegations. Political affiliations. What does it all mean? I'm a Liberal myself."

"The suggestion," said Miss Toup, "was that it was undesirable for the headmaster of a school—a State School— to hold extreme or openly avowed political views."

"Oh, you're talking about Mr. Wetherall. What's he done now? I thought you were a Conservative, Mr. Wetherall."

"I should like to put it on record," said Miss Toup, "that I did suggest that Mr. Wetherall should not attend this meeting. Apparently, however, he feels---"

"Please don't mind me," said Mr. Wetherall. "Just imagine I'm not here."

"That's all right, then," said Mrs. Griller. "Now tell us what he's done."

"May I ask you a question," said Miss Toup. "Are you a member of the Communist Party?"

"No," said Mr. Wetherall.

"Have you ever been a member of that Party?"

"Yes. I was once. I think it was eighteen years ago."

"Have you entirely severed your connection with it?"

"Entirely."

"And your political convictions?"

Now Mr. Wetherall had only got to say "yes." He realized it clearly. The matter could then hardly be taken further. There was a limit to the lengths which even Miss Toup could go; and, though not the most sensitive of women, she must have realized that the rest of the committee were not with her.

Unfortunately he had become suddenly and unaccountably so angry that none of these cool arguments carried any weight with him at all.

"I refuse to answer the question," he said.

"Ah," said Miss Toup, exactly like a bullying barrister who has at last extracted an admission.

"And I shall ask the chairman to rule that it is a most improper question."

"I—well—ah," said the Colonel.

"I must say I agree with Mr. Wetherall," said Mr. Hazel. "This is a school committee, not an inquisition of consciences."

"Well—if that's your view—" The Colonel turned to Mrs. Griller, in the evident hope that he could protect himself behind a majority opinion. But Mrs. Griller was out of her depth.

"If Mr. Wetherall will assure us," said Miss Toup smoothly, "that he is no longer an advocate of communism, I, for one, should be quite satisfied."

"I thought I had already made it plain that I left the Communist Party a very long time ago."

"You ceased to subscribe to its funds," agreed Miss Toup. "What I, for one, would be interested to hear is whether you ceased to subscribe to its opinions."

"Well, that's a plain question," said Mrs. Griller. "What do you say?"

"It's a question that the committee has no right to ask," said Mr. Wetherall, "and which I have no intention of answering. And I demand the protection of the chairman."

The Colonel looked unhappy.

"Then I move," said Miss Toup, "that the best method of dealing with the matter would be to minute the discussion without arriving at any conclusion."

"A minute—yes—perhaps the secretary—"

Mr. Wetherall, being himself secretary of the committee, obediently took up his pen.

"In what form would you like the minute?" he inquired.

"I should suggest," said Mr. Hazel, " 'A most improper question as to his personal political beliefs having been put to Mr. Wetherall, he very rightly refused to answer it.' "

"This is hardly the occasion for flippancy," said Miss Toup.

"I am perfectly serious," said Mr. Hazel. "I regard the matter as unpleasant, uncalled-for and out of order."

"Come, come," said the Colonel hastily (and, in the circumstances, rather belatedly). "We don't want any unpleasantness."

During the lunch break Mr. Wetherall telephoned his wife.

"It was the craziest meeting I've ever attended," he said,

"and when you consider our committee, that's no mean record."

"You don't think they were serious?"

"Serious about *what?* What do they think happens next? That's what made it so stupid."

"You say Miss Toup started it?"

"Yes. But Colonel Bond knew all about it. He was in it too."

"Supposing they report you?"

"For goodness' sake," said Mr. Wetherall. "Who to?"

"I don't know."

"If they were trying to goad me into handing in my resignation—or assaulting Miss Toup—it was mismanaged. They oughtn't to have warned me beforehand. If it had been sprung on me, I might have gone off the deep end."

"Well, I don't like it," said Mrs. Wetherall.

Mr. Wetherall didn't like it either. There were one or two things worrying him. Not the least was the absence of the Donovans. There was nothing he could do about that. They had no telephone and he was tied to the school all day.

At half past six that evening, when he was reaching for his hat and coat, he heard footsteps along the corridor and the red head of Sammy Donovan appeared in the gloom.

He was glistening with excitement.

"Oh, Mr. Wetherall."

"Where have you been all day? And where is Peggy?"

"She's home."

"What's wrong with you all?"

"Nothing's wrong," said Sammy. He sounded important, complacent and excited. "We can't move out till after dark. Even after dark's not easy."

"What on earth are you talking about?"

"It's Patsy. You heard what he did?"

"I heard something."

"You know you tipped him off about Jock's Café and Pop Maunder."

"Jock's Pull-In for Carmen," said Mr. Wetherall slowly. "Yes, I believe I did say something. What about it?"

"Patsy went round and busted Pop up—to make him sing."

"Sing?"

"Talk. He bounced him up and down on his head till he talked. He can get very mean, these days, Patsy."

"Yes," said Mr. Wetherall. He thought of Sergeant Donovan as he had last seen him. "Yes. But why—?"

"He got slung out of the police for it. Well, he's not actually slung yet, but he's going to be."

"What has all this got to do with not being able to go out?"

"The boys'd do him if he went out, Mr. Wetherall."

"Then why don't they come in and get him?"

"They couldn't do that. There's a lot of Irish in our street and they like Patsy, see."

"I see," said Mr. Wetherall. He tried to think dispassionately. "What do you want me to do?"

"Patsy wants you to come and see him."

Mr. Wetherall hesitated.

"It's quite safe," added Sammy tactlessly. "I'll show you the way."

"I wasn't thinking about that," said Mr. Wetherall. "If the truth were known I expect there's nothing to prevent us walking up to the front door—or Patsy walking out, for that matter."

"He tried it yesterday. Got fed up with sitting in the house and slipped out for a drink. There was three of them waiting for him at the end of the road."

"What did he do?"

"He ran," said Sammy, with a gap-toothed grin. "Patsy don't often run, but he ran this time."

"All right," said Mr. Wetherall. "If he really wants me, I'll come."

It was a curious journey. Immediately after crossing the Walworth Road they turned into the forecourt of a big block of Council flats, and walked across it, to the blind end, where one of the iron railings was missing. After squeezing through, they crossed what looked like a builder's yard, climbed a low wall, crossed another yard and came up against a further row of spiked railings. Again, one of these proved to be loose. Mr. Wetherall got the impression that he was moving along a well-used highway.

The next obstacle was a line of back garden walls which ran up to, but did not quite meet, a higher blank wall behind them.

"We gotter squeeze here," whispered Sammy apologetically.

They squeezed for about fifty yards. The gap grew narrower and narrower. Mr. Wetherall was about to protest when he found himself out in the open again.

"We gotter climb here."

The first step was a dustbin top, the next a ledge, and then the guttering along the top of a row of garages. Mr. Wetherall was beyond caring.

They creaked across a flat garage roof, lowered themselves onto the corresponding ledge on the other side, and dropped to earth.

"Our back garden," said Sammy. "Mind the chrysanthemums."

In the kitchen the Donovans were assembled.

Mrs. Donovan was a smaller, plumper version of Peggy. Her hair was gray, but she had the same steady eyes. When she spoke Mr. Wetherall realized that, like all the best families, the Donovan family was a matriarchy. And while the younger Donovans spoke pure cockney, there still lingered, at the rear of Mrs. Donovan's speech, a faint lilting tone. It was nothing that could be expressed in phonetics. It was as indefinite as an echo and it was a reminder that she had not always belonged to those dark streets, but had been born within sound of the surf on the West Coast of Ireland.

"I'm pleased to see you, Mr. Wetherall," she said. "I hope the boy has not been too rough with you. Go and brush your trousers, now, Sammy." Sammy muttered but obeyed. "It was my idea you should come here. I told Patsy he ought to speak before anything happens."

"Before anything *else* happens," said Peggy.

The person who had not spoken so far was Sergeant Donovan. He was sitting at the head of the table, in the same disquieting attitude of repose. Now he looked up and said, "You heard I got into trouble."

"Sam started to tell me."

"It was Maunder. He gave me some back talk, see. Mentioned Doris. Then I hit him."

"Did you hurt him?"

"Yes." Sergeant Donovan looked surprised. "Yes. I hurt the little bastard right enough."

"Tell Mr. Wetherall what he said to you afterward."

"When I'd finished with him he started talking. He hadn't got no more tick left in him than a busted clock. So he told me things—about his end of the racket. He didn't know a lot, but he told me all he did know."

"And have you passed it on?"

"No one's asked me yet. Next thing I knew old Clark was round here, telling me I'd been suspended. You could've knocked me down."

It was the speed of the thing that had surprised Mr. Wetherall too. He was not surprised that Patsy should have got into trouble. Sooner or later, in any police force, a policeman who bounced suspects on their heads would be likely to be looking for another job. It was the speed with which Sergeant Donovan's mouth had been shut that he found astonishing. Then, remembering the letter to the newspaper he began to have a faint idea of how it had been handled.

"Tell Mr. Wetherall what Pop told you," commanded Mrs. Donovan.

"You know he runs a café, Mr. Wetherall, for rail men and transport drivers."

"Yes, I've been there."

"There's a yard at the back for parking lorries. You seen that? All right. Now say you're a railway worker who's got a vanload of hot stuff. Two or three cases of tea, or tinned ham, or a crate of poultry, or whatever you like.

You drive into Pop's parking place—better, perhaps, to wait till it's dark, but you could do it by day if you had to—and you park your lorry with its back up against Pop's back door, and you go in and sit down at one of the tables Pop serves himself. When he comes to take your order you tell him what you got for sale and fix a price. Two cases of tea, say, at five pounds a case. No one's to tell what's happening. You might be arguing over the prices on the menu or the result of the 3:30. And that's all there is to it."

"That's all?"

"When the driver goes out to pick up his lorry two cases of tea are gone from the back and there's ten pounds in notes under the driver's seat."

"I see," said Mr. Wetherall. It seemed simple and fairly foolproof. He thought back to his visit to Pop's café. It could have been going on all round him. He would have been no wiser.

"Where does the stuff go then?"

"Into Pop's storeroom for a day or two. Then the boys come and collect it."

"Red and Sailor and Guardsman and the rest?"

"That's right. Your boy friends. They run two or three lorries of their own. Quite legitimate. My guess—it's only a guess—they run the stuff up Central somewhere and store it."

"You don't think Pop's is the only place of its kind?"

Sergeant Donovan leaned back in his chair. "I'm damned sure it isn't," he said. "And I'll tell you something else, Mr. Wetherall. As soon as you shut one they'll open another. The word gets round—"

"Then as I see it, the people who are essential to the running of the thing are Red and his crew."

"They're just a heap of muck," said Sergeant Donovan. "If you got rid of them tomorrow there'd be another lot doing it the next day. There's no shortage of muck in this town, if you're prepared to pay the rates for dirt."

"Yes. But this happens to be the particular heap of muck who are doing the work at the moment."

"That's right."

"Who are they working for?"

"If I knew that," said Sergeant Donovan, and the gust of his anger blew him to his feet, "if I knew that I shouldn't be arsing round here wasting—" He caught a look from his mother. "I'm sorry, sir," he said. "It's got me down."

"That's all right. I really wanted to know. Is there any sort of lead up from this crowd to the man above them? If I follow what you said, these men collect the stuff and dump it somewhere, and distribute it to the Luigis and others. And they collect the money from them, and get tough with them when it's necessary. But unless they're the people actually running it—"

"Not them. They haven't got enough brains to run a Sunday School."

"Then they must pass the money on—less their cut—to someone else. Perhaps they don't all know who it is, but *someone* must know what the arrangements are."

"They may know. They won't talk."

"Guardsman might talk," suggested Mrs. Donovan softly.

There was silence in the little kitchen. A draft from the window was swinging the unshaded electric bulb and chasing the shadows across Sergeant Donovan's scarred face.

"He's had a two-stretch," went on the old lady. "He'll collect a handful next time."

"Something in that," said Sergeant Donovan. He sat down as abruptly as he had got up. "Mother means that if Guardsman was actually took, on the job, he might talk to save his skin. He's had a full prison sentence already. It'd be five years penal servitude next time he was caught."

"Caught doing what?"

Sergeant Donovan thought seriously about this.

"Assaulting the police," he suggested at last with a smile.

Ten minutes later Mr. Wetherall was back in the Walworth Road. Sammy, who had escorted him, brushed him down, and said, "If you want any help, Mr. Wetherall, don't forget me."

"All right," said Mr. Wetherall, and he meant it. It had gradually become plain to him that he was involved in a business where a bald head full of brains might be less use than courage and red hair.

TEN

Fleet Street and Pall Mall

On the following morning Mr. Wetherall paid two visits in the Fleet Street area.

The first was to a twenty-four-hour café in St. Columbus Street much used by newspapermen. At two in the morning it was usually crowded but was emptyish at more conventional times. Here, at a scrubbed wooden table in the corner, he found Todd.

Five minutes' talk brought Todd up to date. Mr. Wetherall poured it all out, in no sort of sequence—the failure of the identity parade, the row in committee, the conversation with his solicitor, the trouble over Sergeant Donovan—and Todd sat, stirring his coffee, his head tilted, his eyes bright.

For no particular reason it was one of the pictures which was to remain in Mr. Wetherall's mind when more significant matters had faded.

When he had finished, Todd drank the last dregs of his coffee, spooned out about an inch of damp sugar, and said, "Down in the forest something stirred. Could be a tiger, could be a bird. Or could be a red herring. Plenty of life in this jungle."

"You think it all hangs together."

"Of course it does. It's the technique. If you'd listened you'd have heard me telling you about it the other night."

"Even my troubles in committee?"

"Certainly."

"I refuse to believe that Miss Toup is a member of a gang."

"I doubt if she realizes it herself," said Todd. "And the fact that you can say that shows what a darned clever crowd you're up against. Or else it's just because your ideas are so old-fashioned that you're incapable of grasping what's happening. These boys don't sit round in cellars, in hoods. They're big business. They know how to use friends and influence people. Look here—I've no more idea than you have how it was worked but suppose—just for the sake of supposing—that someone, some influential person who was vaguely 'something in the City' approached your Miss Toup and said that he happened to be a trustee of a large fund which could only be used for educational purposes. He himself had heard of the South Borough High School—and the good work which Miss Toup was doing on the committee—and would like to make a handsome donation to the school. There was only one snag. His fellow trustee was a very staunch Tory. He wouldn't countenance giving a penny to a school where the headmaster's politics were suspect. They had heard that Mr. Wetherall—it was doubtless only a rumor—was actually a member of the Communist Party. Could she find out the truth of the matter? Perhaps if she raised it in committee, etc., etc., you see what I mean."

"Yes," said Mr. Wetherall slowly. "I should think that she'd be very susceptible to an approach like that. She's got a hide like a hippopotamus and about as much brain as a bee. What about Sergeant Donovan? The same technique?"

"I'm not sure. They may have played off the wrong foot

there. They had to move very quickly. And when you move
too quickly you're apt to put yourself out of position for
the return shot."

"I don't understand."

"Well, it was awkward. They so much prefer to play this
game at businessman level. Influence and blarney and
threats and bluffs. Sergeant Donovan went and spoiled all
that. He waded in and used his fists. And what's more, he
turned up some real information. There was only one thing
to do. They had to put him on the spot. Raise a public
stink, so that whatever he'd found out no one would dare
to use it. A normal citizen would have gone to the Commissioner and lodged a complaint. They couldn't do that.
Too risky, and too slow. So they go to their patent poison-
pen man and get him to write to the press. That blows
it up all right. The police were bound to act on that. Only
thing is, as I said, in their anxiety to move quickly they
may have moved too quickly."

Todd did not develop this. He tilted his chair until he
was balanced crazily on the back legs. His mind seemed
suddenly to have moved two squares forward.

Mr. Wetherall was on the point of asking for further
explanations when another thought distracted him.

"Any luck with Annie?"

"Annie?" Todd moved back to the present with an effort.
"Why, yes. I think I've solved Annie."

"For goodness' sake—!"

"It was an exercise in empirical logic. Like a crossword
puzzle. Your first three answers are guesses. The fourth fits
them all, and locks the thing together. First a fact about
which there's no doubt. All 'the boys' use the private bar at
the Double Four. It's a sort of thugs' clubhouse. I've seen
them all now. Last night I spotted little 'Pretty,' the Jamaican, a sweet boy with the nicest smile. I imagine he used
to smile just that way when he sat on his mammy's knee,
castrating the cat, or whatever kids do before bedtime in
Jamaica. Second thing is this. You remember me saying I
didn't think it'd be a good place for handling stolen food

and drink. Correct conclusion, wrong premise. They don't handle food. All they hand over to Annie is money. She's cashier and paymaster."

Mr. Wetherall nodded. Since he had had his talk with Sergeant Donovan he had been working the thing out for himself, and that was how he saw it must go.

"I take it they've got a central warehouse of some sort," he said. "They take the food and drink there by lorry from the collection points—places like Jock's Café, I mean—and they distribute it from there to the restaurants. That's right, isn't it?"

"That's right. The people who are really running the show never touch the stolen stuff at all. They just get the money."

"You mean the boys pay it over the counter to Annie and she—what does she do with it? Take it to Mr. X, the next man up?"

"I don't suppose she takes it personally."

"Posts it, then."

"Yes. I think that's how she'd do it."

"That makes it a bit awkward, doesn't it? If we want to get any further we shall need Post Office help."

"I had an idea about that, too," said Todd. "I told you I'd been doing some thinking. Remember, Annie's no fool. And it's absolutely essential that the link between her and Mr. X shouldn't be spotted. She wouldn't just package up the pound notes and send them off openly to him. She'd want some sort of cover. Well, she's got one ready made. It's the sort of stupid thing that's so damned obvious no one sees it at all. It's that patent medicine merchant. What would be easier? Everyone knows about Annie and her patent medicines. She writes to him quite openly. She sends him money from time to time. I expect it's the sort of firm that gives you money back on the bottles. That would be another excuse for sending off packages."

"It could be," said Mr. Wetherall. "There's nothing to show either way. And it still isn't going to be easy to prove."

"If it had been easy," said Todd, "it wouldn't have been right. This isn't an easy league we're playing in."

"Who is the medicine man?"

"It's a company. Holoman's Cures, Ltd. Somewhere off the North Pentonville Road."

"Holoman's. I'm sure I've heard the name."

"They advertise a lot." Todd glanced down the advertisement page of his evening paper. "They're not in today, but you often see them. 'Lumbago, Sciatica, Blood Pressure, Boils and Fallen Arches. Why waste money on the doctor when Holoman's can kill you just as quickly.' That sort of line."

"I wasn't thinking of advertisements," said Mr. Wetherall. He was folding back his copy of the *Kite*. "It was in the jobs column I thought I'd seen the name somewhere. I cut these out for my boys if they look promising. I'm pretty certain—yes, there you are. And it was in yesterday, too."

"Smart Boy wanted," said the advertisement. "General dispensing, packing and clerical work. Salary by arrangement. Prospects. Apply the General Manager, Holoman's Cures, Ltd., 5 Strudwick Road, N. 7. Only written applications will be considered."

Mr. Wetherall and Todd looked at each other.

"It's certainly an opening," said Todd. "Had you anyone particular in mind?"

"Sergeant Donovan's brother, Sammy. He's a smart child, with eyes on both sides of his head. And one blessing, we shan't have to explain it all to him. He knows most of it already."

"Yes, that sounds all right."

"The next thing is to make sure of landing the job."

"Keep his price low enough and fake up some good references. What with National Service, boys aren't all that easy to get nowadays. Come to think of it, you'd better not write him a reference yourself. If it *is* the same crowd the mere sight of the name of the South Borough High School will make them leap like mountain goats."

"I'll get him one from his scoutmaster," said Mr. Wetherall. "That always goes down well with an employer."

"All right. And I'll back it up with a good social one. What would you fancy? A judge or a bishop? We've got both on the payroll."

As they got up to leave Todd said, "You're sure Sammy's got his wits about him?"

"He's a sensible boy," said Mr. Wetherall. "A good boxer at his weight, and as sharp as they come. After all, it isn't as if we wanted him to do anything very startling. Just to keep his eyes open and see if he can spot any funny business. Why?"

"A sudden attack of gooseflesh," said Todd.

Mr. Wetherall's second call that morning was in Hoopmakers Court and he was fortunate enough to find Mr. Bertram in his office. It is true that he had taken the precaution of telephoning to make an appointment, but an appointment was not always a guarantee of Mr. Bertram's presence. He was a one-man firm, and if something more important cropped up a client had to wait and like it.

He listened attentively to what Mr. Wetherall had to say, breaking off only twice to answer the telephone, and once to sign a bundle of pink forms which the boy brought in.

"There isn't much you can do about it," he said at the end.

"But she was making a dead set at me—insinuating the most frightful things. Isn't it libel or something? Supposing I lose my job?"

"She told the committee you had once been a member of the Communist Party."

"Yes."

"As you had?"

"Certainly. But—"

"She went on to ask you if you were still a Communist."

"Yes."

"Which you're not."

"Certainly not."

"But you refused to tell her so."

"It was none of her business."

"Certainly it was her business," said Mr. Bertram calmly. "What's a school committee for if it isn't to look into the character of the headmaster?"

"Politics is nothing to do with character."

"In any event, she'd be completely covered by the defense of privilege—unless you can prove that the whole thing was done from spite."

"No. I don't think it was quite that. But I don't see why she should be privileged and not me."

"I can't explain it," said Mr. Bertram. "It's not logical, but then the law of defamation is not in the least logical. It's just one of those things you'll have to take my word for."

"All right," said Mr. Wetherall. "It doesn't seem right that she should be able to get at me without me getting back at her. Still, if you say so. There's one thing. Isn't there some place near here where you can find out all about companies?"

"Any member of the public is entitled to make a search at the Registry at Bush House."

"And you can find out who runs a company and what sort of business they do."

"You can ascertain the names of the directors," said Mr. Bertram precisely, "although I am afraid that will not always tell you who runs the company. As for the business being done, that would depend on whether the company has to file its accounts. Some do, some don't."

"I see. I should imagine that this company would be just about as secretive as it could possibly be. But I'd like you to see what you can get. Would you be able to do that for me?"

Mr. Bertram reflected.

"It would really be just as easy for you to do it yourself," he said. "It's not the sort of thing you need a solicitor for at all. However, I'm sending the boy down to the Stamp

Office before lunch, so if you want me to, I'll have him
look in and see what he can pick up. I'll drop you a line on
Monday."

"A Mr. Todd to see you," said the club waiter to Mr.
Pride.

Mr. Pride sighed. "You didn't tell him I was here?"

"Certainly not, sir. I said I would ascertain."

"Who is he? Did he say?"

"I did gather, sir, that he was from the press."

"Oh." Mr. Pride clothed himself with indifference as a
novice puts on a white sheet. It caused the waiter, who was
a student of human nature, considerable pleasure. "Well.
Perhaps I'd better see him then."

"I put him in the Small Card Room."

"I'll be along in just a minute."

"Very good, sir."

"The penalty of fame."

"Quite so, sir."

The Small Card Room was so called because it had
been used, at the turn of the century, to accommodate a
few members who preferred the new and noisy game of
auction bridge to the dignified solemnities of whist, but it
was now chiefly used as a repository for bound numbers of
the *Illustrated London News* and the *Estates Gazette*. Mr.
Pride found Todd waiting for him, seated on a table,
swinging his legs.

"Mr. Pride?"

"Yes. I'm afraid—"

"I'm from the *Kite*." He presented his card.

"Oh, yes. I expect you want to ask me about my Syrian
letter." Mr. Pride settled himself happily into one of the
chairs. "I am aware that the views I expressed were somewhat revolutionary—"

"It wasn't your Syrian letter, Mr. Pride. Although, speaking for myself I found it very stimulating. But our readers
were interested in—what shall I call it—your metropolitan
letter."

"My—?"

"I'm sure you remember the one I mean. Your letter criticizing the conduct of a sergeant in the metropolitan police." Todd unfolded his notebook with a vigorous snap. He was not looking in the direction of Mr. Pride, but a picture of Queen Victoria opening the Fishguard Ferry afforded him an excellent reflective surface.

After a short pause Mr. Pride said, "Oh, yes. Scandalous. Perfectly scandalous. What can I tell you about it?"

"Well, now. Perhaps you could give us some of the background. For instance, how did you find out about it?"

"My sources of information—"

"I take it you weren't an eyewitness."

"Good gracious me, no."

"Then someone must have told you about it."

"As I was about to say, I fear I cannot divulge my sources of information. Being a newspaperman yourself, I'm sure you will understand."

Todd let that one go.

"I must admit," he said, "that it wasn't exactly the source of the information that interested me. Speaking as—er—one newspaperman to another, it was the *speed* of your information that I found intriguing."

Silence fell in the Small Card Room.

"I'm not sure that I follow you," said Mr. Pride at last.

"I'm a newspaperman," murmured Todd. "It was the mechanics of the thing that interested me. The particular weekly paper you wrote to comes out on Tuesday. Its day for distribution to news agents is Monday and it is 'put to bed,' as we say, on Sunday night. In the normal way nothing could be included which was received after teatime on Sunday. Even that would be cutting it fine."

"What about it?"

"Nothing, really. Except that the outrage of which your letter complained took place late on Saturday night—about twelve hours before you wrote the letter."

"If you think," said Mr. Pride a little breathlessly, "that

by making observations of this sort you are going to bam-
boozle me into revealing my sources of information—"

"Of course not," said Todd. "By the way, when did you
post your letter?"

"I—I walked round with it."

"Very public-spirited of you." Todd made a note in his
book.

"The sooner these matters are given publicity the better."

"I quite agree with you. You write a good many letters
to the papers?"

"Not a great many. The difference between me and
other writers to the papers is that my letters are *always*
published."

Mr. Pride gave a slight smile as he pulled this one off,
and it stung Todd into an indiscretion.

"There are other ways in which you are unique," he
said.

"Several, I expect. Which had you in mind?"

"Other writers to the papers write solely for the pleasure
of seeing their views in print. At least, I had always supposed they obtained no more—er, no more material re-
ward."

There was a further silence. Mr. Pride seemed to be
seeking for speech.

"Perhaps you would explain what you mean."

"I think my meaning was quite clear."

"And I understand your not caring to repeat it. There
is a law of defamation in this country."

"There are other laws too," said Todd. "Simpler and
older laws. I seem to remember, 'Thou shalt not bear false
witness against thy neighbour' and also 'Thou shalt not
steal.' "

Without waiting for a reply he turned on his heel and left
the room. As he went he retained an impression of a very
white face and a pair of blazing eyes.

"He was angry all right," reported Todd on the telephone
to Mr. Wetherall. "But, if you see what I mean, angry in

the wrong way. There was a lot of fright mixed up with it. I'm going to keep on at the little beast. If I'm right, he's a loose end that the other side have left hanging out, and the harder we tug him the better."

At about the time that Todd left the Augean Mr. Bertram rang the bell for his assistant.

"I've changed my mind," he said. "I'll go down to Bush House myself."

"If it's only stamping and a company search I can do it," said the youth resentfully. A trip to Bush House meant a nice break, and possibly a cup of coffee too.

"No," said Mr. Bertram. "There may be more to it than that. I'll go."

He reached for his bowler hat and tittuped thoughtfully down the stairs and out into Fleet Street. Around him the traffic roared. So far as Mr. Bertram was concerned, it roared unheard. His thoughts were elsewhere.

Principally, he was thinking about Mr. Wetherall; about the facts which he had mentioned and, even more, about the facts which he had plainly suppressed.

Mr. Bertram was nobody's fool. Anyone who has prospered as a one-man solicitors' firm in the heart of London must have his wits about him and his ear pretty close to the ground. Names meant a lot to him. The knowledge of who was who and who did what was his stock in trade.

Quite often, on the way home to his house in Kingston, he would pick out some small item of news in his evening paper and would wonder, as he looked round the crowded carriage, if there was anyone else, reading the same news, who knew what it meant. Why Sir Archibald Hearty had resigned as managing director of the Mucilage Galleries or the reason for the youngest Gaiter boy joining the board of Imperial Glue; or even why Captain Corrigan had sold all his race horses and gone to live in Ireland. Probably not; and Mr. Bertram, being a solicitor, would have been the last person to have enlightened them.

Musing thus he arrived at Aldwych and turned into the

uninspiring southwest wing at Bush House. He paid his shilling, filled in a form, and sat down at a table. He had not long to wait, and presently he was opening a thin blue folder headed "Holoman's Cures, Limited."

He produced a piece of paper and a pencil and jotted down a few notes, his tongue flickering between his lips as he wrote.

Formed in 1945. Authorized capital of one hundred pounds. Issued capital five pounds. Registered office at 5 Strudwick Road, N.7. The usual memorandum—which generously permitted a company with three pounds capital (and ninety-seven more in reserve) to do anything from promoting a luxury hotel to running a liner. Normal articles. Nothing in the Charges Register. No accounts.

One of the issued shares was held by Mr. Henry Holoman, one by Mrs. Anita Holoman, three by Mr. Arthur Herbert. The directors were Mr. and Mrs. Holoman. The secretary was Mr. Holoman.

Mr. Bertram's pencil paused for a moment in its scribbling. Far down in the distant, undusted recesses of his mind a memory had stirred. He was unable to pin it down. Such memories were like quicksilver. If you tried to grasp them, they were gone. He pursued it with a growing sense of frustration. A futile attempt. Perhaps he would remember it later, when he had stopped thinking about it.

His pencil resumed its scribbling.

It was Todd who got the news, in the young hours of Monday morning, as he was beginning to think of going home to bed. The sub who brought it up was worried. "You knew the man, didn't you?" he said. "Then perhaps you can suggest what we're going to call him."

"You couldn't print anything I should call him," said Todd savagely.

"We thought of 'clubman' but that's a bit dated."

"Call him a journalist," said Todd. "That covers almost everything."

So that was how Mr. Wetherall (and a lot of other people) read about it over their Monday-morning breakfasts.

Tragedy at Pinner [it said]. Journalist killed.

A heavy transport lorry, drawing a three-ton trailer, on long-distance haulage ran out of control at Pinner yesterday evening when the steering locked. Fortunately the streets were not crowded at the time. The lorry mounted the pavement and hit and killed Mr. Marshall Pride, who was a well-known figure in journalistic and literary circles. The lorry passed right over him and death must have been instantaneous. The breakdown gang were still at work an hour later trying to lift the wreckage.

ELEVEN

North of the River: Sammy at Holoman's

Mr. Pride's death was announced on Monday morning; on Monday afternoon Sammy started work at Holoman's; on Tuesday evening he wrote a letter to his sister Peggy.

"This is a queer sort of place and no mistake," he wrote, in his well-formed cursive hand, "if I had known the job meant staying nights I might have thought twice about it Mr. Holoman is a case he looks like Boris Carloff only worse Mrs. Cameroni she is the woman who does for us here is deaf but not a bad old girl I think everyone else is round the bend except me I get off Saturday p.m. and will be with you for tea Dont eat all the sandwich spread before I get there your loving brother Sammy."

Sammy sealed this with several loving kisses and determined to slip out and put it in the box at the corner of the road as soon as Mr. Holoman had departed up west on business. So far as he could gather he usually went out in the evenings and was not expected back before eight.

Precise information was hard to come by. First there was Mrs. Cameroni, who acted as housekeeper to the establishment, got the meals, tidied up and fussed round generally.

She seemed a decent enough person and for some time, under the impression that she was his employer's wife, Sammy had addressed her as Mrs. Holoman. Nor had she corrected him; simply because, as he had discovered by accident that afternoon, she never heard him; being not only deaf but, like many deaf people, defiant of her infirmity.

Then there were the girls.

Sammy had had great hopes of the girls. There were two of them, a floppy blonde and a thinner girl with mouse-colored hair and a band round her teeth. They formed the packing-room staff.

Sammy was fond of girls, in a general sort of way. He liked them better in quantities than singly. He enjoyed the chi-hying and the repartee and the general give and take.

Accordingly, during the lunch interval, he had made his way into the packing room. The girls had suspended their packing of Mother Mankeltows Mucilage of Molasses and were sitting on a bench eating sandwiches out of a bag.

At first all had gone well; indeed, from the beginning almost too well. Sammy's opening remarks had been received with smiles. Even his ordinary conversation was smiled at. Everything was smiled at. Neither girl seemed to have a great deal of conversation in return. The blonde girl did nothing but smile. The mouse-colored girl squeaked and said something which sounded like "Ham for lunch" but she mouthed her words so that it was difficult to establish anything beyond the fact that it was an effort at good will.

After a few minutes of this Sammy withdrew.

"Just my luck," he said to himself. "Two girls, and both of them barmy." In fairness he added, "They seem to get through their work all right." He had never seen such workers.

He had restored his spirits by standing himself an expensive lunch, which he could not afford, at the Corner Dining Rooms.

The morning had been spent copying addresses into a

book. When he got back after lunch he had been summoned to the presence and introduced to the more important branches of his work.

"There are certain basic mixtures," explained Mr. Holoman, "that we use in most of our preparations."

He was a tall man, thin but with obvious strength in his long bones. He had the mottled, peach-veined face of an old country clergyman, white tufts in each nostril, and the shadow of an imperial in the unshaven patch under his full lower lip. His least prepossessing characteristic was his head of hair. If it had been a wig, thought Sammy, it wouldn't have been so bad. But since it clearly wasn't a wig, it looked somehow abnormal and horrible, a wolf's pelt of thick black and gray hair. He had black hairs on the back of his hands, too. His eyes were hot brown, and his voice was like treacle. It reminded Sammy of the voice of a minister whose services had once attracted large congregations in the New Cut, until he had disappeared as a result of overenthusiasm in training female members of the choir.

"I shan't bother you with all our little technical secrets," went on Mr. Holoman. "But I can see you're a smart boy, so I might as well tell you at once that you will find that most people are fools where their own health is concerned."

Sammy nodded. He felt interested in spite of himself. Such a diagnosis agreed very well with his own observations. He had an aunt who had spent all her money on an Elixir of Life. It had done her no visible harm, but at ten shillings the bottle it had consumed a great deal of money which, in Sammy's view, she might more profitably have saved and left to her nephews and nieces.

"There's one born every minute," he agreed.

"We have just finished the diarrhea and prickly heat and are preparing for the coughs and colds. In the profession we refer to them as catarrhal afflictions." Mr. Holoman smiled genially. "We use nothing but simple wholesome ingredients. Phenol—" he indicated a large stoppered jar full of a pinkish disinfectant—"and sodium chloride." This was a cardboard box.

"Looks just like salt," said Sammy.

"I shouldn't wonder if you were right," said Mr. Holoman. "Our standard gargle and throat spray, two shillings and sixpence the bottle, contains one measure of phenol—measure it out in that little glass jar—to four measures of sodium chloride. You can use a tablespoon for that. The rest is aqua pura."

"Where do I get that?"

"Out of the tap."

"Do you mean you can sell that stuff for half a crown a bottle?"

"It is often difficult to meet the demand for it."

"Cor," said Sammy. His respect for Mr. Holoman increased.

"There are, of course, certain overhead expenses, connected with advertising and the like, which you would not appreciate. There is the bottle itself—a scandalous price these days, though we usually succeed in getting them back by offering a small rebate. One of your jobs will be to clean the returned bottles. See that you do it thoroughly. Our clients are not of the highest class, and we had a bottle returned the other day nearly one third full of gin, which I can assure you was *not* in it when it was dispatched. Finally, and possibly of more importance than anything else, there is the label. One to each bottle." Mr. Holoman extracted a gummed label from a cardboard box. It was quite an imposing and well-printed affair. It had "Holoman's Special Gargle Mouthwash and Throatwash" in old-fashioned lettering and a portrait of a man with a long beard, an eyeglass and a high collar. On the left of the portrait was a list, in small print, setting out the honors and awards which had fallen to the gargle in its long life (First prize, Palace of Health, Chicago, 1888. Grand Prix, Exposition de Santé, Bruxelles, 1893, etc.). On the right in larger print was a summary of the conditions which it was guaranteed to cure or alleviate (Catarrh, Hay Fever,

Tonsilitis, La Grippe, Pleurisy, Asthma, Biliousness, Constipation and Consumption).

"The label is most important," said Mr. Holoman. "I should say of paramount importance. And you must be particularly careful to place the right label on the right bottle. Your predecessor had to be asked to leave after an unfortunate incident in which he sent out a dozen of Embrocation for the Legs and Thighs labeled as Blood Tonic. Strictly, and between you and me, the difference in the ingredients was not large, but there was a principle at stake."

Sammy had spent an interesting afternoon. He was no ball of fire at mathematics but it didn't need an accountant's brain to see the margin of profit in selling salt and water at two and sixpence a bottle. A certain amount of outlay would be needed for printing and advertising, but as soon as that was paid for—

Sammy swam away into a happy daydream and inadvertently doubled the dosage of phenol in a whole boxful of gargle, which, as Mr. Holoman sharply pointed out, halved the profit, since phenol was virtually the only ingredient which cost anything.

After tea he was introduced to another branch of the trade.

"Ointments, or unguents, as you must learn to call them, are in a way an even better line than medicine. Certain of the more tiresome and restrictive of the various acts of Parliament that hamper the druggist, do not apply to ointments, and there are other considerations with which I will not weary you."

"I'm not tired at all," said Sammy, and he meant it.

"Splendid," said Mr. Holoman, with a smile which lifted the lip and revealed a row of small, sharklike side teeth. "Youth is the time to learn. The trouble about unguents is that it is more difficult to persuade people that they stand in need of them. With medicines it is different. With a little effort anyone can believe anything about their own insides. *Omne ignotum pro magnifico.* With the external parts it is more difficult. I therefore devised what has turned out to be one of my most successful dual remedies. It is to cure harshness, roughness, staleness or irritation of the skin. It is also effective against eczema, ringworm, corpulence and baldness, but these are only by the way. Its main purpose is that you should at once apply it if you feel any uneasiness of any sort about your skin. We send it out in two caskets, at half a crown each, with full directions for use. You apply a little from the brown casket, and that brings out the latent condition. In other words, if you had itched a little before, you will now begin to itch like anything. This is not surprising when you consider that the ointment in the first casket contains a high proportion of powdered rosa canina, known to the ignorant as itching powder. Five minutes later, when you can bear it no longer, you apply some ointment from the green casket, and the itching stops at once. You are absolutely cured. This line has been so successful that I fear our rivals have paid us the compliment of imitation. Some people have no idea of commercial morality."

Later, when Sammy was thinking of packing up for the day, Mrs. Cameroni blew in. She was a large, cheerful, untidy woman and to Sammy she represented the only homely touch in the place. If she hadn't been deaf, he decided, she'd have been quite good value.

In self-defense she had acquired a certain facility for lip reading, but principally she followed a system of guessing what you would be likely to be saying. Conversation was a lottery.

"Lovely evening," she said.

"Scrumptious," agreed Sammy.

"That's right. Keep cheerful. Your first job, I expect."

Sammy nodded.

"Work hard and you'll do all right. He don't pay badly. Not but what he can afford to, the money he makes. Comes rolling in. Rolling." Mrs. Cameroni held her hands six inches apart to indicate the width of the roll.

"Seems a pretty good racket to me."

"You want to leave those girls alone, though. They're not quite—you know. You wouldn't believe it, one of 'em had a baby just before she came here. It's not right, you know. A girl like that. She ought to be stabilized."

"They're both barmy, aren't they?"

"Lovely stuff. Why, I'm telling you, he gave me a bottle the other day, free and for nothing. Two and ninepence it'd have cost me in the shop. I rubbed it on my leg, and I was soon skipping round, I can tell you. Felt as if I was on fire. You just keep your mind on the job, put the bits in like he tells you, and shake it up well, and you'll make your fortune too. It's just what a smart boy like you wants. Get into a profession. Well, I mustn't stand here gossiping all day. Got my husband's supper to cook. Works all day at the National Gas Board and the temper he's in when he comes home in the evening, you wouldn't credit it. Talk about gas!"

After Mrs. Cameroni had gone, Sammy took another look into the packing room. The two girls were finishing for the day, too. One was carefully making up her face at a mirror, the other was sitting on a chair, in a startlingly disengaged attitude, as if someone had put her down there and forgotten about her.

Sammy went back to his room and sat for a few minutes swinging his legs. He heard the clatter of feet and the banging of the door as the two girls left. He was alone in the house. He was in charge. It was part of his job to look after things in the evenings when Mr. Holoman was out.

It was the part of the job he cared for least. He could stand up to anything his weight on two legs, but silence and loneliness were more insidious enemies.

Better start doing something, he told himself, or you'll be getting the heeby-jeebies. Even those girls would have been better than nothing.

Doing something? It suddenly occurred to Sammy that this was the moment for investigation.

"Don't get into trouble," hadn't Mr. Wetherall said, "but keep your eyes open. Watch out for letters and packets—

particularly any with the W.C. postmark on them. See if
you can find out what's in them. Notice when Mr. Holoman
goes out and try and remember if he says where he's been.
Take a note of what visitors come to the house."

All right. He would keep out of trouble. But there was
no harm in snooping around a bit. The house was empty
and he would hear Mr. Holoman's key in the lock in plenty
of time to stop doing whatever he might be doing. His
spirits rose.

There were really only two places for investigation. On
the ground floor there was Mr. Holoman's office and upstairs there was his bedroom. The rest of the house seemed
too open for secrets.

The office was the more promising of the two, but here
Sammy suffered a check. The door was locked. And not
just an ordinary, old-fashioned morticed lock, he noticed
(which any of the downstairs keys might have fitted), but
a bright, efficient little lock inset, two-thirds of the way up
the door; new, and quite outside Sammy's limited attain-
ments as a burglar.

He cast his mind back to the short time he had spent
in the office when he had first arrived. He seemed to remember that the window was barred. He went out into the
scrubby garden at the side and had a look to make sure.
It was barred, all right. New-looking bars, and too close
together even for a boy. Upstairs, then.

The house was quiet, and yet, when you really settled
down to listen, not entirely quiet. There were very faint
creakings and rustlings with occasional rather human gur-
glings from the old-fashioned water system. Strudwick Road
itself was quiet, but distantly from the Holloway Road
came the sound of cars.

The bedroom door was not locked. In fact, it stood ajar.

Overcoming a sense of outrage at investigating so private
a matter as someone else's bedroom, Sammy went in.

It was full of the usual sort of stuff you expect to find
in bedrooms. A double bed, a dressing table, some flowers
on the mantelshelf. Signs, Sammy supposed, of the invisible

Mrs. Holoman. Now that he stopped to notice it, the room smelled faintly of woman.

There was a mahogany chest of drawers with comb and brushes and an old leather collar box on top, which was plainly Mr. Holoman's territory, and Sammy concentrated first on this. The bottom drawers were full of things like flannel shirts and sensible ankle-length pants, all neatly laundered and folded. The smaller drawers looked more interesting. The left-hand one was full of socks. One pair looked unnaturally bulky and Sammy picked it out. It was heavy, too. Which was explained when he unrolled it and a small bright-looking automatic pistol fell out onto the floor.

Sammy picked it up, remembering to use his handkerchief, rolled it back into the socks, and replaced the socks in the drawer. His confidence had increased. Ordinary people, he argued, did not keep automatic pistols rolled up in their socks.

In the other drawer under the collar and handkerchiefs were a lot of papers. They looked quite ordinary—bills and such-like—and they looked as if they had been in the drawer some time. They were not hidden in any way. Sammy fingered them doubtfully. He hadn't time to read them, and it would be too dangerous to take them away. Underneath the papers there was a square of photographs. It was the sort of thing you got from a photographer who took a lot of small pictures and you picked out the ones you wanted and had them enlarged. What was in the drawer was not the whole sheet. It was a piece torn out of it. Sixteen snapshots of a woman, in early middle age. Not bad-looking, in a hard way. Mrs. Holoman, Sammy guessed. She looked the sort of woman who would smell the way that room smelled.

Sammy hesitated again. If he cut off one of the portraits it was bound to be noticed. Equally so if he took the lot. Compromise. There was a pair of scissors on the dressing table. He picked them up and snipped off one complete row of four portraits.

As he put the scissors down, he thought he heard a faint sound in the passage outside.

In a flurry he crammed the photographs into his pocket, shut the open drawer, and tiptoed to the door.

All he could hear was the steady slam, slam of his own heart.

There was still one more place to search, and he might never have such a chance again. The hanging cupboard.

He edged over and tried the handle. The door was stuck, but not locked. He gave it a jerk, and as it came open his heart somersaulted up into the back of his throat. There was a very tall man standing there. At least it looked like a man. Really it was only a freak of arrangement. The hat on the shelf, the dark coat and trousers hanging from the hook, and the shoes sticking out under the trousers. Sammy had had enough.

He slammed the cupboard door and bolted out of the room. There was no one in the corridor, and no one downstairs. He went to the front door and opened it. In the short time he had been upstairs dusk had crept over North London, bringing up with it a light haze from the river. Each of the street lamps looked out through a gauzy veil of mist.

He came to the conclusion that he was safer in the street than in the house. He knew that he was not supposed to go out and leave the house empty (or was it empty? He supposed it was empty). Some sort of excuse was wanted. He felt in his pocket the letter he had written earlier in the evening. That would do. No one could blame him for going out to post a letter to his sister.

He set off down the street.

In spite of his preoccupation he kept his eyes open, because he could no more help observing than he could help breathing.

Strudwick Road was not a very interesting road. It was akin to streets he knew in South London, but more elderly, more changed in decay. The gentility which had once reigned was still there; in the houses, with their false fronts like toupees, their ornamental urns, their unnecessary porticoes with the high front steps, which had once raised the gentleman in the parlor above the slavey in the basement.

Had he known it, it was in that district, and in just such a house, that another famous purveyor of patent medicines had lived; and Pentonville Prison, in which Dr. Crippen had died, was not many hundred yards from the end of Strudwick Road.

"Wotter dump," said Sammy. He dragged his feet round the complete block, up Strudwick Road, turned right into Austerberry Road, and right again into Mutlow Terrace. Here he was momentarily cheered by the sight of the entrance gate and turnstiles of the Elephants Football Club. He had never got around to watching them play, but they were his League favorites. It gave the place a feeling of home.

At the end of Mutlow Terrace, running at an angle into the Holloway Road, was a short street of shops, small grocers, stationers, tobacconists and the like. They kept no exact hours, and most of them were still open.

Sammy went into a stationer's and bought a large envelope. Into it he pushed the letter he had already written to Peggy, together with the folded row of photographs he had taken from Mr. Holoman's bedroom. Then he stuck down and addressed the large envelope. The Post Office was shut, but there was a stamp machine which sold halfpenny stamps. Sammy bought what he judged to be sufficient stamps and posted the letter.

That was one small item off his conscience and he felt the better for it, but he still had no particular wish to go back into the house. The sight of a telephone kiosk gave him an idea. A friend of his who, at the balance of sundry transactions, had owed him ninepence had liquidated the debt by showing him a system by which, with a certain amount of practice, you could ring up from a public telephone without actually putting any money into the machine.

Sammy rang up the school, but got no answer. He then tried Mrs. Wetherall's home and learned from Mrs. Wetherall that her husband was out at a meeting of the

Save London Committee, and not expected back until much later. Feeling that he had nothing to lose Sammy next tried the office of the *Kite*, and, after some delay, got put onto Mr. Todd. He explained to him what he had been up to.

"He had a gun in his sock drawer, did he? Was it loaded?"

"I didn't look, Mr. Todd."

"Just as well. If it was an automatic you'd just as likely have shot yourself. Any chance of getting into that office?"

"It's always kept locked, except when Mr. Holoman's in it."

"Keep trying," said Todd. "The money's the important thing. Watch what he does with the post in the morning. That should give you a line." He was about to ring off when another thought struck him. "I think you'd better ring me up every day. When would be best?"

"I get off about four for a cup of tea."

"All right. Ring this extension between four and six every day. If I'm not in there'll be someone to take a message. And look here—all this ringing up must be costing you something. I don't see why it should come out of your pocket. Let me know at the end of the week—"

"Don't worry about that," said Sammy handsomely.

When he had finished telephoning he decided to watch the bus stop in the Holloway Road to see if he could spot Mr. Holoman coming back. Luck was with him, and he saw him almost at once, getting off a trolley bus, carrying a small suitcase.

Doubling round the back way Sammy got into the house in plenty of time to be sitting quietly in his own room when Mr. Holoman arrived.

Shortly afterward they had supper together. It was cold stuff, which had been prepared and left for them by Mrs. Cameroni. It was an odd, grown-up sort of meal of meat and pickles and brown ale, and Sammy rather enjoyed it. Mr. Holoman had brought back two evening papers, and they read one each, propped against pickle bottles. There was a good deal less of "Don't put your elbows on the table, don't drink with your mouth full of food" than Sammy was used to at home. He felt he was getting on in the world.

Everything was left on the table, presumably for Mrs. Cameroni, when she came in the morning to cook their breakfast.

"You'd better get up to your room now," said Mr. Holoman. "I've got some work to do. Don't go reading to all hours. And don't smoke in bed. The last boy nearly set the house on fire."

"All right," said Sammy. He had never smoked in his life.

He went up to his room. It was after nine o'clock. He decided that the thing to do was to wait until about ten o'clock, then turn the light off, but stay awake. The first part was all right. It was the second bit which caused the difficulty. He had had a long and rather exciting day and as soon as he lay down, fully clothed as he was, boots and all, he felt himself dozing off.

"This won't do," said Sammy. He sat up and wedged his back against the bars of the bed. There was an iron knob, which dug into him halfway up his backbone, and he reckoned this should keep him awake all right.

At some indefinite time later he woke with a start. The house was quiet, but the street lights were still on and it was not, he guessed, very late. He was still sitting up. His mouth was dry, and there was a bruise in the middle of his back where the knob had failed to keep him awake. He took his boots off, and sat and listened some more. Then he got up, opened his bedroom door, and went out onto the landing.

The linoleum was cold under his stockinged feet, but blessedly silent.

Suppose that Mr. Holoman came suddenly round the corner and asked him what he was doing? What was he doing? He was going to the lavatory. There was a cloakroom and lavatory just inside the front door. No one could be blamed for going to the lavatory.

The stairs were carpeted, and Sammy got down them,

too, without making a noise. At the turn of the stairs the door of Mr. Holoman's study came into view and he saw that there was a light on. Evidently Mr. Holoman was still at work.

When, with infinite care and precaution, he reached the study door, he realized that there was more than one person in the room. Two at least, he thought. He could distinguish Mr. Holoman's dry, conversational tone, and another, much softer; so soft that it was difficult to tell if it was a man or a woman. Also, there was another noise that worried him. It sounded like someone with a heavy cold, snuffling.

Sometimes words came through.

He heard Mr. Holoman say, "I'm sorry," in the tone of voice of someone who was not in the least sorry. And a thin voice saying, "Just a week."

Without stopping to think much about it, Sammy decided that he must have a look. There was a chair in the hall and he had discovered in the course of his explorations earlier in the evening that by standing on it he could just get his eye to the small fanlight. It was frosted glass, but the frosting was inefficient along the bottom edge and he knew he could see Mr. Holoman's desk.

A few moments later he was in position, his fingers hooked onto the dusty lintel. It proved more difficult this time, probably because he now had no boots on. He strained up on tiptoe, taking his weight on his fingers.

There were three people in the room, and he could see them all.

Mr. Holoman was seated behind the desk. Forward of him, in a chair, sat the woman of the photograph.

The third occupant of the room was a little, gray-haired man, whom Sammy had not seen before. Both Mr. Holoman and the woman were staring at him, and Sammy, unaccountably, felt more frightened than he had ever felt in his life.

The snuffling was explained. The little man was crying.

TWELVE

How Mr. Wetherall
Made Up His Mind and
Suffered a Disappointment

On that same Tuesday morning Mr. Wetherall arrived at
the school in good time.

Among the letters waiting on his desk was a legal-look-
ing one from Mr. Bertram.

He read it, but absent-mindedly. It recorded the bare
results of Mr. Bertram's investigations at the Companies
Office, but did not seem to take matters very much further.

It was evident that Holoman's Cures, Ltd., was one of
those extremely private companies which are little more
than the legal projection of the personality of their founders.
Mr. Wetherall understood, in a vague way, that it was a
device highly thought of in trade to turn yourself into a
private company, and that somehow or other it gave you
immunity from your debts; which was a desirable thing,
come to think of it, in any walk of life.

His thoughts were interrupted by the arrival of Peggy.
She seemed to have something on her mind.

"Had that Toup woman round here last night," she said.

"Miss Toup," amended Mr. Wetherall gently.

"The Dowager Duchess of Toup," said Peggy unabashed. "Do you know what she wanted?"

"I can't imagine."

"She wanted to inspect the classrooms. I told her all the boys had gone home. Balmy. She still wanted to go round. I had to get the keys and unlock all the doors for her. I'd half a mind to lock her in for the night."

"What did she seem to want?"

"She was looking at all the blackboards and notice boards. You know what she's like." Peggy gave a rapid imitation of a short-sighted lady peering up at a notice board. "There was a frightfully rude drawing left over from Mr. Em's biology class. I thought that might choke her off, but she just sniffed. What do you think she wanted?"

"I imagine," said Mr. Wetherall, "that she was looking for evidence of left-wing propaganda."

"Come again."

"She has got it into her head that I am an active member of a subversive group. I expect she thought she would find notices, possibly with small hammers and sickles in the corners, calling on the proletariat to cast off its chain."

"Oh, was that all," said Peggy. She still looked worried. "It's none of my business, but you wouldn't perhaps have been—well, annoying someone, would you? Without noticing it perhaps?"

Mr. Wetherall had known Peggy for most of her life, and it suddenly occurred to him that she was genuinely upset: more than she would have been on account of Miss Toup. They had laughed at Miss Toup often enough.

"What's up?" he said.

Peggy gave him the long, steady Donovan look which always made him wonder whether he had got up without putting his tie on, and said, "Someone propositioned me last night."

"He did what?"

"It wasn't a him. It was a woman. I haven't known her

long. I thought she was all right, only evidently," Peggy's mobile nose was wrinkled, "she isn't."

"Who was it? And what did she say?"

"I don't think I'd better tell you who it was, really. It wouldn't do any good. She was only passing it on from someone else."

"All right. Just tell me what she said."

"She told me I could make some money. Quite a lot of money."

"Oh," said Mr. Wetherall. "How?" He tried not to sound shocked, but was aware that he wasn't making a very good job of it. "I mean, don't tell me if you'd rather not."

"I expect I'd better tell you," said Peggy. "It was cash down, on the nail, if I'd go to the police and say you'd been fooling about with me."

There was a long silence.

"And what did you say?" said Mr. Wetherall at last.

"Oh, I told her to take a running jump at herself," said Peggy lightly. "What did she think I was, I asked her. If I went to the police every time people made passes at me, they'd have to call up the Specials."

"Well thank you very much anyway," said Mr. Wetherall. "Don't you think you ought to tell me this woman's name?"

"I don't think it'd do much good, really. I'd say she was in on the job fifth hand. In fact I only passed it on because I thought you might have been treading on people's toes without knowing it. Someone's certainly got it in for you."

"Someone certainly has," said Mr. Wetherall. "Would you mind checking all those bills? The last three lots have been added up wrong, and all in his favor, I notice. I don't know if Williams imagines that because we're a modern school we can't do simple arithmetic."

When Peggy had gone Mr. Wetherall sat for some time staring at the calendar on his desk. He did not seem to be worrying about the date, which had not, in fact, been altered for about a month, but he was reading, with close attention, the gilt lettering across the top which said "Get Your

Scholastic Supplies from Skimbles" and lower down "Courtesy and Service Combined with Economy."

He might hide it from other people, he thought, but it was no use trying to hide from himself the fact that he was badly shaken.

He had been a schoolmaster, and a headmaster, long enough to know the peculiar pitfalls which lie open beside that path.

The first malicious whisper; the inevitable busybody; then the inquiries, which hurt everyone; the children questioned by police officers who knew as much about children as he himself knew about murderers; the court proceedings, the case (as often as not) dismissed; and then the clatter of tongues, the "No smoke without fire" brigade—and another promising career moved quietly into balk.

How many teachers, how many people known personally to him had gone out on that tide?

He recalled that when he had first come to London he had listened to a friend, a very old hand in the trade, who had told him of two resolutions that he himself had made and kept; never, whatever the salary and prospects offered, to teach in a school with girls in it, and never, if he could help it, to see his pupils alone out of school. Even if you had to give private tuition, he said, give it as a class, not to individuals.

It was absurd that such precautions should be necessary. He remembered he had thought that the man was exaggerating, but had lived to discover the contrary.

And now, suddenly, this unexpected angle to the attack.

He felt more than shocked, he felt frightened. There is something unnerving about hidden malignancy when it comes to light. The mine in the path, the blade in the pocket, the poison in the food.

If his enemies disliked him so much, if they were prepared to go to such lengths, where would they stop? They had foundered this time on the exceptional rock of Peggy's integrity. He didn't think they were the sort of people to make the same mistake twice.

In his considerable distress and confusion he could only find one fixed light, one point which was absolutely clear. He was in a position where there could be no standing still. A sitting man was an easy target. Either he went on or he got out.

That afternoon Mr. Wetherall set his history class to write an account of the Battle of Leipzig, and turned his problems over in his head.

He looked so grim that the class worked with great diligence and produced essays of unusual distinction.

When Mr. Wetherall got home that evening he found a note from his wife and a letter from Major Francis.

Spelling had never been Mrs. Wetherall's strong point and her husband was not therefore unduly alarmed to read that she had gone out "to the anti-natal clinic."

"Dear Folks," wrote Major Francis. "How I wish you could be out here now. The fall's the best time of year. The colors of the leaves have to be seen to be believed. Don't believe what you see on the Travelogues. They don't give you the half of it." Somehow Mr. Wetherall felt vaguely comforted as he read it. It was agreeable to think that someone could get excited about the color of leaves. "When I said that I wished you could be out here," the letter concluded, "I wasn't just being polite. I really do wish it. Could you and Alice not come over here for a long vacation? Nothing under six months would be worth your while, and maybe you don't have school holidays that long, but if you called it a cultural study tour I expect your governors or committee, or whatever it is, would give it their blessing. Why not try it? Just give that great mind of yours to it, Wilfrid. I seem to remember you weren't the man to let difficulties stop you once you'd set yourself on a project."

Not the man to let difficulties stop him?

His mind went back to Major Francis. A big, blond, rather silent man, who wore rimless glasses with an air of serious purpose which camouflaged a very kind heart. A widower; shy to start with, but thawing remarkably once you got to know him. He had been billeted with the Wetheralls for most of two years at Leamington Spa, and a sad coincidence of loss had drawn them very close.

First there had been the time—he didn't like to think of it even now—when Alice's first child had died unborn. No reason in particular that the doctor could see. Just the strain of life as it was being lived at that time. A microscopic war casualty. (That was what made this one so doubly important. All must go well this time.)

Then there had been that bleak Monday when the news had come about the Major's only son who had been doing his pilot training at Fort Shilo. Exactly what Mrs. Wetherall had found to say to Major Francis her husband had never discovered. He had kept out of the way, pleading overwork. It was an excuse that really had some validity in that mad time, when horizons were short and everyone was doing the work of three, and seemed to thrive on it. Perhaps everything that had happened in England since had been a reaction from that period.

He fidgeted round for a bit; wondered if he ought to do something about putting the supper on, but decided that anything he did would certainly be wrong and would have to be done again; thought about a cup of tea but decided that by the time the kettle had boiled his wife would be home; picked up the *Times* and tried to finish the crossword puzzle which he had started at breakfast; thought a little about his own problems, and came to the conclusion that, since he had already made up his mind, it was a waste of time thinking any more about them.

When his wife came home she found him asleep.

Next morning Mr. Wetherall caught the ten-o'clock express from Waterloo.

He started out, as if to go to school, by catching his usual bus, jumped off at the traffic lights before the school stop, and walked along Albany Road until he was quite certain that no one was taking any interest in him whatever. Then he picked up a cruising taxi and drove the short remaining distance to the station.

At twelve-thirty his train slid into a sleepy West Country town, and made its first halt. Mr. Wetherall climbed out. He had a telephone call to make from a box on the platform, and then he walked out into the town.

It was a wonderful autumn day. A herd of year-old bullocks was being driven down the main street, bunching and clowning. No one paid much attention to them. It was the sort of a town that had long ago got past worrying about year-old bullocks. Moving in the other direction came a file of girls, in straw hats with red ribbons, marshaled by a big lady in tweeds. Compared with the bullocks the girls looked junior league, but may have been more dangerous. There was a tar sprayer at work in one of the side streets.

Mr. Wetherall drank in the sights and sounds and smells. A true Londoner, he regarded the country as a perpetual open-air entertainment; a nonstop variety show, always there and to be seen for the price of a railway ticket.

Bells were sounding from the Abbey as he turned up Cornmarket Street, right at the War Memorial and right again into Rowan Street.

Halfway down on the left, unchanged since he had first seen it twenty years before (practically unchanged in the three centuries before that), stood the Old House of John Walters. Only the gilt lettering on the notice beside the door was fading a little.

SCHOOL OF ART.

PAINTING, PASTEL AND ETCHING.

PRINCIPAL, LLOYD AP-LLOYD.

He pulled the dangling iron bell, which looked like a stage prop but worked.

A maid appeared and showed him into a study. It was not a large room, and was further diminished by the tangle of drawings which hung from its walls, professional reproductions of old masters fighting for life with photogravures of Tintagel and Stonehenge, the many products of Mr.

Ap-Lloyd's prize pupils and the water colors of Mr. Ap-Lloyd's wife.

Mr. Ap-Lloyd himself appeared, and grasped Mr. Wetherall's hand. He was a small, Lloyd-George-pattern Welshman with white hair.

"Wilfrid. I'm so glad. Come and have a drink."

"A drink?"

"Some sherry. Molly has been looking forward to this."

"How's Peter getting along?"

"Splendid. Quite splendid. That was a really good turn you did for us. I hope you haven't come to take him away?"

"No. Not if he wants to stay."

They found Mrs. Ap-Lloyd in the drawing room. She was twice the size of her husband, and shaped in two bulges, one above the other, like a gazogene. She had the kindest heart of any woman known to Mr. Wetherall, who kissed her affectionately.

"There you are," said Mr. Ap-Lloyd. "Tell me what you think of it." He tipped some sherry from a decanter into a glass.

"Ha—hum," said Mr. Wetherall.

"That's right," said Mr. Ap-Lloyd, "if you don't know, don't say. It's a very curious survival, wine snobbery. A product of the time when all gentlemen drank wine, and it was a gentlemanly trait to understand vintages. Nowadays nobody knows a damn thing about it, but they all keep it up. We had Canon Trumpington in here the other day. I gave him a glass of this and asked him what he thought of it. Do you know, he smacked his silly old lips, twiddled the glass round, and said, 'Delicious, delicious. A real old fino. Not too sweet but not too dry—' "

"What is it?"

"South African," said Mr. Ap-Lloyd smugly. "And I don't mind taking a bet—"

"Don't start bullying Wilfrid the moment he gets here," said his wife. "Particularly after what he's done for you. Such a boy."

"He's doing all right, is he?"

"All right? He's a furore. He's the fashion. People have quite stopped going to the cinema to see Ronald Colman. They come here instead, to be taught art by Peter."

"My dear, don't exaggerate."

"He's grown the sweetest little silky beard, so fair that you can only see it in the strong side light. He wears corduroy trousers and—my dear, his shirts. I've never seen anything like them. A dozen of them, and all pure silk. When I unpacked them I felt sure he must be a prince in disguise."

"Actually," said Mr. Wetherall, "I think they are part of a consignment stolen from a London railway terminus."

"Well, that's romantic too, isn't it?"

"Molly talks a lot of nonsense," said Mr. Ap-Lloyd. "But, joking apart, Crowdy's an extremely promising draughtsman. Really, he's more than promising. He's got a very mature technique and a sort of eye for line which you can be born with, but you can never learn."

"You really think he's good?"

"More than good. With a bit of practice and encouragement he might be great. But that's all in the future. At the moment he's extremely useful to me. Assistants are almost impossible to get hold of. I'd like to take him on with a proper contract. I can pay him a living wage while he's completing his training. It's no kindness. He'll be worth a lot more soon. Can you fix it with his family? I promise I won't exploit him."

"I'm sure you won't," said Mr. Wetherall. "The only trouble is he hasn't got much family. However, I shouldn't let that worry you. He's old enough to make his mind up. Can I have a word with him now?"

"He's in the studio. Go along, you know the way."

It took a moment for Mr. Wetherall to recognize Peter Crowdy. If the interval had been ten months instead of ten days he could not have been more surprised.

"That's a lovely beard, Peter."

Crowdy smiled. "It's part of the uniform," he said. "All

great artists have beards when they're young. Glad to see you, Mr. Wetherall."

"You won't be when I've done with you." Mr. Wetherall backed the words with a smile, but he saw the boy stiffen up.

"Come on," he said roughly. "Sit down and get it over. Just imagine you're having a tooth out. Three hard pulls and away it comes."

"O.K.," said Crowdy. They both sat down on the window seat, under the big window, and looked at each other.

"If I tell you," said Crowdy, "does it mean I shan't have to tell it all over again—to the police?"

Mr. Wetherall nearly said "Yes," but the northern light was too uncompromising.

"You know I can't bind the police," he said. "But I promise you I'll do what I can. And I'll tell you one thing. It won't just be the local coppers. I'm going right up to the top with it, if I have to. If what I tell them helps them to get their hands on the people they want, I don't imagine they'll be too fussy about the early stages, especially now that—"

"Now that Dad's dead."

"Yes."

"It wasn't an accident, was it? He was killed."

"Yes," said Mr. Wetherall. "I don't think there's any doubt about that at all."

"All right," said Crowdy. "Here it is. You know Dad had a job in the forwarding office at Crossways goods station. I don't know if you know how a forwarding office works. Say you're sending a sewing machine from Brighton to somewhere in London. You hand it over to the railway at Brighton Central. It gets entered up in a book and you get a receipt. Brighton sends it to Crossways, with particulars. One of the forwarding clerks at Crossways labels it the correct way—'Carriage Forward' or 'Cash on Delivery' or 'Carriage Paid' or whatever it might be and arranges for it to be put on the proper lorry or van or whatever it may be going out to that district—O.K.?"

Mr. Wetherall nodded. It seemed reasonably clear.

"Well, that's how it worked."

"How what worked?"

"The racket. There was Dad and three or four others in it. More, by the end. It got a bit out of hand. It was too easy. They had labels ready with their own addresses on them—or, anyway, addresses they could use. They just slapped these onto promising-looking parcels, with a 'Carriage Paid' label, and the carriers delivered them. The carriers weren't in it, see. They just followed the labels and notices. Easy as falling off a log."

"What sort of stuff?"

"Cases of spirits, tea, wireless sets, cartons of cigarettes, sewing machines, lawnmowers. Anything takes your fancy."

"I see." Mr. Wetherall pondered for a moment. "I suppose the person who had dispatched the goods sooner or later produced his receipt and made a fuss and then the railway had to pay up."

"That's right." Crowdy giggled. "Do you know, one chap who was in on it—he sold typewriters—used to tip us off whenever he sent one by rail to a customer and we simply *labeled it back to him*. Dad said he got to recognize one machine. It came round six times."

"Hmph," said Mr. Wetherall. "What did they all do with the stuff?"

"That was the crazy part," said Peter. "A lot of it they didn't really want at all. It was stealing for the sake of stealing. I know one man had four wireless sets buried in his allotment. Of course, if it was food or drink or smokes they sold them—sold them to—sold them to a local—"

"I know all about Jock's Pull-In," said Mr. Wetherall. "How did you come into this?"

"It was on account of the labels. The only way the railways had of checking at Crossways was the number of forwarding labels—'Out' labels they called them—that each clerk used. They had to tally with his record book—like a bus conductor and his tickets. Of course, they couldn't enter the phony deliveries, and if they'd used official labels on them they'd have been short in their tally at the end of the day. So Dad got me to make some up for them. I drew the originals, and one of the gang had them photographed on special paper."

Light dawned.

"That's what you were doing that evening."

"That's right. You didn't half give us a fright."

"Hmph," said Mr. Wetherall again. It was clearly the moment when he ought to tackle the moral side of the business. He felt at a loss. Perhaps robbing a railway didn't seem as immoral as robbing a person. It had cost Peter's father his life, and Peter was talking about it as if it were some sort of game.

Mr. Wetherall gave it up.

"Behave yourself," he said. "I've got to get back to London. I've got a job to do."

He did quite a lot of thinking in the slow train which took him back.

There was a chemical simplicity about the way things were falling out. He was the catalyst. He provoked reactions in others.

Luigi, Sergeant Donovan, Mr. Crowdy and Peter; even Mr. Pride and Mr. Bertram the lawyer. All had spun for him their single strands. All had their parts preordained in the matter. All had played them for his benefit. Now he could see the pattern. Not all of it, but enough to see that it was a pattern; enough to be certain that something ought to be done about it; enough to realize that it was too big for him alone.

He needed professional help, and he thought he knew where he could look for it.

As the train crawled toward London he outlined his plans to himself. Soon the heaviness of the afternoon and the movement of the train subdued him. He fell asleep, and into the grip of such a sharp and hideous nightmare that he woke with a scream, to find an elderly lady, who must have got into the carriage at Basingstoke, regarding him anxiously.

"Such a horrid look on your face," she said. "I nearly pulled the cord."

"Indigestion," said Mr. Wetherall hastily.

"Those train meals," she agreed sympathetically.

It was not until after tea on the following day that he could get away from the school. He reached the *Kite* office at about half past five, when the great machine was beginning to hum into first gear. Once there, it took him another half hour to get as far as Todd.

"I'm sorry," said Todd, "but I've been dealing with a lunatic. You get lots of lunatics in newspaper offices. When this particular one gets past the desk sergeant I have to deal with him. Now, what's on your mind?"

Mr. Wetherall explained. It took time, as always in that office, but Todd was soon interested enough to disconnect the telephone and lock the door.

"I see," he said at the end. "That's quite a comprehensive picture, isn't it? There's not a great deal of what you might call concrete proof, but add it to what I've got, and it sounds like sense. The thing is, what are we going to do about it?"

"I thought I might have a word with that editor of yours," he said, "and see if he'd get the paper onto it."

"You thought what?" said Todd faintly.

"I thought—"

"Yes. I heard. And how did you imagine, just as a matter of interest, that you were going to set about it? If a Cabinet Minister wants to see him he gives him a week's notice and hopes for the best."

"*You* must be able to see him."

"If he wants to see me—and if I can persuade him that I have got anything to say worth his listening to—and if I'm prepared to risk getting the sack if I was wrong about it."

"Go along," said Mr. Wetherall. "It can't be as difficult as all that."

"I can see you've never worked in a newspaper office," said Todd, giving him a dirty look. "All right. I'll do it. If you hear a dull crash it'll be me bouncing."

He went reluctantly out, and Mr. Wetherall was left to his own thoughts.

About half an hour later the house telephone rang. Mr. Wetherall removed the receiver, gingerly.

"You still there?" said Todd's voice. "Well, hold on a bit longer. I'm not there yet, but I'm advancing."

Half an hour later the telephone rang again.

"Go and get yourself something to eat," said Todd. "You remember that café I took you to. Go there. It'll be a bit more crowded at this time of night, but if they try to give you the 'house full' ask Joe for the *Kite* table. There's always room for one more."

Mr. Wetherall had been sitting at the *Kite* table for nearly two hours before Todd turned up. He had had some sort of meal and had then started ordering and drinking cups of coffee. This had caused no comment. The table was full of a succession of customers, some of whom came to eat, some to drink coffee, and some just to talk. Nobody took any notice of anybody else. Even men who were being talked to usually went on reading their late editions of the evening paper.

When Todd arrived the rush had slackened so they had a corner more or less to themselves.

"He won't do it," said Todd.

"No help at all?" Mr. Wetherall fought down a sinking feeling.

"He's sympathetic. In fact, he was very nice about it. But there was no shifting him. You can't argue with the old man any more than you can argue with Table Mountain. It's a question of watching his moods and getting under cover when it rains. What he said was, he isn't going to start a crusade. It isn't his line of country. It's pure crime—better dealt with by the police. If there's some point the police can't get at, for legal or social or some other phony reason, then a newspaper can sometimes go for it and clear it up. He says, as far as he can see, there's nothing here the police can't deal with."

"I see," said Mr. Wetherall.

"Cheer up," said Todd. "We're still with you. Something may happen yet, you never know. If you get knocked off you'll get a wonderful obituary. I'll have sausages, Joe, sausages and bacon. Two rashers. Don't talk to me about rationing. We all know where your stuff comes from."

Joe grinned and withdrew. Mr. Wetherall finished his fourth cup of coffee thoughtfully.

THIRTEEN

Whitehall: A Lecture by Chief Superintendent Hazlerigg

The fine autumn weather had broken and Mr. Wetherall approached Scotland Yard from the river entrance in a downpour of rain. Apart from the three impassive policemen at the gate, the rain cascading sleekly off their black capes, there was nothing to distinguish the building on the embankment from any other office block.

Mr. Wetherall wiped his feet on the mat, furled his umbrella, and handed himself over to a hall porter.

"You have an appointment?"

Yes. Yes. He had an appointment with Chief Superintendent Hazlerigg.

"Fill in the book please."

Mr. Wetherall wrote down the date, getting it wrong first time, and having to do it again, and then his full names. Under the column headed "Object of Visit" he put "Interview." He wondered (as he had wondered before on such occasions) exactly what purpose was being served. Supposing his name had been Popski and he had come with a bomb in his brief case to blow up the building, he could scarcely have been expected to have entered these particulars in the book.

"This way, please."

He followed a young policeman. They walked along three or four miles of corridor, up some steps, over a sort of enclosed bridge and down some steps and stopped at a dark brown door with a number on it.

The room was no different from any other government office except that it was neater than most; almost severe in its rectitude.

The man who got up from behind the desk was unmistakably a policeman, although he could also have been a farmer. He was thickset and had a red-brown face and grizzled hair. He had the tolerant look of one who has spent a lifetime coping with the unpredictable climate of England. Perhaps the only remarkable thing about him was his eyes. They were that shallow gray which, like the gray of the North Sea, can change without warning from friendliness to bleak wrath.

At the moment they looked friendly.

"Sit down, Mr. Wetherall." He indicated the easy chair opposite the desk. "I'm so glad you've come. I heard about you from Huth and I hoped I should be seeing you sooner or later. He tells me you're the head of South Borough High School. And you were at Battersea? I expect you remember Cusins."

"Franky Cusins, or his brother Lefty? I remember both. The finest boxers we ever had. Franky had a foot shot off in Sicily. Were you—?"

"No, no," said the Inspector. "All the schooling I had I picked up at a little village school at Sendelsham—that's in Norfolk. Closed down now, I hear. Most of the old village schools are going. More's the pity. Still, I suppose you don't agree with that. You're probably in favor of big schools. You've got one of the biggest in London."

"In reason."

"Centralization. That's the cry nowadays. Centralize everything."

"Even crime," suggested Mr. Wetherall, just to see what would happen.

"Even crime," agreed Hazlerigg impassively. "You know that's one of my jobs. Organized crime."

"Superintendent Huth said something about it."

"It's not a nonstop job, you understand. I get an outing from time to time. But by and large you can take it I hold a watching brief on the black market. A lot of these offenses aren't really police matters at all, Mr. Wetherall. They're jobs for the Food Ministry and their men look after them. 'Snoopers' the papers like to call them, but you don't want to pay much attention to that. They're good men, most of them, doing a long day's work and collecting quite a few hard knocks into the bargain. But very often it comes to crime." Hazlerigg tilted his chair confidentially forward. "You know, there's something about black market that always brings crime in sooner or later. Maybe it's a couple of smart barrow boys—one thinks the other is trespassing on his pitch and blood gets spilled. Nothing much in that. Or else it's something worse, like blackmail."

"Blackmail?" said Mr. Wetherall sharply.

"Why certainly. There's a lot of scope for that. A restaurant proprietor, you see, gets short of a line and some smart Alec fixes it for him on the side. All right. Next time the restaurant owner is offered the same commodity and he doesn't happen to want it. Perhaps there's no demand for it—or he can get plenty of it honestly. Then the supplier says, 'You can take it or else—' "

"Or else what?"

"It depends if the buyer has got money or not. If he's well off he'll be forced to buy—at a bigger price this time. If he's a little man, they just run him out of business, as an example to the others."

"They run him out of business all right," agreed Mr. Wetherall. He was thinking back to that evening at Luigi's when it had all started. Less than three weeks ago, actually. It seemed a good deal longer.

"Violence, blackmail," went on Hazlerigg. "But those are

just side crimes. The root crime is plain stealing. That's what it always boils down to. An increase in all forms of stealing. It works both ways. First, a man finds a profitable line of scarce goods. I say 'finds.' Maybe the first time he did get his hands on them more or less honestly. He sells them on the black market and makes a thundering profit. Naturally he wants to do it again. Only this time he just can't get hold of the stuff. Sooner or later he'll be buying in the stolen goods market. Stealing for himself, or buying off a receiver, it comes to the same thing in the end. Or just look at it from the other side. You're not a trader at all. You're a railwayman or a Post Office worker or a lorry driver. You're not overpaid, and goods—valuable goods, some of them—pass through your hands every day. You could steal them—easily—just like that—if you wanted to. What stops you?"

He seemed to be waiting for an answer, so Mr. Wetherall gave his mind to it.

"Discounting," he said, "the surprising decency and honesty of the ordinary man, I should think the chief preventive is the fear of being found out."

"All right. But say that you're pretty certain you won't be found out. Your experience has shown you that the ordinary checks aren't going to catch you—or perhaps you know a way round them."

"Well—in that case I take it the next consideration is, what chance have I got of making a quick safe profit."

"Right. That's where the organization comes in."

"And that, I take it," said Mr. Wetherall slowly, "is where you come in."

"Yes," said Hazlerigg. "That's my job."

He got up, unlocked a filing cabinet, and took out a set of cardboard folders.

"That's where we come in," repeated Hazlerigg. "We can't control the main situation. We're not a Ministry of Economics. As long as there are shortages there's going to be a black market. All we can do is to see that the other end of it isn't made too easy. If individuals cheat a little, and get a little on the side for themselves, we have to leave it to the Food Officials. But if they sell for profit, that brings it straight to us. And, above all, if they get organized at the selling end."

"And have they got organized?"

Hazlerigg opened the first folder. "They're organized all right," he said. "In confidence, they're a damned sight too well organized. I had three of the biggest caterers in the country in here yesterday. Bellengers, Hyams and the P.S.D. You've probably never heard of them. They're wholesalers and they supply most of the restaurants in the metropolitan area. They're absolutely aboveboard themselves, of course. But they say they can't compete. They're losing customers every day. All right. They're in it for money. We won't waste any tears over them. But that's only one end—"

He opened a second folder. "It's the other end that's terrifying. First of all, if I told you how high the railway losses by theft had jumped last year—which I'm not allowed to—I doubt if you'd believe the figure. It's astronomical. But that's not the worst of it. I just want to show you a cutting. There's nothing confidential about it. It appeared the other day in a well-known newspaper and I've no doubt it's absolutely accurate."

"Strike Threat" the cutting was headed. "Railmen at Bradstreet Goods Depot threatened to strike at midnight last night in protest against the employment of two men who, they say, gave information to the police and helped them to check pilfering. The strike threat was called off after a meeting lasting more than two hours pending a full station meeting of all the men this morning when further decisions might be reached. Bradstreet Depot is one of London's chief points of distributing meat and fish."

"Do you like it?" said Hazlerigg. "Does it amuse you? Nearly a thousand men to go on strike because two of them were honest and had the guts to demonstrate it. That particular strike didn't come off. As a nation I don't think we're quite corrupted yet. But give it a year or two and if this sort of thing goes on we might just as well put the boards up—Final Performance. The Old Firm Going into Liquidation."

He shut the folder, straightened up, and said with a smile that went straight to Mr. Wetherall's heart, "That's why we are not ashamed to ask for any help we can get."

"Yes, of course," said Mr. Wetherall simply.

He had told the story so many times that he was becoming good at it. Having a sympathetic listener made a difference.

Hazlerigg did not interrupt him at all, but when Sergeant Donovan's name cropped up he got out an entirely new and rather bulky folder. He may also have pressed a buzzer, because as Mr. Wetherall finished speaking a sergeant put his head round the door and Hazlerigg said, "Would you get hold of Superintendent Blacking, please. He's somewhere about."

The Sergeant withdrew.

"I can't say how grateful I am," he went on, "that you should have come forward to tell us this. What you say fills in some big gaps. That item about Crossways in particular. Now if you'll bear with me for a couple of minutes I propose to put you further into the picture. It's not entirely unselfish. As I said I want your help, and if you're going to help you'll have to hear things which mustn't go outside these walls. We'll start at the bottom. There's a lot of pilfering going on. It's uncoordinated at that level. It always has been and, so far as I can see, it always will be. There's no great master brain organizing gangs of looters. It's haphazard. People like Crowdy think of a bright idea about diverting railway goods. Things are stolen in transit from lorries. Smart types hang around American Air Force stations in Norfolk and get mess waiters to sell them duty-free canteen stock. Men go round the countryside in motor vans lifting chickens and turkeys and slaughtering cattle. The other day they even lifted a dozen ducks from the pond in Hyde Park. There's another crowd that specializes in forging used coupons, which go to dishonest retailers who sell them rationed food in bulk and use the false coupons to square their accounts with the Food Office. All well-known, well-tried methods, and if they receive no particular encouragement we can keep them in bounds. In fact, at the beginning of last year I almost thought we were in for a spell of peace and righteousness. The graphs were going down. Now they're in reverse. And simply because someone has had the wit and the knowledge to organize the distribution end."

Mr. Wetherall thought about what Todd had told him. It looked as if the fancies of Fleet Street and the facts of Whitehall were marching in step for once.

"That's the outline," said Hazlerigg. "They have established receiving centers in different places round London. There are two or three cafés with lorry parks of the Jock's Pull-In type. Those concentrate on food. You know how they work. Then there's a certain wholesale wine and spirit store in North London that we've had our eye on recently. The principle seems to be the same. You go in with what looks like a lot of 'returned empties,' money passes across the counter, and you come out carrying two or three wrapped bottles. Nothing wrong with that? Except that the 'empties' were really full bottles of Scotch or rye and the bottles you came out with were empties or dummies—and you received money instead of paying it. Damned difficult to spot. We only got wind of it when one of our men happened to get curious about the number of vans and cars with Norfolk registration plates that stopped near this particular shop. Then there are the stolen cigarettes."

"I suppose they run a cigarette shop for those."

"Too risky," said Hazlerigg. "Think again. Too many people in and out of a tobacconist and no excuse for carrying parcels in and coming out without them. Any ideas? Well, the biggest receiver of stolen cigarettes that we know about is a dry-cleaning establishment in Clerkenwell. So much for the receiving end. Each of these receivers is cleared about once a week. The clearing is done by whichever gang happens to be currently in favor."

"That's where Red Whittaker and his friends come into it?"

"Yes. It seems to have been Whittaker for some months now. His lot'll go on doing it until they blot their copy books by getting too obvious or too greedy—or by getting into trouble with the police on some other count. Speaking for ourselves we'd prefer to keep it at Whittaker for the moment—because then we do know where we are."

"Which was no doubt why you were so unenthusiastic about my charges against Whittaker the other day."

"Partly," said Hazlerigg cautiously. "Partly. There were other considerations as well."

"All right," said Mr. Wetherall. "Let it go. Where do they take the stuff next?"

"That's one of the things we would give a good deal to find out. And it's not going to be easy, without giving our hand away. These boys are expert drivers who know London backward. They've got fast, nippy little vans, and they don't mind how much time or trouble they take to make sure they're not being followed. One time, when they got the idea we were following a van, they abandoned it, with all its contents, in a cul-de-sac near King's Cross. We didn't touch it. We just put men into a nearby building to watch it." Hazlerigg grinned. "After a month," he said, "we gave them best on that one. However, I expect we shall spot the central dump sooner or later—unless they keep moving it round, which is a possibility. When we get there we shall find the answer to one or two further little problems. Among other things I expect to find some sort of printing press."

"Coupons?"

"No. Too risky. It's labels. A lot of the stuff they steal is well-known, proprietary stuff. They find it pays to relabel it. Partly to make it difficult for their customers to check back on them, but chiefly, I believe, because some of the restaurants they sell to are of the 'near honest' variety. Not jet black, just a shade of off-white. If you present them with what are patently stolen goods they'll jib—but offer them a case of tinned ham with an unknown label marked 'Produce of Panama' and they'll kid themselves that it's all right and accept it."

"There's a suggestion of psychology at the back of that," said Mr. Wetherall.

"I don't know about psychology. But I'd say that there was someone in the background with a detailed knowledge of how the food industry works."

"All right. What next?"

"The next step, I have no doubt, is Annie. When the boys have sold off the stuff to the hundred and one restaurants and cafés on their visiting list they pack up the cash into sizable bundles and pass it over the counter in the private bar of the Double Four in Lauderdale Street."

"And she passes it on to Holoman."

"I think that's right."

Mr. Wetherall felt a quickening of excitement, tempered by the thought that he might have delivered Sammy over to the enemy. "Do you think, then, that Holoman is the man who runs the whole show?"

"Could be," said Hazlerigg. "Could be. And yet, I don't know. It's early to say. There's one thing we've got to prove —and I mean prove in such a way that it'll stand up in a court of law—and that's the connection between Whittaker and Holoman."

"Or Annie and Holoman."

"Yes. That could work either way. Annie could be just a post office, and Whittaker could take his orders from Holoman. Or Holoman could send the orders to Annie, who passes them on to Whittaker. My only objection to that is that I can't see a tough boy like Whittaker taking his orders from a woman."

"You haven't met Annie," said Mr. Wetherall. "I've met her and I can believe that part easily. But I don't see how you'll ever prove it. If Whittaker hands the money to Annie and Annie posts it to Holoman and Holoman gets rid of it somehow to someone else—"

"It's not easy," agreed Hazlerigg, "but it's not as difficult as all that. We're almost ready to pick this particular bunch of wildflowers. And when a big show like this begins to break up, it always breaks up from the bottom. You find a flaw, slip in a wedge and," Hazlerigg held up one thick hand, "you wham it with a hammer and the thing falls apart—if you see what I mean."

"Roughly."

"You've got to find the flaw, of course, and pick the right wedge."

"Yes," said Mr. Wetherall cautiously.

"In this case, you've suggested the answer yourself. Or rather, if what you tell me is right, Sergeant Donovan seems to have it all worked out for us. A minor character in Whittaker's lot known as Guardsman is the flaw. The wedge is Sergeant Donovan himself. And we—" Hazlerigg heaved himself up to his feet—"are the hammer. Come in, Blacking. How are you keeping? This is Mr. Wetherall."

Superintendent Blacking grinned like a little white alley cat and shook Mr. Wetherall's hand.

"I'd just got as far as Sergeant Donovan," said Hazlerigg.

Superintendent Blacking said, "Yes."

"We are in rather an unhappy position there. He's not been one of our successes. I'm not saying that's all his fault. There have been mistakes on both sides." Mr. Wetherall intercepted the look which passed between Hazlerigg and Blacking and, having met Inspector Clark, understood it perfectly. "However, we won't go into that just now. It's been a queer setup from the start. You know Sergeant Donovan was used by us as an undercover worker. That's perfectly true. He brought in a lot of information. The stopping of one nice little racket in petrol can be chalked up to his credit. Then, we know, he started taking money. He handed over money to us, too, though not, I can't help feeling, absolutely all of it. Then, the information he produced started to get less valuable. Well, there were two ways of looking at that. There was the nasty way—which we didn't want to think. Or the reason could have been that his game was becoming known, so he wasn't able to find out much. So we took him off the job. If we'd been sensible we'd have moved him out of the district altogether—"

"Would this have been before or after his wife got killed?"

"A few weeks before." Hazlerigg looked again at Blacking, who said, softly, "It was never proved that the two things had any connection."

"It was pretty obvious, I should have thought," said Mr. Wetherall sharply; and when both men looked up at him, he felt uncomfortable.

"Well, we'll not argue about it," said Hazlerigg. "But either way it doesn't make things any easier now we want to use the Sergeant."

"Use?"

Again he caught Hazlerigg looking at Superintendent Blacking and realized that a proposition was going to be put up to him, and that they were afraid he would not approve.

"I won't pretend this is a plan we're keen on," said Hazlerigg, "but we just can't think of a better. Here's Sergeant Donovan, more or less treed at home. I mean, we could get hold of him easily enough by sending a police car, but that's not the point. He may be more useful where he is. Then there're the Whittaker boys waiting for him to come out of balk so that they can hit him. Sooner or later he'll come out. We'd like him to do it in our time, not theirs. That's all there is to it."

Light began to dawn.

"You'd like me to fetch him out."

"This is what we had in mind. We thought you might slip in the back way as before. It would be natural enough for you to go and see him. Tell him about going to see Peter Crowdy, and that Peter has given you a lot of information. No harm in telling him about the parcel-labeling racket— that should appeal to him. But drop in the extra item that you think you may have discovered the address of the central sorting house. Something Peter heard his father say before he was killed. You can wrap it up any way you like. The address we want you to give him—" Hazlerigg scribbled on a bit of paper—"is an old factory on a site off the North Circular Road. It's a factory that's got certain features about it that have made it useful to us before. All you've got to do is to get it into his head that this might be the place. Suggest that you'd like to go with him and have a look at it. Then tip us off when he starts out. We'll do the rest."

Mr. Wetherall picked up the piece of paper and sat for a few moments turning it over in his fingers. "Yes," he said, at last. "Yes, and no. I'm agreeable to putting myself in your hands. You're not asking me to do a great deal, and if you think this is the best way of bringing things to a head, then I'll do it. But I'm not going to do it blind. I must know what the idea is."

"It might be easier for you to do your part if you didn't know too much," said Hazlerigg. He was still friendly.

"You may be right, but I still want to know."

"All right," said Hazlerigg. "You've got the right to know. As soon as Sergeant Donovan moves out, one of our contacts will tip off Whittaker and tell them where he's going. Whittaker's boys will either follow him, or get there first. When they catch him they'll beat him up. Then we shall intervene—but not too soon—and hold them all for assault. Donovan's still technically a member of this force—he's only under suspension. The charge will be assaulting a police officer with intent to kill. That's a damned heavy charge. Then we shall work on Guardsman and promise him consideration if he'll give us all we want on Whittaker."

"Which he will," said Blacking, beaming quietly. "In about five minutes."

"When we've got Whittaker fixed, we'll offer *him* consideration if he leads us to Holoman."

"I see," said Mr. Wetherall.

"You insisted on knowing, or I wouldn't have told you. If you think it's rough on Sergeant Donovan—"

"I'm not worried about Sergeant Donovan at all," said Mr. Wetherall. "In fact, it's practically the plan he suggested himself—"

He fell silent again. He was thinking of a lot of things rather confusedly. He thought of Luigi and old Mr. Crowdy, and Peter Crowdy and of quite a lot of other boys he had taught. But chiefly he thought of Peggy.

"All right," he said. "When would you like me to do it? The sooner the better, I take it. What's today? Thursday. I'll get in to see Sergeant Donovan after tea tomorrow. You can expect to hear from me sometime in the evening."

FOURTEEN

North of the River: Trouble

Friday was a short day at Holoman's. The girls knocked off at four o'clock and by half past four Sammy was sitting in the dining room with a cup of tea, thinking about things.

On the one hand he had just discovered that he had lost the boxing medal which he always carried as a lucky charm in his waistcoat pocket. On the other hand his wages, two rather used-looking pound notes, were safe in his wallet; and by twelve o'clock next day he would be free for the week end. On balance, it seemed all right.

He finished his tea and turned over the pages of a magazine. It was one that the blonde girl had left behind and it was, so far as Sammy could see, devoted entirely to Love. There was a picture on the front of a man with a dark mustache pushing a lady into a cupboard ("Beasts of Belgravia"). No murder and no football. Sammy abandoned the paper and concentrated on kicking the chair leg and whistling.

Presently Mr. Holoman put his head round the door.

"I'm going out," he said. He seemed preoccupied. "I'll be

back by six. Don't go away. There may be a telephone call. You can take a message."

"Right char," said Sammy.

The front door slammed. He turned to the evening paper. Elephants at home against Manchester United. That was going to be a game. Two unbeaten sides. Oh boy.

It was ten minutes before the significance of Mr. Holoman's parting remarks dawned on him.

There was only one telephone in the house and it was in the study.

Feeling curiously weak about the knees he got to his feet and went out into the hall. The study door was not only unlocked, it was open.

He stopped to think. He could sneak in now and search round quickly. Or, better, he could go in openly, turn all the lights on, and pretend to be waiting for that telephone call. If he left the study door open he would hear Mr. Holoman's return in plenty of time to clear up any mess he might make while searching. The study window looked out on the side garden. It was not directly visible from the front path.

"Can't lose," said Sammy to himself. "What a turn-up for the book."

He marched in briskly, switched the lights on, and looked round him.

There was plenty of scope for a search. There was a filing cabinet. There were two cupboards, both, as it turned out, unlocked and both full of papers. And there was the desk itself, which had half a dozen drawers down each side and a lot more small ones inside the top.

"Take a fortnight to look through this lot." He picked out a sheaf of papers from the filing cabinet. They all seemed to be connected with Mr. Holoman's patent medicines. Instinct told him that he was on the wrong track.

He came back to the desk and sat down. The roll top was open. It looked somehow more personal than the cupboard. He opened one of the small drawers at random. It was full of bank statements and check stubs. He noted the name and branch of the bank, and tried another drawer. This one contained a hip flask of brandy and three packets of Vegan-ine tablets. The next drawer was a very small one. It was set in the foot of the pillar, and he would not have spotted it if it had not happened to be standing open a fraction.

It was not exactly a secret drawer. Rather, one that had been constructed so as not to catch the eye.

In it lay a bright ring of keys. Two were small keys which might have fitted a drawer or cabinet, and the third was, quite obviously, a safe key.

Sammy took the ring out, and twirled it thoughtfully round his finger while his eyes roved. He was looking for the safe. By now he had stopped straining nervously for approaching footsteps. The fever of the chase was in him.

Unless, he concluded, it was hidden behind some panel or picture on the wall—and it didn't seem quite that sort of house—the only possible place was the brown wood cup-board built into the corner of the room beside the desk. The door was locked, but he knelt down to it and found that one of the small keys fitted. And there was a safe in-side the cupboard.

He didn't know a lot about safes, and was confused at first by the fact that there were two keyholes, at an angle to each other, but he soon got the hang of it, snapped back the lock, twisted the handle and pulled open the door.

There were more papers in the safe; but what caught his eye was the big drawer at the back. The second small key fitted.

Inside the drawer was more money than he had seen be-fore in his life. A few fivers, but mostly ten-shilling notes and pound notes, in bundles, secured by rubber bands and stacked on top of each other. He noticed that most of the notes had a well-used look, as if they had been through several pockets and tills since they had left the bank.

At that moment, and out of the corner of his eye, he noticed something else.

It was on the carpet, to the left of him and behind him.

It was a well-polished shoe.

He looked up and found Mr. Holoman standing over him.

"When I invited you," said Mr. Holoman softly, "to take an interest in the business, you will appreciate that I did not mean quite such a personal interest."

"No—I mean, yes," said Sammy.

He had been in one or two bits of trouble in his short life, but nothing quite so dangerous as this. Instinct told him to get out into the open part of the room, but he was caught between the end of the desk and the side wall.

He got up off his knees and turned round, but there was no room for maneuver.

"What exactly are you doing?"

"I was waiting for a telephone call, like you said."

"And you thought, perhaps, that I kept the telephone in the safe?"

"No—well—as a matter of fact I saw the keys."

"You must have good eyes," said Mr. Holoman blandly, "considering the drawer was shut."

"Well—I opened the drawer to look for a pencil, and I saw the keys."

"There is a certain fascination in hearing you improve your story as you go along. Is this yours?"

He shot out his hand and Sammy saw his boxing medal.

"Yes," he said. "I lost it."

He reached out to take it back but Mr. Holoman tipped it neatly into his own waistcoat pocket. All his movements were strong and precise, like those of a conjurer.

"I thought it might be yours. You left it outside this door some nights ago. Also some grubby little fingerprints on the edge of the fanlight. What were you doing? Trying to see what there was to steal?"

"I never—"

"What were you doing?"

Sammy remained silent.

"I see," said Mr. Holoman. "Well, I hope you do better at the police court."

"I never took nothing."

"No?" The hand snaked forward, went inside Sammy's jacket, and came out holding a wad of notes.

Sammy stared.

"I never put those there," he said at last. "You're trying to frame me."

"A thief."

"I never—"

Mr. Holoman took another step forward and grasped Sammy by the lapels of his jacket. His hands gripped the coat and the shirt and the vest underneath. He shook the boy gently.

"A little thief."

"Let me alone. Take your hands off me."

"A dirty, common little sneak thief."

The shaking increased in violence. Sammy put his hands up and tried to push Mr. Holoman's arms away. He might as well have tried to shift a pair of steel connecting rods. He suddenly realized how strong Mr. Holoman was.

A little wave of panic rose and subsided.

"Let me go."

Mr. Holoman stopped shaking him and appeared to consider the request. "And why should I let you go?" he said.

He was so close that Sammy could smell him; a wild dog smell, of sweat and power and beastliness.

"Get the police then, go on, get them."

"Why should we trouble about the police? I've got a much better idea. I come into the room—" Mr. Holoman marked each sentence with a fierce little jerk. "I find you robbing my safe. I try to lay hold of you. Ah, you dodge away. You jump for the door. But you trip up, and you hit your head on the corner of the desk. Hard—very hard—"

He was positioning himself with the nice judgment of a man felling an awkward tree.

Sammy opened his mouth to shout. His throat was dry, because he knew now that Mr. Holoman meant to kill him.

In that tiny moment of silence they both heard the click of the front-door latch, and footsteps in the passage.

With a swift, pouncing movement Mr. Holoman threw himself behind the desk, dragging Sammy with him. As he dropped into the chair Sammy was practically sitting on his knee.

The footsteps had halted. The study door opened cautiously and Mrs. Cameroni looked in.

"There now," she said, "I thought I saw a light."

"What do you want?" said Mr. Holoman.

"Help," said Sammy.

"Could have been burglars," said Mrs. Cameroni.

"Let me go," shouted Sammy. "Leave me alone. Fetch the police."

"There's a lot of it goes on. I don't know that you can blame the police. It's the films."

Both of Sammy's wrists were locked excruciatingly behind his back, and one of his legs was pinned to the desk by Mr. Holoman's knee. His other leg was free and he stamped on Mr. Holoman's foot.

Mr. Holoman grinned crookedly and said something between his teeth.

Mrs. Cameroni's button eyes had been swiveling busily round the room.

"Look at all that money," she said. "Lying about. It's a temptation."

"Help," roared Sammy. "Help, help, help, help."

"You ought to keep it in the bank or the Post Office Savings."

"All right," said Mr. Holoman. "You can get along now." He jerked his head toward the door.

"I come back to see if you was short of tea."

"Fetch the police," screamed Sammy. He got one arm free for a moment and knocked a desk calendar flying. But Mrs. Cameroni had at last realized that she was not wanted. She was already making for the door. When she got there she paused for a moment, looked back, said something that sounded like "young blood" and went out carefully, shutting the door behind her.

They listened to her steps shuffling off down the passage toward the kitchen quarters, and heard another door shut.

Sammy thought: "She's still in the house. She hasn't gone away altogether. She's still here." And again, "She's seen me and Mr. Holoman together. She's seen I'm alive. He's not going to be able to do—what he said he was. He'll have to be more careful now."

Some such thought seemed to have occurred to Mr. Holoman. He was sitting, holding both of Sammy's wrists easily now, in one big hand. The boy's arms were twisted up behind him to such an angle that it seemed improbable that they could go any further without something snapping.

Mr. Holoman used his free hand to restore some order to the desk and his person. He seemed to be thinking.

"You let me go," said Sammy.

"Keep quiet."

"Let me go."

Mr. Holoman exerted a slight upward pressure. The tears stood out in Sammy's eyes.

"Any more out of you," said Mr. Holoman, "and I'll break both your arms, and glad to do it."

Sammy opened his mouth, then decided to shut it again. It was a good moment for saying nothing. That left the next move to Mr. Holoman.

They could still hear the sounds of Mrs. Cameroni banging round in the kitchen.

At last Mr. Holoman seemed to make up his mind. He moved off toward the door. Sammy moved with him. Any variation in the position of his arms was torture.

They marched along to the end of the passage and Mr. Holoman opened a door.

Sammy knew what it was. He had been in and out of it before. It was the store cupboard where the ingredients for Mr. Holoman's medicines and ointments were kept. It was a large cupboard—almost a small room, with a great number of shelves up and down either side. It had a stone floor and no window. The door was a thick one. It might almost have been designed as a lock-up.

Mr. Holoman pushed the boy in and then let go of him. Suddenly released he stumbled forward, and finished up, half squatting, half kneeling, against the far wall.

Mr. Holoman stood in the doorway and looked down at him thoughtfully.

When he spoke there was a detached coldness in his voice that warned Sammy that he had made up his mind to do something evil.

"If you shout or make any attempt to attract attention, or break out," he said, "I shall tie you up and gag you. I shall tie your arms and feet together in the middle of your back. It's a method invented by the Japanese police."

Sammy said nothing. He was gently flexing his misused arms.

"It won't be comfortable. In fact, it will be very uncomfortable. There was a man once—I had to leave him tied like that for twelve hours. Do you know what happened? We never got his arms or legs straight again. Think of that. Just twelve hours. He was crippled for life."

Still Sammy said nothing.

Mr. Holoman went out, slammed the door and turned the key in the lock. His footsteps went softly away down the passage.

Todd felt an immediate twinge of uneasiness when Sammy failed to ring him up by six o'clock that Friday evening. It was the first time he had missed doing so. For Todd had spent some time that afternoon talking to Mr. Wetherall; and although the fact that they were using a public line had dictated a certain discretion, he had picked up enough to realize that, in Mr. Holoman, they might be trying to cast their net over a very dangerous animal.

He gave it fifteen minutes more, then scribbled a message for his second-in-command, seized his hat and coat, and set off up Fetter Lane.

It was an unpleasant evening, raw and airless at the same time, with low clouds overhead and hardly a stirring of wind. It promised a very dark night, with fog as well, perhaps. He boarded a trolley bus at the terminus beside Smithfield Market. The evening rush was over and he was bowled quickly northward, past the Mount Pleasant sorting office, through the squalid jungle of King's Cross, along the Caledonian Road past the dark fortress of Pentonville Prison and back again to the lights of the Holloway Road.

Here he got out.

He found Strudwick Road without difficulty and seven o'clock was striking as he stopped outside the gate of No. 5. For the first time since he had started out it occurred to him to wonder just what he was going to be. Schoolmaster, salesman, welfare worker, political canvasser, pools tout. In his shabby raincoat, his indeterminate, friendly face under the ruins of a trilby hat, he might have been almost anything.

His experience as a reporter had taught him that it was generally a waste of time to make up any story in advance. Wait and see who opens the door was the best rule.

He advanced cautiously up the path, between the bushes. There was a light in the hall. It shone dimly out through the stained glass of the door. The front windows on either side of the door were dark. He pressed the bell, then stopped and listened.

There was life somewhere at the back of the house. Someone was moving about. He waited hopefully, but nothing more happened. He put his finger on the bell push again and kept it there for a full minute.

In the kitchen Mrs. Cameroni had almost finished what she had come to do. She was packing something into the bottom of an old black bag. When the bell first sounded she was actually inside the larder and heard nothing. On the second occasion a faint thrumming did assail her unresponsive eardrums. The sound was familiar and she glanced up irritably at the box of telltales above the sink.

Someone at the front door now!

First it was one thing, then another. What an evening. She laid her black bag carefully under the dresser and threw a dishcloth over it. Then she started off down the passage.

From inside the storeroom Sammy heard her coming. He took a deep breath. Ten minutes before he fancied he had heard Mr. Holoman go out. He had been moving very quietly, but the front door had a distinctive squeak and Sammy was pretty certain that he had heard it open and shut. On the other hand, his experiences that evening had already taught him the important truth that because you hear a door open and shut it does not necessarily mean that anyone has gone through it.

He had no desire to be tied up in a Japanese bundle, but this might be the last safe chance that he was going to get of attracting attention.

As against that, even if Mr. Holoman *was* out, the person who had just rung the doorbell might easily be a friend of Mr. Holoman, and therefore evilly disposed.

He thought he would compromise.

As Mrs. Cameroni came opposite his door he put his fingers to his lips and gave one piercing whistle.

Outside in the passage Mrs. Cameroni scarcely slowed down.

She certainly heard something. A faint but distinct tintinnabulation. Since she knew she was alone in the house the only conclusion she could arrive at was that the impatient person outside the front door had started whistling. Let him whistle. What did he think she was? A canary?

She flounced forward, flung the street door open, and said, "Well?"

"Good evening, madam," said Todd, raising his hat and switching on the full power of his smile. "I'm so sorry to have bothered you."

Mrs. Cameroni, of course, did not hear a word, but she was sensibly mollified. She had a weakness for young men who smiled that way.

"It's no good," she said, "I can't do anything for you. Barring me, there's no one in the house."

"I was looking for a young friend of mine, Sammy Donovan."

"He's gone up to town. Goes every evening about now. He goes up to his club."

Todd felt baffled.

"Just a boy," he said. "Red hair."

"I expect it's medicine you want," agreed Mrs. Cameroni. "Urgent, too, I suppose."

Again Todd's professional experience came to his rescue. He felt in his pocket, got out an envelope, and wrote in block letters: WHERE IS SAMMY?

Mrs. Cameroni glanced out of the corner of her eye at what was written and said, "I heard you right enough the first time. He's gone out."

"Where?" Todd shaped the word very carefully with his lips.

"Not long ago," said Mrs. Cameroni. "Can't have been gone long. Quarter of an hour I should say. Can't be more than twenty minutes ago he was in there—"she jerked her head toward the study—"playing with Mr. Holoman."

"Playing!"

"Romping. He was sitting on Mr. Holoman's knee."

"Good gracious." It didn't sound sense to Todd. There had been nothing kittenish about the Sammy he remembered.

"You don't know *where* he went. *Where?*"

This was over her head. He took the envelope and wrote it down.

"Nothing to do with me," said Mrs. Cameroni. "I was in the kitchen. Minding my own business."

It was clear that the interview was drawing to a close. Todd seized the paper again and wrote, "If you want help, ring me at Central 96999."

Mrs. Cameroni looked surprised.

"Why should I want help? No one's doing anything to me."

"You're lucky," said Todd pleasantly. "Really I can't think why someone hasn't strangled you a long time ago."

He waved his hand to her. She stood staring after him. His last message seemed to have upset her.

Todd walked quickly down the road. He made for the callbox which he had noticed at the corner and put a call through to Mr. Wetherall. As he heard the bell continuing to ring he imagined the flat must be empty, but at the last moment the instrument gave a "clunk" and Mrs. Wetherall came on the line. She sounded out of breath.

"I heard the bell as I was coming upstairs," she said. "Who is it? Oh, it's you, Alastair. I didn't recognize your voice."

"It's the fog," said Todd.

"I'm afraid Wilfrid isn't in." She sounded faintly upset. "He telephoned me about an hour ago from the school. He had to go round to see the Donovans. I thought he'd be back by the time I got home."

"The Donovans? Did he happen to say why?"

"No. What's it all about?"

"I wondered if Sammy might have turned up. No one up here seems to know where he is."

"I don't think it was anything to do with Sammy. Something about Sergeant Donovan."

"I'll ring again in an hour," said Todd.

The fog had been getting thicker as he was speaking. When he came out of the box he could no longer see across the road.

Back in the kitchen at No. 5 Strudwick Road Mrs. Cameroni had rescued her black bag from under the dresser. The contents still showed a tendency to clink as she moved, so she took a newspaper, rolled it into a ball, and crammed it down inside. Then she turned out the light and walked to the front door. She sniffed at the fog, which was not yet quite so thick up at that end of the road, and pulled a scarf over her head and ears. Then she went out, banging the door behind her.

She was halfway down the path when she saw the figure coming along the pavement opposite, passing under the lamp. There was nothing wrong with her eyesight.

With remarkable agility she hopped off the front path, into the shrubbery.

The gate slammed and Mr. Holoman stalked up the path, passing within a few feet of where she was standing. He seemed to be in a hurry.

His key clicked in the lock and the door opened and shut again.

Mrs. Cameroni came out of the shrubbery and shuffled away, out of the garden and down the road.

It seemed to her an awful lot of trouble for two tins of bacon.

It was Peggy who conducted Mr. Wetherall to Ratcliff Lane that evening. When it came to squeezing through fences and climbing over walls she seemed even more agile than her brother. Mr. Wetherall did not give his full attention to what he was doing. He was beginning to feel a distaste for what lay ahead.

He recognized the necessity of it, but he could not be happy about what he was letting Sergeant Donovan in for. Three weeks ago he might not have minded so much. Three weeks ago he had not been subjected to that particular treatment himself.

"Mind the wire," said Peggy. "They put it up since you came here last. It's meant to stop the cats."

The Donovan kitchen looked somehow warm and homely. Ratcliff Lane was suffering under an electricity failure and Mrs. Donovan had lighted an old, oil-smelling lamp. She had also made some tea, for which Mr. Wetherall was thankful. It was a damp, unpromising night.

While he was drinking it Mrs. Donovan said, "Show Mr. Wetherall that letter you had from Sammy."

"Seems all right," said Mr. Wetherall when he had read it. "He was bound to be a bit homesick to start with. Hullo, wherever did you get that?"

He was staring in astonishment at the strip of photographs that had fallen out of the envelope.

"It was in Sammy's letter," said Peggy. "He didn't say

anything about it. He must have put them in after he had written it."

"What's up?" said Sergeant Donovan.

"I really think," said Mr. Wetherall slowly, "that we ought to get in touch with Sammy without delay."

"He's coming home lunchtime tomorrow," said Mrs. Donovan.

"There's something up," said Sergeant Donovan. "What's wrong? What is it, Mr. Wetherall?"

"We must find out where Sammy got those photographs. It's a woman called Annie. It's difficult to explain—but she's a barmaid in a public house in Soho. It's thought to be a sort of pay office for Whittaker's people."

Sergeant Donovan said, "If Sammy got this photograph up at Holoman's place—"

"I don't see where else he could have got it from."

"That's right."

"Then we ought to hand it over to Scotland Yard at once."

"Scotland Yard," said Sergeant Donovan softly, lifting one corner of his mouth.

Mr. Wetherall recognized that he had got ahead of himself.

"Well—the police—somewhere safe."

The Sergeant turned the photographs slowly over in his hand.

"Now look here," said Mr. Wetherall with sudden authority, "tear it in half. You can keep half if you want, but I'm going to have the rest. It's not safe here, so let's split the risk."

"Go on, Patsy," said Mrs. Donovan. "It's a good idea."

Almost reluctantly Sergeant Donovan tore the strip down the middle. Mr. Wetherall pocketed one piece and said, "You almost put it out of my mind what I came to tell you about. I saw Peter Crowdy on Wednesday."

"Well now," said Sergeant Donovan.

"You saw Peter," said Peggy. "I am glad. Is he all right?"

"Happy as a sandboy. He's grown a sweet little beard."

Peggy giggled. "It looks very fetching. He's teaching art and being made love to by all the girls in—well, perhaps that had better remain my secret. Anyway, you can take it from me he's safe and happy for the time being."

"And I expect he had a lot to say to you when you saw him," suggested Sergeant Donovan.

"Yes. We had a talk. He explained one or two things that I'd been wondering about."

He told them about the Crossways scheme. It did not seem to occur to any of his listeners that they should present any moral judgment on it.

"What a boy," said Peggy.

"Neat, that," said the Sergeant.

"Sure, there's nothing new about it," said Mrs. Donovan. "It's a trick the boys used to play at Connemara station."

"There was another thing he told me." Mr. Wetherall hoped that the switch from truth to lies did not sound quite so obvious to his audience as it did to him. "And I think it might explain, in part, why Mr. Crowdy was killed."

There was no doubt about their interest.

"It was one of the van drivers who was a friend of Mr. Crowdy's. As I understand it, the drivers weren't in the scheme at all. They were sort of innocent agents. But this one—Peter never told me his name, and come to think of it I don't suppose his father told it to him—suspected something. Eventually Mr. Crowdy took him into his confidence, and he got involved, too. The usual drill was that anything salable—food or drink or cigarettes—was kept hidden in an old shed under one of the railway arches. Mr. Crowdy had the key. Whittaker or one of his crowd picked it up when they could and paid cash down and took it away in one of their vans. That was how it usually went. Only on one occasion there was a hitch—the van couldn't turn up, and there was a lot of stuff piling up in the shed, and the Crossways men were getting nervous. So, rather against his will, Whittaker let Mr. Crowdy's van-driver friend do the actual delivery. He was made to swear every sort of oath of secrecy—but, of course, he talked—to Mr. Crowdy."

"That's likely enough," said Sergeant Donovan. "None of that sort can keep a secret better than a four-year-old child. Do you think that's why they killed Crowdy? Just because he knew where this place was?"

"Not that alone," said Mr. Wetherall. "I think he was sickening for a severe attack of conscience. I got that impression that night when he was talking to me. He was about ready to blow the whole works. They wouldn't have liked that anyway—but they liked it a good deal less when they realized he knew the address of their central dump."

"Yes," said Sergeant Donovan. "I expect that was one reason. Another would be that he was an old man, and couldn't hit back. That's the sort they enjoy killing, Mr. Wetherall."

There was a bitterness in his voice that was deeper than any spite or rancor. It had gone down into his own self and become part of him.

Mrs. Donovan spoke quickly, as one who wishes to turn an awkward moment.

"Did Mr. Crowdy tell Peter where the place was?"

"That's just what he did," said Mr. Wetherall gratefully. "And Peter told me." He felt in his pocket for the plan he had drawn. "It's an old factory block, near the North Circular Road—" He pointed the place out.

He had expected many different reactions to his bombshell. The one thing he had not anticipated was indifference.

"I'm afraid that's out of date," said Sergeant Donovan briskly. He got to his feet as he spoke. "We'll let you into a little secret." His glance included his mother. "We know where their place is. A friend of mine found it out for me —oh, about a week ago. The place you've got there must be the last one they used. This is near St. Pancras—over a paint factory. I've been meaning to pay them a visit for some time. What with one thing and another I've had to put it off. Just before you came we decided that tonight was right for it. You couldn't have a better night. I know these evening fogs. It's going to be so thick soon they couldn't stop you, not if they linked arms across the end of the road. You could crawl between their legs and they wouldn't see you."

As he spoke he was putting on an old raincoat and winding a scarf round his neck.

Mr. Wetherall's mind was racing in helpless circles like the screw of an upended motor boat.

"Should I—would you like me to come with you?"

"There's no call for you to get mixed up in this," said Sergeant Donovan. He had his coat on now. It hung straight and heavy, and there was a curious bulge in both pockets. "You've done your bit. You keep clear. Give me a quarter of an hour to draw them off, and you can walk out and go home."

Without another word, or a look behind him, he was gone, and they heard the front door shut softly.

Five minutes later, and it was one of the longest five minutes he had ever known, Mr. Wetherall had extracted himself, and was out in the street again. The fog was blinding. The nearest possible callbox would be somewhere along the Walworth Road. He broke into a shambling run.

FIFTEEN

North of the River: The Paint Factory

Even before Mr. Wetherall had finished speaking Hazlerigg had a second telephone in his hand.

"Give me E Division on this line," he said. "I want the DDI or his Assistant. Then I want Operations. And send Duffy up here. Please be as quick as you can."

A buzzer sounded.

Hazlerigg said, "Operations. Will you get three crews moved out into the St. Pancras area. I can't tell you exactly where they're to go, because I don't know myself, yet. And see if you can get one of the cars with an L Division man in it. It may be useful to have someone who can spot Sergeant Donovan. Donovan. Yes, that's the chap. Tell me as soon as the cars are standing by."

And, to a red-faced giant who came into the room a few minutes later, "Good evening, Duffy, I want to use your local knowledge. They say you know the St. Pancras district backward."

Sergeant Duffy grinned. "I've pressed every inch of it with my flat feet," he said.

"I want to find a paint factory. It's been described as being 'near St. Pancras.' I expect it may be a disused factory —or maybe partly used."

"You mean the ground floor a paint factory and the floors above it vacant."

"That's exactly the sort of thing."

"It's not all that easy, sir. You won't find anything big in that area at all. All the big factories are outside of London. But there's quite a few little places. Places which mix up paint for builders—mostly cheap sorts of white paint and undercoat. A few of them make varnish and stain. Some builders will buy any old muck so they can save on their tenders. Then there's one or two places that store paint. Regular old death traps. You remember, sir, we tried to get 'em all under license, but it didn't come off."

"I think he said 'factory.' Not 'store.'"

"Hm. Well, the best thing I can do is fetch you a street map and show you the ones I can remember."

At that moment the DDI of E Division came up on the telephone and Hazlerigg told him what he wanted.

"I've got Duffy here," he said. "Picking out likely places for us. I want you to check up on any addresses he gives us. It's pretty urgent."

The DDI said something.

"I agree," said Hazlerigg. "We could do without the fog."

Ratcliff Lane was a cul-de-sac, and correspondingly easy to watch. Sergeant Donovan was, of course, aware of this, but he also knew that the sort of men Whittaker would be likely to use would be bad, unenthusiastic players without either the patience or the stamina for a long game.

On a night like this, anyone told off to watch the end of the lane was more than likely behind a pint pot in the nearest saloon bar.

Nevertheless he went carefully, moving quite silently on his rubber-soled shoes, keeping to the middle of the road. After a few right and left turns, he breathed more freely. He was approaching the Walworth Road. The great over-head lamps blazed down, each shedding its cone of milky drifting light, hindering more than helping the traffic, which was here wedged in a tight blaspheming line from the corner of Albany Road right up to Blackfriars Bridge.

Happy in his obscurity, the Sergeant padded along the pavement, and made his way to the entrance of the Walworth Road tube station. He booked a ticket for King's Cross.

Had he realized it, he had taken all his precautions at the wrong place. The net which had been spread for him was of an altogether different kind, broader-meshed, more carelessly flung and correspondingly more difficult to evade.

Even as he moved to the head of the escalator, a newspaper vendor, with one leg and one wooden stump, hauled himself off the upturned crate on which he was perched beside the booking office, and hobbled across to the line of telephone kiosks inside the station entrance. He knew Sergeant Donovan by sight. He had also heard the whisper that had gone round. He had no idea what it was all about, except that there could be something in it for him. If not money, then tolerance of some sort. He dialed a number, introduced himself as Len, and, after some delay, spoke to a man called Ted. From the background of shouts, screams and rifle shots one might have supposed that Ted was on active service on a noisy sector of the front. (In fact he was proprietor of an amusement arcade near the Tottenham Court Road.) Ted sounded strictly disinterested, but thanked Len for his trouble. Len returned to his evening papers full of the particular satisfaction which comes from having kicked someone who cannot possibly kick you back.

Sergeant Donovan was by this time boarding his train. It was not full. As he sat down in an empty seat at the far end of the carriage he was careful to arrange his raincoat on either side of him so that what was in the pockets rested squarely on the seat.

At King's Cross he got off the train and climbed up and out into the fog again.

Old Chaos reigned at the crossing of the five roads outside that station. At the center of a tangle of traffic two lorries stood, headlight to headlight, like two intractable cats endeavoring to outstare each other. Up the road lights were flicking on and off. Horns were sounding. Drivers were getting out of their cars to unbosom themselves.

The Sergeant grinned. He might have grinned even harder had he known that no fewer than three police cars were locked in the confusion.

He took a quick look around him. It was an empty precaution, for his nearest neighbors were dim ghosts. Then he plunged into a side street.

Away from the lights it was a little easier to see. He was now entering the peculiar area which is the hinterland of the great terminus stations. An area of tiny streets flanked by high walls; streets which often end abruptly where the great rail arteries cut across them; an area of little squalid shops, ramshackle garages and dangerous eating places; a place of steam and soot and frustration.

The Sergeant made his way forward with some confidence. He had served his apprenticeship in E. Division. At one point he unlatched a wooden gate, passed under a tunnel lined with dripping tiles, went down a flight of ironshod steps, squeezed through a narrow opening and came into an alley beyond.

Here his pace became slower. He knew that he was very near his objective. The white fog blanketed all sound. He might have been alone in the world.

He was feeling with his fingers along a wall made of upended railway sleepers. Twenty yards along he found a gate. It was shut and padlocked. He tested the padlock thoughtfully and decided it was beyond him. Then he felt for the top of the gate. It was just within reach. His fingers touched an iron stanchion and he guessed that there would be two or three rows of rusty barbed wire along the gate top.

That was not much of an obstacle for an active man. He grasped the bottom of the stanchion, used the padlock as a toehold, and heaved himself up. There was a tricky moment as he balanced on the gate, straddling the barbed wire, to reverse his grip. Then he dropped quietly down into the obscurity of the other side.

He was in a cinder-covered yard. Ahead of him loomed the building. It was a two-storied affair of brick which had once been yellow and was now the color of slow death.

The Sergeant felt his way round to the right, turned a corner to the left, and was stopped by a high boundary wall. Then he turned about and reversed the process, coming back to the same wall, or a continuation of it. He had an idea that behind this wall must lie the canal.

After that he turned his attention to the ground-floor windows. They were small and steel-framed. After a moment's hesitation he took out a silk handkerchief, wrapped it tightly round his bunched fingers and knocked in a pane of glass.

The noise seemed to die in the fog.

Carefully he pushed his hand in and undid the catch.

"Curse the fog," said Hazlerigg mildly.

"That's all the paint factories, and all the stores," said Duffy. "They seem to be O.K. Unless it's a lot further from St. Pancras than we think."

" 'Over a sort of paint factory near St. Pancras,' " repeated Hazlerigg.

He stared out of the window at the drifting curtain. It was yellowing now, as the grime of London settled upon it.

Suddenly Duffy made the noise of one who has had an inspiration and said, "Quigleys'."

"What's that?"

"You couldn't really call it paint. They make some paint. Chiefly it's boat varnish and printer's ink."

"Where is it?"

Duffy pointed down at the map on the table.

"That's in St. Pancras all right," said Hazlerigg. "Backing onto the canal."

"What made me think of it," said Duffy, "was that I remembered that Quigleys' never used more than the ground floor. It was an old building they took over. Too big for them, you see. In my day the top story was used for hides."

"Could be what we want," said Hazlerigg.

He got onto the DDI.

"I'll send a man just as soon as I've got one," said that harassed official. "They're all out in the fog now."

Hazlerigg rang off and tried Operations.

"I'll chance sending a car straight there," he said to Duffy. "I've got a feeling about this."

The Junior Inspector in charge of the Operations Room reported back a minute later.

"I've given the order," he said. "It may take a little time to carry out. I'm told there's a sort of private hell going on at King's Cross."

The room Sergeant Donovan was in was full of varnish. The darkness was full of it, a sweet, sickly resinous smell. Without using his torch he picked his way to the door and found it unlocked.

From the hallway a flight of shallow wooden stairs ran up, with one turn, to the first-story landing. Here there was another door, which was locked. There was a white card tacked onto it and he smiled gently as he read the words GENERAL TRADING ENTERPRISES.

The door was old and ill-fitting and the lock was a catch lock. He produced from his top pocket a flattened cone of stiff talc and inserted the small end between the jamb and the door edge. A gentle pressure and he felt the tongue of the lock give way. The door opened inward.

There was a further short passage with partitioned rooms on either side, and beyond that a very large storeroom.

This was full of stuff. Most of it was in crates and cartons but some was spilled out onto benches and tables. Sergeant Donovan, picking his way among the jumble, used his torch more freely. A wooden box with the label of a well-known whisky distillery caught his eye and he bent to inspect it.

As he did so he heard the sounds which told him he was not alone.

Someone was coming up the stairs; worse than that, there were people inside the room already, near the door.

There was very little time to do anything. He jumped toward the ladder which his torch had shown him at that end of the room and went up it. It was a short ladder, four or five steps, leading up to a sort of loading platform, with crates on it. He had no hope of hiding. He just wanted to get his back to something solid.

The platform ended in double doors, which were shut and barred. He turned with a grunt of satisfaction. He could hear men below him moving in the darkness.

Then all the lights went on.

Some of the fog had got into the room and hung in shreds round the overhead lamps, but there was plenty of light for Sergeant Donovan to see his pursuers. There were five of them, all looking up at him with the bleak intent look of a pack who have had a long run but are close on a kill.

He knew every one of them.

There was Guardsman, with his scrubbed cheeks, his immature nose and knowing eyes. Beside him, like a banner, the red mop of big Whittaker and Sailor Jackson with his black hair, white face and dead eyes. Behind them stood the coffee-colored boy from Jamaica. His face alone had a sort of excitement in it, out of keeping with the solemnity of the others. The ex-boxer Prince was the fifth. He had just come through the door. As the lights came on he shut it behind him and came forward, blinking his single, puffy eye in the sudden glare.

As they closed on the platform Sergeant Donovan, instead of retreating, came forward to meet them. He put his foot out and kicked the ladder away. It fell onto the floor with a noise which emphasized the silence.

Without a word Jackson stooped to pick the ladder up.

"I wouldn't do that," said Sergeant Donovan.

He had taken his right hand out of his pocket and was holding something lightly and lovingly in it.

All movement in the room ceased.

"It's powerful stuff," said Sergeant Donovan. "Makes the old Mills grenade look like a penny cracker. Incendiary too, as well as explosive. And while we're talking about fires, I hope you've none of you forgotten what you're standing on top of. Did you ever watch varnish burn? All right, Whittaker, I can see you've got a gun. What good do you think it's going to do you? The pin's out. Take a look. No deception. It's a short fuse, too. I've only got to open my fingers and there'll be just three seconds between you and the bonfire."

He spoke slowly, relishing his words.

"You weren't thinking of going, were you, Prince?"

Four heads jerked round. Prince had taken a few furtive steps back toward the door.

"I could toss this beauty right into your lap from here. Like to see if you can catch it? I've got another with me in case you miss. Three seconds be plenty. That's right. Back you come. All nice and cozy."

"Look here," said Whittaker. He seemed to be the only one who had a voice. "We don't want any trouble. You clear out and we'll let you go. Is that right?" He looked quickly at the others. There was a murmur of agreement from everyone except Jackson, whose hungry eyes had never left the man on the platform.

"May I take that as a firm offer?" said Sergeant Donovan, coming a further step forward, to the very edge of the platform. "How very generous. Perhaps you'd care to put it in writing? Or get down on your knees and sing it. You big yellow gasbags. Take a look at yourselves. You're frightened. I can see the guts running out of you like rain. Perhaps you're thinking you can talk yourselves out of this one. Or buy yourselves out. I haven't heard any mention of money yet. Nothing to say, Guardsman? You're not on parade now. What about you, you little brown bastard? You're not dealing with a woman this time. Do you understand enough English for that? You've come to the wrong party. There's no woman here to be tied up, and gagged, and suffocated."

The strong light shone down, picking out the lines on Sergeant Donovan's scarred face.

"Did you think," he said at last, almost conversationally, "that I was really going to let any of you go?"

It was not in Sammy's nature to sit still for long. Anyway the cold forced him to move.

He had heard Mr. Holoman return some time before and all thought of shouting for help had drained out of him. He had no desire to lie in that cold damp place, his limbs twisted grotesquely behind him, hardening gradually into a knot that no one could untie.

There had been a cripple of that sort, he recalled, who had lived near them in Ratcliff Place and who had propelled himself round on a trolley, and Sammy remembered now with shame the occasion, one Guy Fawkes night, when he had lit a Chinese supercracker behind him to find out how fast he could be made to move.

One blessing, the electric light worked. He was not in darkness.

He started by examining all the jars on the shelves, taking each one down in turn, opening it and sniffing the contents. What was in his mind was that he had once seen a film about a man who had been locked up in a storeroom by an enemy agent and who had discovered some sticks of gelignite and had succeeded in blowing the door down.

He re-examined the jars but none of them (apart possibly from the essence of cascara) looked even remotely explosive.

It was while he was up at the far end of the room that he heard the voices.

They were odd voices; so distant, so clear, so disembodied, that they might have been sounding inside his own head.

"Bleak," said the first voice. "Bleak is the word I should

use. It's not the sort of climate that suits everyone. Take my sister. The one who went to live at Westcliffe. She could never stand it. That girl was born with asthma."

The second voice was deeper. Possibly it was a man's voice, if disembodied spirits differentiated between man and woman. "When he goes away," said the second voice, "do you think he makes any arrangements? He's the only one who's allowed to sign for the petty cash. You'd imagine he'd sign a check before he went. What do you expect me to do, Mr. Stanley, I said, raise a loan from the bank every time I want to go to the lavatory?"

Sammy was entranced. There were lesser voices, too, voices which said things like "There now" and "Well, fancy that, so did mine": but the two leading voices overrode them.

Sammy took another look at the end wall.

There was no window but, as he saw now, there were two ventilators, one in each corner. It was undeniably through these holes that the voices were coming into the room. More, when Sammy stood on a stool and applied his ear to the vents it appeared that the man's voice was coming through one and the woman's voice through the other. It was because he had been standing in the middle that he had picked them both up.

Wireless? Neither of them sounded like any program he had ever listened to. Then was he hearing, by some trick of sound, people talking in the houses on either side?

Sammy set himself to consider the layout of No. 5 Strudwick Road.

The cupboard he was in occupied the space between the dining room and the kitchen. The house was semi-detached—its other half section, No. 7, lying beyond the dining room. Therefore, while the voice from the right-hand ventilator could, by a fluke of construction, be coming from No. 7, bypassing the dining room, as regards the left-hand any such explanation was impossible. There was the width of a garden between him and No. 3.

There was no back garden in the proper sense of the

word; it was all front and side. In other words, thought Sammy, his mind suddenly springing to attention, the wall he was listening at formed part of the outer wall of the house. Take it away and you would step straight out onto the pavement of Motlow Terrace. Even so the problem remained.

For why, in heaven's name, thought Sammy, should two groups of people be standing, on a night like this, some three yards apart from each other, discussing general topics with the idle persistence of people who had a night to kill.

As he put the question the whole glorious answer presented itself.

There was only one sort of person who would stand through the night in any weather (the worse the weather the more persistently they would stand). And it was on Friday evening in winter and in a road like Motlow Terrace that they would be likely to be found.

Sammy could see it as clearly as if the wall had suddenly rolled up, like the curtain at a theater. The whole road would be full of the supporters of the Elephants Football Club, waiting for the morrow and Manchester United.

As the truth dawned on him, Sammy's heart began to thump. Thousands of potential allies, separated from him by less than twelve inches of brickwork.

He applied his ear to the right-hand vent again. "Dead ignorant," said the relentless voice. "The doctor told him, 'You can take game but you can't take fish.' You know what he said? 'I'll have crab. Crab's game, isn't it?' "

Sammy even picked out the laugh which followed. There was balm in the sound.

He sat down and thought furiously.

The obvious thing to do was to shout or whistle or poke something through the hole. Anything to attract the attention of the crowd. Perhaps he might write out a message on a spill of paper and push it through the hole. There was no lack of paper. The shelves were lined with it. He had no pen or pencil but there must be something in one of the jars he could dip his finger into for ink. Or he could write in his own blood.

But even as he thought of them, Sammy could see only too clearly the weakness of all these ideas. He knew what would happen.

If he succeeded in attracting someone's attention, and if that someone was sufficiently interested to do anything about it, he would come round to the door and ask Mr. Holoman what it was all about. And Mr. Holoman, who was a horribly plausible man, would say, "Oh, that's my little boy. I'll see he doesn't bother you any more. So sorry you've been troubled." And ten to one the man would be satisfied and would go away, and then Mr. Holoman would come along and—Sammy's arms and legs already ached in anticipation.

Dare he risk it?

On the other hand, dare he not risk it? Mr. Holoman had already tried to kill him once, and, if he could safely do so, would have as little compunction about trying again as he would about cracking the top off a soft-boiled egg.

And then, quite suddenly, the plan was there, fully formed.

With fingers that trembled in spite of himself, Sammy pulled off one of the pieces of stiff white paper which lined the shelves and rolled it into a thin tube. Then he cast his eye round for the jar he wanted.

Mr. Jeffery was a keen supporter of the Elephants, and, like all their keenest supporters, was a fanatic. He took a perverse pride in the sufferings he endured. For important matches he could cheerfully stand for eighteen hours in any weather. The worse the weather the greater the attraction. (Did they not still talk among themselves of that night of snow in 1947 when five women had collapsed and a family party of four had entirely lost their voices and been unable to do anything but wave their arms when the Elephants came through that celebrated replay into the Final?)

A bit of fog was nothing. The braziers were alight, and voluntary helpers with cans of tea were passing up and down the queue and Mr. Jeffery, taking a deep breath, had just said, "We must be clear in our definition of free will" when he felt it. It was no more than a breath of gritty air on the back of his neck.

It came again.

Mr. Jeffery took out his handkerchief and rubbed his neck. Almost at once the most alarming symptoms developed.

"Just as if it was on fire," he said afterward. A burning, irritating, itching torment. He must have called out, because the next thing was that his wife had struck a match and was examining him anxiously.

"I do believe you've got scarlet fever," she said.

"Nonsense," said Mr. Jeffery. "I had scarlet fever when I was four. Ouch! Don't touch it whatever you do."

"If you'd allow me," said their neighbor in the queue, a pleasant young man to whom they had already spoken, "I'm a medical student."

A third spectator produced a torch. The young man took a long look and was about to pronounce the word "urticaria" (which would have been the first, though not the last, incorrect diagnosis of his professional career) when another voice in the crowd said, "Here it comes, whatever it is."

Sure enough, plainly visible in the light of the torch, its passage marked by the disturbance of the fog vapor, a jet of something was originating from a hole in the brickwork beside them.

The medical student who was holding the torch exclaimed something and pointed to the back of his own wrist.

On it were spots of brown powder.

Handing the torch to Mr. Jeffery he drew a clean handkerchief from his pocket and wiped the powder carefully away. The back of his hand was already beginning to look inflamed.

He turned to Mr. Jeffery with a grin. "It's nothing to worry about," he said. "You know what it is? Some joker's blowing itching powder at us through that hole in the wall."

"Blowing what?"

"Itching powder. That's the popular name. It's quite harmless. It's a sort of powdered berry."

"I don't care what sort of powdered berry it is," said Mr. Jeffery stiffly. "He's not going to blow it over me."

The sentiment of the crowd was with him there. It was felt that the dignity of the Elephants was at stake.

"A bloody poor joke," said a large man in tweeds, who had been fortifying himself from a hip flask. "I suggest we send a little deputation round to sort the joker out."

This suggestion found favor too.

"There's a policeman at the corner," said the medical student. "He'd better come along as well."

Accordingly when, in answer to a loud and persistent ringing at his doorbell, Mr. Holoman came to the door he found no fewer than four men on his step, one of them a police constable.

Mr. Jeffery outlined the case for the prosecution.

"Oh dear," said Mr. Holoman. "Oh dear, yes, I'm afraid that must be my boy Sammy. Such a mischievous child. I'll certainly see he doesn't get away with this."

"Well then, gentlemen," said the policeman pacifically, "if Mr.—?"

"Holoman, officer."

"If Mr. Holoman promises to deal with the boy."

"Hm," said Mr. Jeffery.

"I don't believe there is a boy," said the man in tweeds suddenly. "He's got a bloody shifty face. He's lying. He did it himself."

"Really," said Mr. Holoman angrily, "I can assure you—"

"Let's see the boy," said the man in tweeds. "I'll believe'm when I see'm."

"Show the dog the rabbit," suggested the medical student.

"Really, there's absolutely no need—" began Mr. Holoman.

"I think, after all, I *should* like to see the boy," said Mr. Jeffery.

"Come now, sir," said the policeman. "Just produce the boy and the gentlemen will be satisfied."

"I'll be satisfied when I've seen him given a bloody good walloping," said the man in tweeds.

After embracing the opposition with a calculating look, Mr. Holoman stalked down the passage, turned the key in the storeroom lock, and jerked the door open. Sammy, crouching ready just inside, came with it like a bullet. Mr. Holoman grabbed, and caught a handful of red hair. There was a moment of tension, but the hair was well-rooted. Sammy slid to a halt with a squeak.

Mr. Holoman transferred his grip to the boy's sleeve, had time to mutter, "Just you remember what I told yar," and then dragged him back toward the front door.

"Well, now, gentlemen," he said smoothly, "here he is. As a matter of fact I'd locked him in as a punishment for something he did earlier this evening. I never imagined he'd be up to more tricks."

Everybody now looked at Sammy, who was perfectly silent.

"What have you got to say for yourself?" asked the policeman.

"Speak up, boy," said Mr. Holoman, "and tell the gentlemen you're sorry."

"He'd be a lot more sorry if I had my way," said the man in tweeds.

Still Sammy said nothing. Nothing that he could say was going to be of any use. His fear had reached a point where Mr. Holoman seemed more than human. In a match of bluff the older man had all the weapons.

With sudden determination he swung out his left foot, and kicked Mr. Holoman as hard as he could on the ankle. Mr. Holoman swore and loosened his grip for a second. Sammy dived between the medical student and Mr. Jeffery, handed off the man in tweeds, wriggled under the policeman's arm and disappeared down the front path into the fog.

If the gate had been latched he would have been caught but it opened to his touch.

He scudded off down Strudwick Road with the pursuit hard behind him.

Even as he ran he realized that his hope of safety lay in avoiding the main road. Among lights and people the shouts of his pursuers would quickly lead to his recapture. The fog both helped and hindered him. He turned at the bottom of the road, and right again. He could still hear the steps of more than one pursuer. At the end of the road there was a choice of ways and he took the right once more. Quite suddenly he realized that he was in a cul-de-sac.

Ahead of him a brick wall blocked the way.

Without pausing to think he jumped up onto the nearest garden wall, felt for the top of the high wall, and pulled himself up onto it.

Next moment he was over and hanging by his hands. Then he let go.

It was a good deal further down than it had been up. He hit a steep bank, rolled down it fast, and came to rest on something hard.

As he lay there winded he heard, away to his left, in the fog, a sharp crack.

"Shooting," he said to himself. "That's the limit. They've started shooting now."

At that moment the ground on which he was lying started to vibrate to a slow rhythm and he felt that he was near a heavy moving body. Then, out of the darkness not three feet away a tall shape passed, ringing and thudding. The red glow of a banked fire. The hiss of escaping steam. The smell of hot oil. Then, further off, the report of a second fog signal and he was alone again in the darkness.

The realization that he was lying actually on one of the

tracks of a main railway line dawned slowly. Then he got to his feet and started shakily across.

It was not until he had gone too far to turn back that the dangers of what he was doing occurred to him.

The width of the track seemed endless. It would be the main north line into London. Was any of it electrified? Sammy thought not, but he slowed down still further, lifting his feet carefully over successive rails. As he crept across great engines seemed to be moving quietly in the fog to destroy him.

He lost count of the rails he had crossed when suddenly there was another wall in front of him. A low one, this time.

He dragged himself over it onto grass; took one step forward, was slipping, and was up to his shoulders in water.

After that railway a canal was nothing. Sammy struck out with the confidence of one who has swum from before he could remember. Then he was climbing out onto cinders. It felt like a towing path.

If he followed it he must come to a gate.

He shook himself and started out. A few minutes later he saw something. First it was a faint lightening of the darkness. Then a glow, as of the early morning sun coming up through mist. Then, still veiled behind the curtain of the mist, a belching of red and orange and flame.

There was a big building on fire, and it was not far ahead of him.

He broke into a trot.

SIXTEEN

Mr. Wetherall
Receives Visitors

When Mr. Wetherall got home to his flat he was prepared to bet that he would be worrying about the complicated affairs of the Donovans for the rest of the evening.

As it turned out, he was wrong.

First he placated Alice, whom the fog and his continued absence had combined to upset. Then he settled down to attack a prime chop which had been sitting in the oven for more than an hour and now looked and tasted like pemmican.

It was at that moment that he noticed Mr. Bullfyne's letter. It was not visibly different from a score of other letters which that energetic gentleman had written to him except that, not being bulky, it could not contain a rejected manuscript. He opened it quite casually.

His shout brought Mrs. Wetherall running.

"Death by Big Ben," he gasped.

"What do you mean?"

"I've sold it. Bullfyne's sold it."

"It's not true."

"In black and white," said Mr. Wetherall. The prime

chop grew colder and harder as husband and wife read and reread Mr. Bullfyne's letter.

"I am happy to tell you," he wrote, "that Messrs. Hobnell and Block want to make a contract for *Death by Big Ben*. I have always had confidence that this novel would find a purchaser ["Hmph," said Mr. Wetherall]. Mr. Bertram Block, who is well-known to me, writes, 'I like *Death by Big Ben* very much. It is an excitable and readable story, and above all, it is a pleasant story. Apart from the word "bloody" on page 156 there is not a word in it which I should hesitate to read to my children. That is my standard of a good detective story.' He offers an advance of £100 on the signing of the contracts and a royalty—" (Here they got lost in a maze of percentages and sliding scales which meant nothing to them at all.)

"Wilfrid!"

"We ought to go out and have a drink."

"A hundred pounds!"

"Perhaps we'd better not go out in this fog. Have we got anything in the house?"

"There's some cooking sherry in the kitchen."

"Wheel it in."

By eleven o'clock they had drunk half a bottle of the cooking sherry and had retired to bed to continue spending the five hundred pounds which was the least they calculated to be coming to them from the blessed Mr. Hobnell and the benevolent Mr. Block.

At ten minutes past eleven they turned out the light and settled down to sleep.

At twenty past eleven the telephone rang.

"Perhaps it's an American publisher," said Mrs. Wetherall sleepily.

It was Todd.

"Have you seen Sammy?" he said.

Mr. Wetherall came back to the present with an effort.

"No," he said. "Why?"

Todd told him.

"You mean he's been missing since six?"

"There's something very odd going on up at Strudwick Road. I was on my way back there, but I've got stuck."

"You mean the fog?"

"Fog and worse," said Todd. "I'm in a callbox near King's Cross. There's a factory on fire and the engines are blocking both main roads. What with that, and the fog, and the jam they had to start with, I don't see this being sorted out before morning."

"Factory," said Mr. Wetherall sharply. "Do you happen to know what sort?"

"Does it matter?"

"Yes."

"All right," said Todd. "Hang on a second. I'll find one of the local inhabitants." He came back. "It's a place called Quigleys'. Paint and varnish."

"Oh dear," said Mr. Wetherall, and rang off before Todd could start asking questions. He found his wife behind him. "You get back to bed," he said. "This may take some time."

He rang up Scotland Yard and, after some delay, got put through to Hazlerigg, who sounded elaborately unruffled (a very bad sign, as Mr. Wetherall would have realized if he had known him better).

"That factory at King's Cross," he said, without preamble. "Is that the one—"

"I'm afraid so," said Hazlerigg.

"What happened?"

"We were sixty seconds too late," said Hazlerigg. "That's what happened. One of our cars was actually outside the factory when it went up. From the flash it looked like a Stillson grenade. Prince says Sergeant Donovan simply pulled the pin out, counted two, and dropped it among the five of them."

"Prince?"

"He was nearest the door. He managed to crawl out. He was pretty well burnt up though. He won't last till morning."

"And Sergeant Donovan. Is he—"

"My goodness," said Hazlerigg, with a sudden gust of anger. "Have you ever seen varnish burning? If we find a bone button between them it's all there will be."

"I see," said Mr. Wetherall. "I'd better let his mother know."

"It would be a help if you could do that," said Hazlerigg. His voice was normal again. "We've got our hands pretty full here."

After he had rung off, it occurred to Mr. Wetherall that he had forgotten Sammy. He hesitated. Hazlerigg had told him that he was busy, but even so it would be easy for him to ring up the local station and send a man round to inquire.

His hand was stretched out for the telephone when his front doorbell rang.

He went down the stairs. They had been attic stairs in the original house, and his private front door was at the foot of them. He turned on the light and opened up.

Outside in the passage stood Sammy. It was perhaps lucky that Mr. Ballo's passage light was dim. It allowed him to take Sammy in by installments.

It was only when the boy started talking through chattering teeth that he realized that he was wet as well as filthy.

"Come up at once," he said. "I'll turn on a bath."

Half an hour later, Sammy, wearing an old pair of Mr. Wetherall's cricket trousers and two sweaters, with a dressing gown over the top, was sitting in front of the fire. He had a long bruise down one side of his face where he had made contact with the railway embankment, but apart from this he looked as good as new.

One o'clock struck as he was in the middle of it.

"Rolls of money," said Mr. Wetherall at the end. "You're quite sure about it?"

"Must've been a thousand pounds."

"Not new notes."

"That's right. Old stuff. Same as these he paid me." Sammy unfolded two notes from his wallet. They had not been good specimens to start with and had suffered further in the canal.

Some words were visible on the back of one of the notes. They had been stamped on with a rubber stamp. Most of it was illegible but the last word was STORES. Well—Hazlerigg could deal with that sort of thing better than he could. He managed to find two newer ones for Sammy, and folded the exhibits away in his wallet.

Another thought occurred to him.

"Where did you get those photographs you sent Peggy?"

Sammy explained.

"They were actually in Mr. Holoman's drawer?"

"And I saw her too, Mr. Wetherall, like I told you, with the other man, who was crying."

"Hm," said Mr. Wetherall. "You'll have to tell it all over again to the police in the morning, so I won't bother you now."

Sammy looked thoughtful.

"Is that right? I've got to spill it all to the police?"

"Certainly. Why?"

"And will they pull old Holoman in?"

Mr. Wetherall reflected.

"Not at once, I shouldn't think," he said. "But it'll give them something to work on."

"I don't mind them working on him," said Sammy, "so long as they don't let him get working on me. I don't want any part of him, Mr. Wetherall. You've never met him. I can tell you, I'm not going back there, not even to collect my things. I'll get Patsy to call in and fetch them. He's big enough to stand up for himself."

"Patsy," began Mr. Wetherall awkwardly. He'd have to do it sometime, and now seemed as good a time as any. "I'm afraid—"

The doorbell made him jump.

"Sit still," he said. "You'll catch your death of cold if you start gadding about. I'll see who it is. It's probably Todd."

As he walked downstairs he felt glad that the explanation had been postponed.

Standing in the passage he found a tall, elderly man with a mat of gray-black hair and a high, peach-mottled complexion.

"Mr. Wetherall?" said the stranger. "My name's Holoman. I think it's time we had a talk."

Mr. Wetherall's first instinct, a reflex of pure panic, was to slam the door and bolt upstairs. Overcoming this he said, "I'm afraid I haven't the pleasure. It's very late. Wouldn't tomorrow—"

"If tomorrow would have done, I wouldn't have come out tonight. I don't think you'll regret giving me ten minutes."

His wife appeared at the top of the stairs.

"Who is it, dear?"

"It's a Mr. Holoman. Holoman." He spoke as loudly as he dared. He remembered that he had left the living-room door open. "It's quite all right. You get back to bed."

When they reached the living room, it was empty.

Mr. Holoman sat upright in the chair beside the fire. He did not remove his close-fitting, old-fashioned overcoat. He carried no hat, and his thin, strong hands with their long finger joints rested lightly at his side.

"Still foggy out," said Mr. Wetherall politely.

Mr. Holoman ignored this. He seemed to be summing up the man opposite him, searching for something that he was unable to find. There was a very faint note of surprise in his voice when he spoke.

"You'll excuse me," he said, "if I cut out the social preliminaries. It's very late and what I've got to say can be said quickly. You've been interfering in my business. You removed one boy out of London. Not that it matters now. Anything he knows is out of date. You sent another boy up to spy on me."

"The score seems a little uneven at that," said Mr. Wetherall. "You had me viciously assaulted. And not content with that, you or your friends have been moving heaven and earth to have me discredited and thrown out of my job."

"All right," said Mr. Holoman. "We'll draw up a detailed balance sheet—but some other time, if you don't mind. At the moment I'm interested in the present, not past. You know what happened tonight?"

"More or less."

"Your friend Sergeant Donovan took the law into his own hands—for the second time—and wiped out five men. Six, if you include himself. He also set fire to a considerable amount of property. It's not under control yet."

"I realize," said Mr. Wetherall, "that it makes things awkward for you."

Mr. Holoman looked at him speculatively. "It could hardly have happened at a more convenient time," he said, "not if we had arranged it ourselves."

He seemed to be serious."

"I should explain that we never trust ourselves to one set of people for long."

"We?"

"The organization I represent. Whittaker was on his way out. Curiously enough the change was to have taken place tonight. You'll appreciate that such a transaction can be tricky. A man like Whittaker is easier to hire than to sack. That is why—" Mr. Holoman showed his teeth briefly— "we were so grateful to Sergeant Donovan."

"I'm sure you didn't come here just to tell me this."

"I came here," said Mr. Holoman, coldly and directly, "to tell you to stop being a fool. Please don't misunderstand me. I'm not giving you a warning. I'm giving you an order."

"And if I don't take orders from you?"

"You'll take it," said Mr. Holoman. "What are you getting out of this, anyway?"

"Getting?"

"Or are you just doing it for the kick it gives you?"

"Certainly not."

"I doubt if you know why you're doing it," said Mr.

Holoman, "unless it's interfering for the sake of interfering. Like a nosy old virgin who can't help peeping to find out what's going on behind the park seat."

"If that's all you've got to say—"

"It's not what I came to say. That chapter's finished now. We're starting a few more lines next week, and to be quite frank we shall have our work cut out dealing with the police. We don't want any more interference from the touchline. Got it?"

"Why," said Mr. Wetherall, and he hoped he said it firmly, "should you assume that I'm going to take the slightest notice of what you say?"

Mr. Holoman unrolled himself and stood.

"I thought I'd made it plain," he said. "Do you want it in words of one syllable? We're handing over tonight to a new crowd. I'd give you the name, but it wouldn't mean a thing to you. They work here and on the continent. Poles, mostly. Deserters from both sides."

"All right. I quite understand. You're taking on a new set of bullies. For my taste they can't be more unpleasant than the last lot. I expect I shall survive."

"I wasn't thinking about you," said Mr. Holoman. His eye wandered across the room.

"What do you mean?"

"When you go out tomorrow morning, are you going to be quite happy to leave your wife behind in the house? She's not entirely fit at the moment, is she? It could be awkward. Suppose men broke in while you were away. They might have to keep your wife from interfering. Tie her up—perhaps."

"They couldn't—"

"They're not a nice crowd. Really, hardly human. They learned things in Warsaw and Berlin. I don't say they'd kill her. Probably not."

The knife was out now.

"You couldn't do it."

"I expect you're right," said Mr. Holoman. "Only since it wouldn't be me, the question doesn't arise."

"I'll have to think."

"You've got no time to think." He looked at the clock on the mantelpiece, which showed a quarter past two. "Even now I may be too late to stop some things."

"I must—"

Mr. Holoman moved to the door. "I'm going to be busy after tomorrow," he said. "I'll take your answer now. Yes or no."

"You leave me no alternative."

"You stop interfering and you stop running off to the police. If you get in touch with Scotland Yard we shall know about it."

"Yes."

"That's all right then. Don't bother to come down. I'll let myself out."

After he had gone Mr. Wetherall stood unmoving. His first coherent thought was, "I suppose Sammy heard all that. It'll save me having to break it to him about his brother."

He went to the door of the spare room.

Sammy was there all right. He was on the bed, fast asleep. Mr. Wetherall put the eiderdown over him and came back to the living room. He was too shaken up to want to go to bed.

He looked at the clock. Todd might still be at the *Kite*. He got through, but heard that Todd had just gone out again.

"Would you ask him to ring me when he comes back?" he said, and gave the number. Then he put the kettle on for a fresh pot of tea.

His head was down on his chest when the telephone jangled.

"Hullo—Alastair."

"It's me, Mr. Wetherall."

"Peggy."

"That's right. A nice thing!" She sounded put out.

"You mean about Patsy?"

"I mean about us. They've burnt our house down. Lucky it was insured."

It occurred to Mr. Wetherall for an instant that he had gone to sleep in his chair, and was dreaming.

"What do you mean? What's happened?"

"Some people just burnt our house down. Got in and piled up the furniture and splashed petrol over it and set fire to it. Ma and me were lucky to get out."

"Are you both all right?"

"I got Ma in with some friends. She's very vexed about it."

"Where are you?"

"In a callbox."

Mr. Wetherall thought rapidly.

"You'd better come round here for the rest of the night. I've got Sammy here. It's too long to explain over the telephone."

"Sammy. That's good. He's all right then?"

"Yes. He's fine."

"Did I hear you say something about Patsy?"

"I started it," said Mr. Wetherall. "Perhaps I'd better tell you that when you get round here."

"He's dead, isn't he?"

"Yes. I'm afraid he is." He had no idea what to say. There was silence at the other end, but he could feel that Peggy was still there, listening.

"He took five of them with him," he added softly.

There was another silence. Then a "clock" as the receiver was hung up.

SEVENTEEN

Scuttle

The early hours of that morning had the qualities of nightmare. Time had ceased to count and chronology was upset.

Certain things must have happened because the results of them became apparent later. For instance, he certainly dictated a cable by telephone, for when he looked at the delivery copy long afterward it was marked "03.18 HRS" as "time of dispatch" and the Post Office rarely make mistakes about facts like that. Other things may have belonged to the land of sleep, if he slept at all. He was uncertain even of that.

There were isolated pictures in his mind. Of Peggy arriving, dressed in an outfit that she had borrowed from a friend and which was slightly too small for her in every particular. Of Mr. Ballo, the Japanese who lived on the floor below, silently opening his door at the moment of her arrival, looking inscrutably out, and silently closing it. Of Sammy waking up and asking to be told what had happened to his brother; and being told and almost immediately dropping off. Of Peggy and Alice asleep side by side in the same bed.

Wakefulness and sleep; tiredness and sorrow; awareness and unawareness.

Mr. Wetherall stirred uneasily in his chair. The clock struck five. A cold light was coming up into the world and the fog was almost gone. The taste in his mouth was beyond analysis or belief.

He went out to the kitchen where the half-empty bottle of cooking sherry leered at him, until he took it and hid it in the cupboard. He then considered the possibility of a cup of black coffee. He wasn't very expert at making coffee, tea being more his mark, but he decided that if you threw boiling water and coffee grounds together in sufficient quantities something should happen.

The telephone rang again.

Alastair at last!

At first he thought it was a stranger, the voice was so carefully modulated and controlled. Then he realized that it was Mr. Bertram.

"And what do you want?" he said. "I thought good solicitors never got up before nine?"

"I want you to listen very carefully," said Mr. Bertram, "because I may not be able to get in touch with you for some time after today."

"If it's important I could come round after breakfast—"

"On no account." Mr. Bertram's voice took on a sharper note like a circular saw hitting a nail. "I am catching the early train for Harwich. I expect to be out of the country for at least a month."

"I see," said Mr. Wetherall thoughtfully.

"Before I go, there is one thing you ought to know. I was only sure of it myself recently. There's no one with you, is there?"

"No."

"Good. Do you remember the name of the third shareholder in Holoman's, Ltd.?"

"I can't say I do."

"I wrote to you about it. His name is Herbert. Mr. Arthur Herbert."

"I think I do remember something now. Mr. Holoman had one share and his wife had another. And there was an outsider, Mr. Herbert, who had about three. That was it, wasn't it?"

"Yes. I don't suppose above half a dozen people know this—it's done through nominees of course—but you can take it from me that Mr. Herbert controls P.S.D."

Again the name struck a chord.

Someone had mentioned P.S.D. to him recently.

"Who—" he began; then realized that he was talking to a dead telephone. Mr. Bertram had gone.

"Exit first rat," thought Mr. Wetherall uncharitably.

The kettle came to a boil and he made the coffee. It was, as he had imagined, quite easy. He wondered why women always made such a mystery of it.

Whether it was the coffee, or the early hour or the lack of sleep, his brain, always a useful piece of mechanism, seemed suddenly to be working with exceptional clarity.

The piece of information that Mr. Bertram had given him fell into place.

There was a game he had watched boys playing. He had never been able to make out the rules. One boy stood apart, in a corner, and the others ran off, as far as they could, and brought things back to him.

He was the boy in the corner. It was an impression he had had before. In this game, if he stood still long enough, everything would be brought to him. Just what he was to do with it all when he got it was another thing.

The telephone rang again.

He lifted up the receiver and a strange voice at the other end said, "Mr. Wetherall?" He said, "Yes," and the voice said, "Go ahead," and another voice started talking.

Twice Mr. Wetherall tried to break in.

"Where?" he said at last. "Where did it happen?"

"Chancery Lane station."

"Where is he now? If I came round now could I see him?"

The voice sounded doubtful.

But without waiting for any more Mr. Wetherall snatched up his hat and coat. At the top of the stairs he paused for a moment. There was no sound of anyone stirring.

He went down, shut his outer door quietly, and bolted down the rest of the stairs. In the lower hall he pulled up sharply. A man in a raincoat, who had been sitting on a chair beside the door, got up to meet him.

"Good morning, Mr. Wetherall."

Mr. Wetherall had to look twice before he recognized a very young detective constable from Mace Street station.

"Good morning, Lloyd," he said. "Am I under house arrest?"

"Not yet, Mr. Wetherall. I'm just here to keep an eye on things. I can't stop you going out if you want to."

"Well, I do. I'm going to Bart's. Tell them upstairs if they start worrying. I hope to be back for breakfast."

"I'll do that," said Lloyd. He had a pleasant, soft Welsh voice.

Outside it was raw. The fog was now no more than a light mist.

Mr. Wetherall dived down into the curious early-morning hush of the Underground. A few workmen and office cleaners were standing about the platform, unspeaking. In spite of the fact that none of them came near him, or showed any interest in him, he caught himself edging toward the back of the platform.

His early-morning mood was all drained out of him.

He changed trains at Tottenham Court Road, where the crowd was a little larger, and again he kept himself carefully out of the way. At St. Paul's station he got out and climbed back into the open air.

In that short space of time the mist had blown away and the sky was full of low, hurrying gray clouds.

He walked past the Old Bailey, crossed carefully, and came by back ways to St. Bartholomew's Hospital. Here he gave· his name and waited in a bleak room, and gave his name again and was shown into another bleak room where a man rose to greet him.

At the back of his mind he had expected some last-year medical student, or young, newly qualified doctor, but it was a gray-haired man with a pinched, ruthless Scots face, whom even Mr. Wetherall had no difficulty in recognizing. It was a face that had been a good deal in the papers recently, during its owner's attendance on Royalty.

"Mr. Wetherall? Todd mentioned your name."

"How is he?"

"It's too early to be definite. But in my opinion he'll live."

"Thank God for that."

"As an agnostic," said the surgeon, "I should say, thank his constitution. When you're dealing with shock, a healthy life and a balanced mind are your strongest allies."

"Can I see him?"

The surgeon looked at him curiously.

"You realize," he said, "that we've had to take the right arm off?"

"No, I didn't."

"He won't see anyone but his nurses for a day or two and I doubt if he'll see them very clearly."

"Of course, I only knew there'd been a bad accident. I'd no idea— Can you tell me how it happened?"

"I can tell you what he said. A reporter, isn't he? I imagine he was on his way home. There's an early train from Chancery Lane. I sometimes get it myself. There wasn't anyone on the platform except him and two other men. As the train came in they moved up on him, picked him up and threw him onto the line."

Mr. Wetherall said nothing.

"Luckily he missed the line rail and fell into the trough. Must have thrown his arm up as he fell. The train went over it."

With fingers that trembled Mr. Wetherall felt in his inside pocket and found a letter which had arrived the day before. He scribbled his telephone number on the back of the envelope, removed the letter and handed the envelope to the surgeon.

"That's my address, and I've written down my telephone number. Ask someone to let me know how he comes along."

Then he was gone.

The surgeon, who had learned enough about the minds of men not to be dogmatic, watched him without surprise.

Mr. Wetherall walked quickly out of the hospital, crossed Holborn, went down the lane that leads into Ludgate Hill, and turned right at the bottom into Fleet Street. He walked with his body thrown forward. His breath was coming in short, dry gasps.

The night commissionaire at the *Kite* was a man who reckoned he had seen everything, but Mr. Wetherall added a new subheading.

He did not look mad, and the commissionaire was an expert on madmen. In spite of a night's beard he did not look particularly unkempt. He was just a medium-sized, ordinary, sober citizen in a raging temper.

"I want to see the editor."

"Yes, sir?"

"My name's Wetherall. Will you tell him I'm here?"

"Would he be expecting you?"

"I can only suggest," said Mr. Wetherall, in his most icily pedantic manner, "that a simple way of ascertaining that would be to ask him."

The commissionaire was not paid his considerable salary for nothing. He took a very deep breath and said, "I'll ring his secretary."

"All right, you do that," said Mr. Wetherall.

The man retired into his sanctum, dialed a number and said, "I'm very sorry, Mrs. Bolton. Do you know anything about a Mr. Wetherall?"

Mrs. Bolton appeared to cogitate. Then she said, "Yes, I think so. In fact, he might be important. Send him up."

The commissionaire was so pleased with his own perception that he actually smiled at Mr. Wetherall and conducted him to the lift.

Mrs. Bolton was Duncan Robarts' personal secretary. She

slept, according to the private tradition of the *Kite,* from Friday evening to Sunday morning inclusive, but at no other time at all. However, she was certainly awake, composed and affable when Mr. Wetherall was shown in.

"Mr. Robarts is coming along," she said.

"I haven't got him out of bed, I hope," said Mr. Wetherall with massive indifference.

"Well, no. He was up. He got up when he heard about Alastair, poor boy. We had things to fix."

"I see." Mr. Wetherall had not had time to wonder how quite such an eminent surgeon had been conjured onto the spot quite so quickly.

"You look all in," said Mrs. Bolton. "Sit down by the fire. Have you had any breakfast?"

"Thank you. I couldn't—"

"When did you eat last?"

"I really don't remember."

Mrs. Bolton must have pressed a bell, and to the man who appeared she said, "Get us some coffee and toast and boiled eggs. Can you eat boiled eggs?"

"Yes," said Mr. Wetherall meekly.

He was in the middle of his second boiled egg and of a long reminiscence by Mrs. Bolton about her family in Banstead when Duncan Robarts stalked in. Small as he was, the room seemed to shrink.

"Don't get up," said Robarts. "We can talk as you eat. How was Todd when you saw him?"

"They've taken his arm off. They say he's going to be all right."

Robarts perched on the edge of the table. It was obvious that he was in a towering temper.

"Once," he said, "I had this thing put up to me—by Todd. I refused to go on. And I still think I was right. As it stood, it was a matter for the police. Now things are different. If we can't look after our own people, we might as well shut up shop. You've been in this from the start?"

Mr. Wetherall nodded.

"There's no need to tell me the story. I know most of it.

Todd sent me copies of his reports. Very good reporting too, but of course I couldn't use them. Now it's different. I want to hurt those chaps. I want to hurt them till they squeak."

Mr. Wetherall gulped his coffee and started to say something, but was headed off.

"I don't mean we're going to run crossways to the police. But they can hoe their own row. There are things we can do they can't. Anyway, we can work up public opinion on our side. Now let's have your ideas."

"Three days ago," said Mr. Wetherall slowly, "I sat in Scotland Yard and listened to Superintendent Hazlerigg. He said that the way to attack these people was from the bottom. He had it all mapped out. You worked from A to B, and from B to C and so on up until you reached Mr. X at the top. It sounded sense at the time. Now I'm not so sure. To start with, all the little A's and B's and C's in this equation were wiped off last night."

Robarts looked at Mrs. Bolton, who said, "Factory fire at King's Cross. We didn't know it was connected."

"In any case," went on Mr. Wetherall, "I don't think it would have worked. These people change their subordinates too fast for the little men to find out much. It's no good cutting off the hundred arms of this monster. You've got to go for the head. At least, that's what I think."

"Certainly," said Robarts. "Certainly. An excellent idea. Always supposing you happen to know who the head is."

"I do know."

Robarts ruffled like a little angry eagle. "Let's hear about him."

"There's no proof at all. That's the way it's been arranged. But to my mind it's as certain as anything that depends on probabilities."

"Tell us who he is," said Robarts. "We'll work up the evidence later."

"His name is Arthur Herbert. He's head of the wholesale food firm, P.S.D. The only direct connection between him and this racket is that he holds three shares in Holoman's company."

"Let's take your word for it for a moment—you might turn up anything we have on him, Mrs. Bolton. I seem to remember the name in some other connection. Company merger or something—if you're right, how do you suggest we set about him? It's apt to be risky in this country, attacking a man with a good reputation. Expensive too."

"Yes," said Mr. Wetherall. "I thought of that."

He talked for nearly fifteen minutes. Mrs. Bolton noted the fact as another record. She had never heard anyone, not even a film star, talk to Robarts for fifteen straight minutes.

"All right," said Robarts at the end. "Let's try it out. It doesn't commit us right away. And I'll get people working on that other little man. You think young Donovan will be able to recognize him?"

"He had a good look at him through the fanlight."

"Get Donovan round here straight away. He can come quite openly. The more people who see him the better. I'll have his statement taken on oath. That's the quickest way of making him safe. And the girl. If we like the look of them we'll take them both on the strength. Would that suit them?"

"It would suit Sammy," said Mr. Wetherall. "He'd be an asset to any newspaper. Peggy too, I should think. She's a good secretary, typing and filing and shorthand and all that sort of thing—and as nice a girl as you could find in the length and breadth of England."

He spoke with such unconscious feeling that Robarts glanced at him for a moment.

"All right," he said. "I'll see they're looked after. They'll be quite safe here. The boy will have to live in a hostel anyway. Mrs. Bolton will fix up Peggy."

That was the way, thought Mr. Wetherall. The press; the only real dictator left in a shrinking world. Pull down that King. Set up that President. Dissolve the Empire. Disestablish the Church. Take a note, Mrs. Bolton—

"And now for you," went on Robarts. "First, how long is it going to take you to do your stuff?"

"I'll get it off my chest today, while it's fresh."

"I'll pay you half in advance and half on delivery," said Robarts, and mentioned a figure that set Mr. Wetherall's tired brain spinning. "That should help you to tidy up your affairs. I take it you will be all right. Yourself, I mean."

"I shall be all right," said Mr. Wetherall bitterly. "After all, I'm not doing anything difficult. All I'm doing is running away."

He used one of the *Kite* telephones to ring up his flat, where he spoke to Peggy.

"Listen carefully," he said, "because we don't want any slip-ups this morning. First tell Sammy to come along to the *Kite*—that's it, the newspaper. It's in Fleet Street. He's to ask for Mr. Andrews, that's the staff manager here. He must be careful how he goes, but as long as he keeps his eyes open and keeps away from the edges of platforms and curbs and that sort of thing, I don't think they can do much to him in broad daylight. Then I want you to go to the school. Take a taxi. Mrs. Wetherall will give you the money. When you get there ring up the committee—you've got all the numbers—suggest twelve o'clock. Some of them may be away, being a Saturday, but get as many as you can. All right? Then one thing more. If you go downstairs you'll find a policeman in the hall. He's a nice young man and his name is Lloyd. Oh, you know him. A friend of Patsy's. So much the better. I don't know what orders he's been given, but ask him to see that he, or someone else, stays on duty till I get back this afternoon. And to-night, if possible. After that it won't matter. We shan't be there. What? No, I can't explain now—"

He rang off quickly.

Peggy had done her stuff. They were all there.

Colonel Bond, looking faintly offended. Miss Toup belligerent. Mr. Fawcus important (it was his first full committee). Mr. Hazel neutral. Mrs. Griller baffled.

Mr. Wetherall found himself inspecting them with unusual tolerance. He supposed that there was something to be said for the way public education was run in England. Not a great deal, but something. Better than Soviet Russia? Possibly. Worse than America? Probably. He did not know. It no longer bothered him.

"I must apologize," he said, "for calling you together at such short notice. But what I've got to tell you is, I think, important, and it's certainly urgent. Monday would have been too late. The fact is—" he took a deep breath—"that I have had an invitation to visit Canada. My wife and myself. It's from a man we knew during the war. I regard it in the nature of an—ah—cultural tow. It seemed to be the chance of a lifetime, and in short I accepted."

Colonel Bond said, "How long are you going to be away?"

Miss Toup said, "When were you proposing to start?"

It was almost a dead heat.

"I am actually leaving my present flat tomorrow," said Mr. Wetherall. "I am not certain of my date of sailing, but it should be sometime at the end of this coming week. In the interval I shall be—er—staying with friends."

"Impossible," announced Miss Toup.

"You must have no end of pull," said Mr. Hazel. "Last year it took me six weeks to book a passage to America—and I believe that's easier than Canada."

"One of the large newspapers is interested," said Mr. Wetherall. "I am engaged on a series of articles for them which will defray—in fact, will considerably more than defray—the expense."

"Quite impossible," repeated Miss Toup. "If you must go off on a jaunt, why can't you wait until the end of term?"

"I'm afraid that the sort of trip I had in mind wouldn't fit into a school holiday. It will be at least six months. The earliest I could be back could be the beginning of next summer term."

"It by no means follows," said Miss Toup—"I speak, of

course, for myself and without the authority of the chairman—but it by no means follows that you will still find the vacancy open. Perhaps Colonel Bond will let us know what he thinks."

"Oh, well," said the Colonel. "Really, I couldn't say."

"Don't let it worry you unduly," said Mr. Wetherall. "I'm not sure that I want to come back."

A moment of absolute silence.

"That's taken the wind out of their sails," thought Mr. Hazel. "Isn't it just like these damned committees? When they get hold of a good man they badger him and chivvy him until he walks out on them. Curse that Toup bitch. The Colonel's a fool but she's pure poison. Well, we shall see. She's not indispensable herself. I might be able to pull a string—"

He made a note on his pad.

"I should perhaps explain," said Mr. Wetherall. "This isn't a matter of school business, and I hadn't thought to mention it before, but I am, in my spare time, a writer."

"Plenty of material here for your first novel," said Mrs. Griller loudly and unexpectedly.

"I am happy to say that my first novel has not only been written. It has been accepted. It was this, coupled with the newspaper offer, that made me bold enough to think that I might be able to make a living with the pen."

"What are the articles about?" inquired Mr. Fawcus, feeling it was time he said something. "Educational, I suppose."

Mr. Wetherall toyed with the idea of saying, "Folly and corruption on committees," but disciplined himself. "Just general articles on current topics," he said.

"You spoke about writing in your spare time," said Miss Toup venomously. "I wasn't aware that headmasters had much spare time. Unless they make it at the expense of the school."

Now Mr. Wetherall had meant to be good.

He had intended to confine himself to announcing his departure and parting on the best terms possible with his committee.

It was at this point that he lost his temper.

"I will willingly pay my royalties into school funds," he said, turning directly on Miss Toup, "if you will yourself contribute any money you have received, directly or indirectly, for attacking my character."

Miss Toup gave a squeak.

"Who put you up to inquiring about my so-called communism? You can't really expect us to believe that you care a brass farthing whether I'm a Communist or a Fascist or a Nudist. It was the purest brand of nosy-parkering and troublemaking. And another thing. Miss Donovan tells me you were snooping round the school a few nights ago. After we'd all gone home. What were you looking for? Hammers and sickles or rude words on lavatory walls?"

"Really, Wetherall," said Colonel Bond faintly.

"And you," said Mr. Wetherall. "You're meant to run this committee, aren't you? If it's the way you ran your regiment I'm more surprised than ever that we won the war. Your job is to keep Miss Toup in order, not to let her bully me—or you. If you can't manage it, I suggest you hand over to someone who can. And while you're at it," he added, with an unkind glance at Mr. Fawcus, "I suggest you stop co-opting alleged outside experts and get a few schoolmasters on this committee, and people who really know how schools are run."

Miss Toup had got her breath back.

"If you think," she said, "that by making vague threats and allegations—"

"Let me tell you something," said Mr. Wetherall, overriding her with effortless ease. "You may not know all that's been going on behind the scenes in the last few weeks. I'm not sure exactly how you got brought into this, and I'm certainly not going to waste time trying to find out. There's a limit to muckraking. But I must give you a serious warning. This little melodrama that you've been meddling in is nearly over. We're in the last act. The small characters have all been seen for the last time. Do you understand that?"

Miss Toup tried to say something, but failed.

"I see you do. Then one thing more. The sort of people I've been contending with have got rather drastic and unpleasant ways of sweeping up minor characters when their spell of usefulness is over. You may not know about Mr. Crowdy. His death didn't feature in the sort of papers you read. But you mustn't overlook what happened to Mr. Pride—"

Her face the color of old parchment, Miss Toup got up and walked from the room.

When the committee had dispersed Mr. Hazel sought a word with Mr. Wetherall.

"Don't take them too seriously," he said. "Have your holiday and enjoy it. I think it's been well-earned. When you get back you may find some changes on the committee."

"It's very good of you, but—"

"I didn't understand a quarter of what you said, but I gather you've been engaged in a sort of private war. What has Miss Toup been doing? Helping the enemy?"

"I think she was tricked into it."

"She's got about as much common sense as a hen, less really. Is that the only reason you're getting out?"

"It's one of them," said Mr. Wetherall. "But I really did mean what I said. I just don't know if I shall come back. To schoolmastering I mean. I've long wondered if I was fitted for it. I'm not a patient or scholarly person. And I'm not half energetic enough for a headmaster. I like boys. But I like them for themselves. I'm not mad to improve them."

"You may be right," said Mr. Hazel with a smile. "All I'm suggesting is that you don't make your mind up now."

The news seemed to have leaked out.

Peggy arrived with a face of fire, and said, "What's this I hear about them chucking you out?"

"Shut the door," said Mr. Wetherall, "and stop looking

like a tigress robbed of her young. No one's chucked me
out. I've resigned."

"Really, or are you just saying that?"

"You must know me well enough," said Mr. Wetherall
primly, "to know that I am not in the habit of just saying
things. I am going to Canada almost at once and I shall be
away for at least six months."

Peggy looked at him straightly.

"Are you coming back?"

"The matter is undecided."

"I suppose old Edgecumb will be running things?"

"I imagine Mr. Edgecumb may be given temporary control."

"Not over me he won't. I shall get another job."

"As a matter of fact I have the offer of one for you. On
the *Kite*."

"Newspapers, huh?"

"Big men. Smooth types. Take a note, Miss Donovan. If
the Foreign Secretary calls—"

"You're not kidding?"

"Certainly not. There's a job for Sammy as well. When
you go along—that is, if you like the idea—ask for Mrs.
Bolton. She'll look after you. For a start, she'll find you
somewhere to put up."

"And you're really getting out? No fooling?"

"No fooling," said Mr. Wetherall. "I've almost gone. You
can go along to see the *Kite* this morning, if you like."

"I'd better straighten things up here first," said Peggy.
"I've still got last week's milk returns to make out. I'd
better get them fudged up—"

"Adjusted," said Mr. Wetherall mechanically.

"—adjusted, before I go."

She whisked out quickly and shut the door.

Mr. Wetherall sat staring after her.

EIGHTEEN

Finale in Hampstead

The big car in which Mr. Wetherall was traveling turned north off the Finchley Road and the noise of the traffic died behind them as they climbed the long straight street, which rises gently toward the Heath.

The driver slowed, and then turned again.

If the previous street had been a tributary, this was no more than a backwater.

The car nosed along, its engine running silently, until the road came to a dead end in a circular run-around of asphalt and turf. Then it turned about and drifted down the other side, the driver watching the numbers.

All the houses were big, all modern, and all expensive, in the style of the thirties, in hand-baked brick and rustic tile. Some of them had wrought-iron porch lanterns and others had little shutters beside the upstairs windows which were plainly not intended to shut but looked very attractive all the same. They all had their ration of garden in front, defined by side path, front path and garage run-in.

The car drew up in front of No. 8 and the driver switched off. The stillness and the peace became absolute.

In the distance, cut off as it were by a wind break, the noise of the traffic came up from the foot of the hill like the murmur of a distant brook which enhances the stillness of a forest glade. Secure behind the buttress of pounds, shillings and pence the houses slept out the massive peace of an English Sunday afternoon.

"Quite a dump," said the driver. "We'll wait here for you."

"I may be a little time."

As he spoke Mr. Wetherall glanced at the occupants of the back seat and the largest of the three men sitting there nodded reassuringly.

"Be sure to shout if you want any help," he said. "We shall hear you."

"It's quiet enough to hear a bomb go off," agreed his companion.

"Oh, I don't think it's going to be that sort of party," said Mr. Wetherall.

The little man who was sitting in the middle of the back seat, like a prisoner between two large warders, looked up and blinked unhappily, but said nothing.

"Good luck," said the driver.

Mr. Wetherall walked up the neat, flagged path to the cream-colored front door and applied his finger to a fat chromium bell push. After a longish pause the door was opened by a maid.

"Mr. Herbert?"

"I'm not certain if he's in," said the maid. "Would you mind waiting in here?"

She opened a door and showed Mr. Wetherall into a morning room.

It was everything that such a room should be, from the wood-block floor to the built-in white wood bookcases. There was not much furniture but any bit of it looked worth a year of Mr. Wetherall's work.

Five minutes later a boy looked in. He was about sixteen, with a lanky body and a pleasant, half-grown face.

"I'm sorry you've had to wait, Mr. Wetherall," he said.

"I know father's somewhere about. They're searching for him now."

"That's all right," said Mr. Wetherall.

"He put off his Sunday afternoon golf when he heard you were coming. I shouldn't think he's done that for any-one else this year."

"I'm sorry to have put him out," said Mr. Wetherall.

He made a grab at his morale, which was slipping fast.

"I don't think he minded, actually," said the boy. "He was down to play a man who always beats him. Dad hates being beaten."

Just then the door opened and Mr. Herbert came in.

"Sorry to keep you waiting," he said.

He was in his early fifties and looked, Mr. Wetherall thought, like a retired soldier. A soldier turned business-man. There was none of the weakness, none of the spiritual fatness that he had secretly expected. It was the face of a man used to command himself and others, of a man neither stupidly kind nor stupidly cruel. It was the face of a man who was very sure of himself.

"I hope Tom has been entertaining you," he said.

Mr. Wetherall agreed that Tom had been entertaining him.

"All right. You've done your stuff. You can vamoose."

The boy grinned and disappeared.

"It's his long leave from school," said Mr. Herbert, "and much as we both look forward to it, it's sometimes difficult to find things to fill up the forty-eight hours. Now what can I do for you?"

Mr. Wetherall had never felt himself in greater difficulty.

He realized that he was being cleverly maneuvered into a position of disadvantage, but it was hard to say exactly how it was being done.

It was not as if he had come out expecting to meet a sub-human character wearing a mask.

On the other hand, he had not anticipated that the man would be wearing an old Etonian tie.

Meanwhile Mr. Herbert was waiting.

Mr. Wetherall drew a deep breath.

"Why did you give up your golf for me?" he asked.

For a second Mr. Herbert looked surprised.

"My message," persisted Mr. Wetherall, "was that I wanted to discuss matters connected with P.S.D. Frankly, I should have expected your answer to be that you only talked business in business hours. Your son informs me, too, that you don't lightly give up your Sunday golf. That's why I was surprised."

"Put it down to the approach of Christmas," said Mr. Herbert genially, but his eyes were wary.

Mr. Wetherall sank back slightly in his chair. He knew now that his hunch had been right. However amiable, however correct, however imposing, the man in front of him was a crook.

"I can explain my business best," he said, "by starting with a story. It's the story of a man who founded and built up, between the wars, a very large and profitable retail food business. It was a business which sold direct to restaurants and hotels and clubs of all sorts, mostly in London."

"Sounds like P.S.D. to me," said Mr. Herbert. "Do you smoke?"

"Thank you, no. The man who actually built this business up never appeared directly as head of the enterprise. Partly, I think, because he had an old-fashioned idea that retail trade was the hallmark of the lower middle classes."

"Touché," agreed Mr. Herbert, lighting his own cigarette.

"Also because he had other interests. He was, I think, a whisky broker in the City. And he was concerned in large-scale tobacco purchase."

"Quite an all-round man."

"As you can imagine, the profits and, of course, the commitments of such a man would have rocketed during the recent war. Equally, he felt the draft very sharply in the years that followed the Armistice. No more of the easy money of the war years. Instead, increased food rationing, whisky almost unobtainable, tobacco taxed to the limit."

"I weep for him," said Mr. Herbert. "What did he do?"

"He took to crime," said Mr. Wetherall.

The words fell into a deep pool of silence, broken only by the brisk ticking of the French gilt clock in its glass case on the mantelshelf.

Mr. Wetherall's heart matched the beat of the pendulum.

(Well, what was it going to be? Flat denial, boisterous laughter, threats?)

"Do go on," said Mr. Herbert. "I'm sure you haven't come to the end of your story yet."

"If you wish. As I say, he decided to take to crime. But he determined to do so in such a way that his connection with it would defy suspicion. A number of people have had that idea before, but I should think that very few have taken the trouble to work it out quite so cleverly or so thoroughly. What he needed first was a reliable ally. And he had just the man for the job—a Mr. Holoman."

"Holoman? The name sounds familiar."

"I expect it must be, seeing that you are the majority shareholder in Holoman's company."

"That's it, of course. The man who runs it calls himself Holoman, doesn't he? It's not his real name, I believe—"

"His real name is Michaels. There's still a record of a court-martial of a Sergeant Michaels, in Germany, in 1919, in connection with a defalcation in company accounts. Incidentally he was acquitted, after an outstandingly brilliant defense. The defending officer was a Captain Herbert."

"Yes," said Mr. Herbert. "Yes." The way he said it, it was quite without emphasis, yet it sounded, somehow, like a qualified admission.

"When this gentleman decided to turn to crime, he thought of Holoman, who, I might add, had not been idle since his lucky escape in 1919. In that time he had served one stiff sentence for blackmail and one for embezzlement and had founded and dissolved no less than three patent-medicine businesses. Two had failed for economic reasons, one through police interference following complaints from purchasers who had bought an embrocation which contained an unfortunately high element of pure caustic. Despite these failures he was still convinced—and I should hesitate to say that he was wrong—that all you need to succeed handsomely in that line is experience and sufficient capital. The experience he had. The capital was lacking. The gentleman I mentioned was therefore well-placed to do a deal with Holoman, who possessed every possible qualification for a crook's middleman. He could reasonably be counted on for loyalty. He knew all the necessary small fry in the criminal world. His wife, a considerable character in her own right, kept a public house in Soho which served as an admirable meeting ground between Holoman and the rank and file. In short, he was the perfect instrument. All he needed was intelligent handling."

"And the intelligence," said Mr. Herbert with a smile, "was supplied by—your hero."

"Certainly. Figure it out for yourself. In his own way he was even better placed than Holoman. The field in which they were pioneering was the organized distribution of stolen food and drink. This man had all the proper contacts. In a legitimate way of business—and his own business, remember, continued on strictly legitimate lines—he knew every restaurateur, hotelkeeper and club caterer in London. He knew what was plentiful and what was scarce. What they could obtain legitimately and what they had to fiddle for. He had a shrewd idea, too, as to which of them would be likely to fiddle."

"It sounds like money for jam," said Mr. Herbert. "And just the sort of thing to appeal to a man who had money already. It's only the rich man who has any incentive to crime these days. If he makes ten pounds honestly he has to give away nine to the state. On the other hand every penny he fiddles he keeps for himself. Yes. Highly profitable, I should imagine. And very difficult to bring home to—your hero. Unless Holoman chose to talk. He doesn't sound to me to be the talking type."

"I agree," said Mr. Wetherall.

"And even more difficult to prove in court."

"Possibly so. However, you will remember the saying that there are two things which can never remain entirely secret—the spilling of blood and the payment of money."

"Hmp," said Mr. Herbert judgmatically.

"Arrange the matter how they would, there was still this difficulty to surmount. At some time and in some way Holoman had to pay over to his employer his share of the profits. His employer was living in a style—" Mr. Wetherall allowed his gaze to wander for a moment round the room— "a style which called for frequent and sizable injections of ready money. He had an expensive household and a wife to maintain and a son and daughter at well-known schools."

"Shall we," said Mr. Herbert, in a voice from which all trace of affability had vanished, "leave our families out of this?"

"No," said Mr. Wetherall, "we shall not."

Mr. Herbert half rose in his seat. "I presume you want to finish this conversation."

"Yes. But so do you. If you hadn't, you wouldn't have let me get as far as this."

Mr. Herbert resettled himself slowly.

"Apart from which, this talk of leaving families out of it strikes me as one-sided. You may not be aware of it, but your friend Holoman paid me a visit in the early hours of yesterday morning. His object was to tell me that unless I ceased to interfere he would arrange for his employees to manhandle my wife—beating up women is one of their specialties. He did not actually add—but the suggestion was there—that she was far enough pregnant for the treatment to be especially effective in her case."

"I see," said Mr. Herbert. His voice was under control again, but it was rough at the edges. "I notice we are dropping the third-party fiction. That's all right. Finish your story. I'm looking forward to the moment when you come to the proof."

"I've very little more to say. You held three shares in Holoman's company. It looked innocuous, but it gave you control of what capital you had loaned him. It did more. If, in spite of all your precautions, and the roundabout way it was managed, and the fact that all payments were in cash—if, in spite of all this it should be possible to demonstrate that large sums of money had passed from Holoman to you—then you had your answer ready made. Any money you got was your share in the profits of the extremely profitable Holoman business."

Mr. Herbert said, "Ah." If he had said, aloud, "So you know that too, do you?" it could not have been plainer.

"One other thing. If you were to preserve the fiction that your only connection with Holoman was that you happened to hold a few shares in his company, then plainly you had to guard against seeing him, or even telephoning him, too frequently. You needed a further intermediary. And that is where, if I may criticize, you were a little bit too clever. You chose a creature of yours—a man called Hellaby."

"Ah," said Mr. Herbert again.

"I believe he's your personnel manager. Something like that. Anyway he was yours to promote or sack, yours to make or break, yours from the soles of his feet to the top set of his state-owned dentures. He would do what you told him and keep his mouth shut. Right. So he would. But what you hadn't calculated on was this. Observing so much profitable fiddling going on all round him he started fiddling himself. Which was quite fatal. Because Holoman caught him at it. And has been blackmailing him ever since. The *Kite* identified Hellaby last night, and he made a statement this morning."

There was a silence.

"And is that all?"

"That's it."

"And do you seriously imagine you can frighten me with some statement made, under pressure, by one of my own employees? No court will listen to it."

"I'm inclined to agree with you," said Mr. Wetherall.

"In fact, I was present this morning at a conference with the legal adviser to the *Kite*. He advised us that our evidence was insufficient to lead to a prosecution."

"I see," said Mr. Herbert, slowly. "Nice of you to tell me."

"That was really why I've come to see you this afternoon. I have brought with me——" Mr. Wetherall dipped into his document case——"a full and factual account of your activities. At least, it's as full as we've been able to make it in the time. It's quite comprehensive. There's a short bit at the end, saying that you've read it through and agree with it. We want you to sign it."

There was a further installment of silence.

"Assuming for a moment that this isn't some elaborate sort of practical joke," said Mr. Herbert, at last, "perhaps you wouldn't mind explaining just why I should do anything of the kind."

"Certainly. If you refuse, the *Kite* is to start publication, almost at once, of a series of articles. I wrote them myself, so I can assure you they are good, strong stuff. And most outspoken. No 'Mr. X' and 'Mr. Y.' Real names and addresses and everything. Perhaps you'd like to see my maiden effort?"

He dipped again into the case and brought out a folder. Mr. Herbert opened it.

"Where did you get that photograph?"

"Is that the one of you and your wife? I don't know. All the big newspapers have a lot of these things in their files. The penalty of fame. There's rather an amusing one of your son winning the high jump at his prep school, but I think that comes in the second article."

"You'd never dare——"

"It's going to save a lot of trouble if I simply repeat to you what Macrea said to us this morning. He said, 'You haven't got enough to found a criminal prosecution, but there's a wide difference between criminal proceedings and civil proceedings, and in my view you've got enough to put up a fighting defense to any libel action you may provoke. You'll have to plead justification and the public interest and go the whole hog. You may even get away with nominal damages. It'll be a jury case, and juries don't love black marketeers."

"It would never come to a libel suit. The court would stop the printing—"

"We considered the point. If it was a book, you might be able to do that, but a daily paper's not all that easy to stop. Suppose you got your injunction on the same afternoon that the first article appeared. It would already be too late. The damage would be done. You'd be forced to sue. And that would afford further opportunities for—shall we say, developing the story."

"I don't believe that any responsible newspaper—"

"Responsible fiddlesticks," said Mr. Wetherall. "This is the mildest of three schemes that Robarts had in mind. What he really wanted was a spontaneous lynching. And I believe he could have organized it, too. You really ought to have left Todd alone."

Mr. Herbert said nothing. He was turning the folder over and over in his fingers, not looking at it.

"Tear it up, if you like," said Mr. Wetherall helpfully. "We've got dozens of copies."

Mr. Herbert looked up. His face was white, but his eyes were ugly. "Have you thought about your own position if you try to go through with this?"

"Hot air and nonsense," said Mr. Wetherall. "If that's the last shot in your locker, we can get down to business. I'm off to Canada—with my wife—in a few days' time. I don't believe that your organization will be likely to bother me much there. And if you're thinking of pressing a button and summoning the boys, I might as well warn you that I've brought my own escort with me. They're all crime reporters. One happens to be a middleweight boxer as well."

Mr. Herbert went over to his chair and sat down.

"What is your proposition?" he said.

"It's quite simple. You sign what amounts to a confession. Then you close down the whole machine. And the existence of this confession will ensure that it stays closed down."

"I see."

"And if you're worrying about Holoman, you needn't. He's going to have plenty of worries of his own quite soon. Whether he, for his part, will be prepared to take what's coming to him and keep his mouth shut—that's a chance you'll have to take."

"And if I sign this document, I have your word that nothing further will happen—provided I keep my side of the bargain."

"That is correct," said Mr. Wetherall, looking at him curiously.

"And I have to rely on your word for that."

"You have to rely entirely on my word."

Even at that point Mr. Wetherall could not avoid the thought that a lesser man would have hesitated longer.

Mr. Herbert picked up his pen.

"Wait a minute," said Mr. Wetherall. He went to the window, threw it open, and beckoned.

A moment later three more visitors were being shown into the room. Mr. Herbert stared hard at the small man who stood between his larger companions, but he said nothing. The small man looked everywhere except at Mr. Herbert.

"Just watch him signing, Mr. Hellaby. Then add your name underneath his as a witness. That's right. You'd better initial each of the pages, too. Splendid. Then we won't take up any more of your time, Mr. Herbert. Don't bother about the maid. We can show ourselves out."

A moment later the front door banged.

From outside came the noise of a car starting up. Increased, diminished and muttered away into the distance.

Mr. Herbert sat without moving. He sat so still that when

the maid came in to lay the tea she thought that the
room was empty.

"Well, that's that," said Mrs. Wetherall. "It's been a
rush, but I think we've fixed everything. Lucky it was a
furnished flat. They're easy enough to get rid of."

"Easier to get rid of than get hold of," agreed her husband.

"If we've a moment to spare for it we ought to have a
little celebration."

"It's not a victory," said Mr. Wetherall. He was cross
and tired. "At the most, a sort of success."

"Well, I call it a victory. And I'm sure you deserved it."
She presented him with a kiss. "And now Timothy's going
to be born a little Canadian. I'm told the hospitals are very
good out there."

"He'll be born in Canada. That won't make him a Canadian."

"Well, I'm sure it's all come out for the best. Though
why you ever had to get mixed up in it all——"

It was people, really, thought Mr. Wetherall. When it
came to the point you'd do things for people that you'd
never dream of doing for patriotism or politics or principles. Unimportant people. People like Mr. Crowdy and
Peter Crowdy, and Luigi, and Sammy and Peggy, and
Alastair Todd—and his own wife, too. But you could
never explain it to her.

"The fact of the matter is," he said, and was aware as
he said it that it sounded silly, "that I've always been
against bullying. Someone starts a thing like this, and he
takes a risk and if it comes off he makes a profit, like any
other business, and it seems all right at his end. But at
the other end, it always seems to come down to plain
bullying. That's really all there is to it."

"What I'm sorry about," said Mrs. Wetherall, "is that no
one's ever going to publish those articles, after you took so
much trouble over them too. I know the *Kite*'s paying for

them anyway, but that's not the same as seeing your name in print."

"You never know," said Mr. Wetherall. "Perhaps, sometime—it would mean changing all the names and places round a bit, of course—but perhaps sometime I might be able to make a book out of it."

THE PERENNIAL LIBRARY MYSTERY SERIES

Nicholas Blake

THE WORM OF DEATH
THE WHISPER IN THE GLOOM
HEAD OF A TRAVELER
MINUTE FOR MURDER
THE CORPSE IN THE SNOWMAN
THOU SHELL OF DEATH
THE WIDOW'S CRUISE
END OF CHAPTER
THE SMILER WITH THE KNIFE
THE BEAST MUST DIE

Michael Gilbert

DEATH HAS DEEP ROOTS
THE DANGER WITHIN
BLOOD AND JUDGMENT
THE BODY OF A GIRL
FEAR TO TREAD

Andrew Garve

A HERO FOR LEANDA
THE ASHES OF LODA
THE FAR SANDS
NO TEARS FOR HILDA
THE CUCKOO LINE AFFAIR
THE RIDDLE OF SAMSON
MURDER THROUGH THE
LOOKING GLASS

E. C. Bentley

TRENT'S LAST CASE

Cyril Hare

WHEN THE WIND BLOWS
AN ENGLISH MURDER

Julian Symons

THE COLOR OF MURDER
THE 31ST OF FEBRUARY

"WE HAVE ONLY ONE TEXAS"

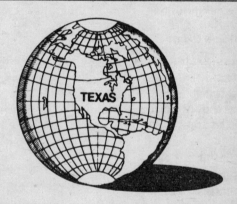

People ask if there is really an energy crisis. Look at it this way. World oil consumption is 60 million barrels per day and is growing 5 percent each year. This means the world must find three million barrels of new oil production each day. Three million barrels per day is the amount of oil produced in Texas as its peak was 5 years ago. The problem is that it is not going to be easy to find a Texas-sized new oil supply every year, year after year. In just a few years, it may be impossible to balance demand and supply of oil unless we start conserving oil today. So next time someone asks: "Is there really an energy crisis?", tell them: "Yes, we have only one Texas."

ENERGY CONSERVATION -
IT'S YOUR CHANCE TO SAVE, AMERICA

Department of Energy, Washington, D.C.